Betrayed

(Book two of the Jenny Watkins Mystery series)

by

Becky Durfee

If you are reading this,
I hope that means you
liked the first one ☺.

Enjoy Betrayed!

Dedication

Once again I'd like to thank my husband Scott for his never-ending support in this process, which is taking up more and more of my time with each passing week. My children/step-children continue to be my inspiration: Hannah Durfee, Seneca Durfee, Evan Fish and Julia Fish—I could not have done this without you. And please take a note of what can happen when you take a chance and follow your dream...

I'd also like to thank my Beta readers: Sam Travers, Sue Durfee, Sarah Demarest, Bill Demarest and Felicia Underwood (look at me throwing around the jargon!) You all catch things I never would have noticed and you point out where my writing doesn't exactly make sense. My stories are better because of you!

Another shout-out goes to my daughter Julia, my cover model, who had to sit in a black sweater on a hot summer day as I took a million pictures that all looked pretty much the same. My graphic designer/husband Scott spent a good long time getting the letters to look just right on the cover, and I appreciate that as well.

A final thank you goes to all of the people who have supported me, friends and strangers alike. I was overwhelmed by the response that Driven received. I never thought in a million years that I'd sell over 50 copies, and I have far exceeded that. Longtime friends (notice I didn't say "old" friends, LOL) have reached out to me, showing their support, and people I've never met have taken time out of their day to tell me how much they enjoyed my book. I have to be honest--that never gets old. Thank you all so much...I can't tell you how much it means to me.

I hope you all enjoy reading Betrayed as much as I enjoyed writing it. ☺

Chapter 1

Someone, somewhere, had been strangled.

Jenny felt the firm grip of hands around her throat as she tried to gasp for a few precious breaths. She punched her gloved hands at the man dominating her, desperate to get away, pinned helplessly to the ground by the attacker's heavy knees. He was filled with such anger, squeezing and shaking her neck, grunting with exertion. But what had she done to him? She didn't even know him. What could have filled him with such rage?

She tried to pry his hands away from her neck as she felt her consciousness fade, aware that this final attempt at survival was going to be futile. This was it. This was how she was going to die…strangled in the middle of the night in a remote area where even if she managed a scream, no one would hear. She thought of all the things she hadn't done yet—the prom, graduation, a wedding—all things she would never do, simply because she'd been in the wrong place at the wrong time.

She looked up into the unmasked face of her killer, illuminated by the headlights of his car. She studied his face, trying to memorize it, hoping to be able to identify him if she did manage to survive. Sadly, she knew that was unlikely. Despite her strong will to pull through this, she felt herself becoming lifeless. Her hands lost their ability to fight, and her eyes closed for the final time.

Jenny sat up straight with a gasp, looking around to make sure this had only been a vision. She was relieved to discover she was sitting at the edge of Lake Wimsat, her easel in front of her, just as she had been before that horrible contact. Unnerved, she recalled the contours of the killer's face, committing them to memory: the pronounced chin, the short sandy hair, his piercing eyes. She realized she would have to be the one to identify this person on the victim's behalf if the time ever came; since she had been contacted, she knew strangulation must have been fatal.

Reaching into her pocket and pulling out her cell phone, she hoped for reception. Relief washed over her when she discover she had the ability to make a call, and she immediately dialed her friend Zack. He had been instrumental in helping her solve her only other similar mystery, and she had promised to let him help with cases going forward.

"Hey, Jenny! How's it going?" he asked upon answering.

"Okay, I guess." Jenny's voice was somber. "I just had a vision."

"For real? It's about time. What was it?"

Jenny swallowed. "Someone's been strangled."

"Oh." Zack's zeal immediately faded. "Who?"

"That's just it," Jenny confessed. "I have no idea. I saw it through the victim's eyes, but I don't know who she was." After a moment she added, "Or he."

"Did you see who did it?"

"Yes, that much I did see. I could definitely identify the guy in a line up, but I don't know what good that does me if I don't know who the victim was. Or where it happened. Or when. For all I know, this happened twenty years ago in Timbuktu."

"Well," Zack reasoned, "let's see if we can figure out any clues. Did anything happen in the vision that might give you an indication of what we're dealing with?"

Jenny let out a sigh. "The victim had to be young. They were upset about never being able to go to the prom."

"Then the victim is a girl—a privileged one."

"How do you know?"

"A dude wouldn't be upset about missing the prom," Zack noted. "A young guy would probably be more upset about dying a virgin."

Jenny gave the notion some thought, and it made sense to her.

"And I assume she's privileged—or at least not under-privileged—because the prom is a middle class concern," Zack added. If she was from a low income bracket, I'd think she'd be more concerned about who was going to take care of her family—who was going to watch her younger brother or care for her ailing mother, that kind of thing.

"Now," Zack continued, "Were there any indications of when this took place? Or where? Was the killer wearing a different style of clothes or something?"

"I don't know," Jenny replied. "It was dark. His clothes were dark. I could see his face because it was lit up by headlights, but that was about it. Although, I did see trees. I was outside when I got strangled, but exactly I'm not sure where."

"Well," Zack concluded, "Hopefully you'll get contacted again and get a little more detail."

Jenny let out a breath. "I guess so. Do you think I should call the police?"

"And say what?"

She leaned back in her folding chair, looking helplessly at her half-finished painting of the lake. "Good point."

"So what else is new?" Zack asked, sensing her disappointment. "How's marriage counseling going?"

"It's going," Jenny replied. "I think the counselor is learning how stubborn my husband is."

"Uh oh."

"Yeah," Jenny said in a melancholy tone as she brushed her hair out of her face. "It's kind of what I expected; the reason we went to counseling in the first place is because Greg is very difficult to reason with. The counselor is not having any more luck getting through to him than I've had." Jenny realized how negative she was being. "But enough about me...how's the new boat?"

"Totally awesome," Zack replied. "I'm on it every chance I get."

Jenny smiled sincerely. "That's good. I'm glad to hear it. Anything else new?"

"Just counting down until the big three-oh. I've only got about a month left in my twenties. Then I'll actually have to become responsible."

Jenny laughed. "Yeah, you are pretty old. Thirty. I've got three good years left before I get there."

"Yeah. Great. You really know how to make a guy feel good about himself, don't you?"

"I do what I can." After some more small talk, Jenny and Zack concluded their call. Jenny looked out at the lake as she put the phone back in her pocket, absorbing the implications of her latest contact. She hadn't been sure if her first mystery two months earlier was going to be her only one, but here she was faced with another contact. Perhaps these psychic visions were going to be a way of life for her now. While she still felt saddened and shaken by the horrible nature of her vision, she had to admit she was excited by the prospect of another investigation.

Her first contact had started with the name of the victim, which at least gave her a starting point for exploration. Now she only had the face of a killer, which provided her with little more than an image to haunt her dreams. This murder could have happened yesterday or thirty years ago, in her hometown of Evansdale, Georgia or on the other side of the world. Jenny surmised that Zack's conclusion was unfortunately correct; she would just have to wait for more insight before she could do anything to unravel the mystery.

No longer in the mood to paint, Jenny packed up her supplies and headed back to her car. She still had some time alone at the house before Greg got home from work, so she could enjoy a little bit of freedom before the tension of her failing marriage took over. She was always so much happier when her husband wasn't around, a notion she knew didn't bode well for her future with Greg.

As she mindlessly prepared dinner, Jenny contemplated the conversation she'd inevitably have when Greg got home. He was not supportive when she discovered that she had psychic ability; he had made that abundantly clear during her last experience. Although he had never voiced it, he was probably quite pleased that a couple of months had passed without any paranormal activity. Perhaps he thought those days of psychic visions were behind them. However, it now seemed like the biggest sticking point in their marriage was about to return.

Greg came through the front door without much fanfare. He set down his bag of ungraded papers and coaching notes, walking wordlessly into the kitchen.

"Did you have a good day?" Jenny asked.

"It was okay," he replied. "Normal." He sorted through the mail on the newly resurfaced kitchen island, deciding nothing was of particular importance. "What's for dinner?"

"Ham," Jenny replied.

Familiar silence followed. Jenny had grown accustomed to the long breaks in the conversation, although she hadn't yet become comfortable with them. She was relieved when Greg went upstairs to change his clothes; the silence was only deafening when he was close by.

When he came back downstairs, Greg scooped food onto his plate as quickly as Jenny could put the dishes on the table. Once the table was full she sat down across from her husband, taking only child-sized portions for herself; she was simply too nervous to eat.

"I had a bit of an interesting day," she began.

"Oh yeah?"

She cleared her throat. "I had a vision while I was painting at the lake." She looked up and waited for a response from Greg which never came. She'd witnessed that same apathetic response from him a million times before, and the familiarity sickened her. It was hard to have a meaningful conversation with a man who refused to acknowledge any news he didn't like. Undeterred, she continued. "Someone's been strangled, although I don't know who."

Greg swallowed the food in his mouth. "That's not really much to go on, is it?"

"No, it's not. But it may be the beginning of something." Jenny wished she was less nervous. "Maybe I'll be contacted again…with a little more detail."

Greg grunted to acknowledge that he'd heard her, silently taking a few more bites before adding, "My algebra class did well on their test today."

Consumed with disappointment and disgust, Jenny quietly said, "That's good."

After the last of the dinner dishes had been washed and put away, Jenny wandered slowly into the living room, casually using the remote to turn on the television before she sat on the couch. She ignored the TV as she once again contemplated her vision at the lake.

Were there any details she was missing? Something that would give her a clue about the victim's identity? With a deep sigh Jenny wished she had the ability to summon contacts instead of just passively receiving them. Waiting had never been one of Jenny's strengths.

At that moment something about the news caught Jenny's full attention. She heard the reporter begin the story.

An Amber Alert goes out tonight for fifteen year old Morgan Caldwell, who disappeared from her home in Braddock late Tuesday night or early Wednesday morning.

A photograph of the missing teen appeared on the screen, and every one of Jenny's nerves tingled.

She knew this was her victim.

According to her parents, she had gone to bed as usual Tuesday night but was not in her bedroom when her mother went to wake her Wednesday morning. Police officials say there are no signs of forced entry or struggle in the home, but her parents insist she was unlikely to run away. Today at a press conference, her mother made a plea for her safe return.

The image on the screen went from a still photograph of Morgan to a recording of a tearful couple making a gut-wrenching statement behind a podium. Morgan's mother could barely speak through her sobs.

Please. If anyone knows anything at all, please come forward. All we want is our Morgan back. And Morgan, if you're watching this, please know we're looking for you. We love you, honey, and we are doing everything we can to get you back. We won't stop until we find you.

Jenny turned away from the screen, unable to look at the parents who had no idea their daughter was already gone.

Just as Jenny was about to succumb to overwhelming sadness, she remembered the advice of her friend Susan, a fellow psychic who had served as her mentor during the last episode. *Don't own it. Your job is not to deliver happy endings, but rather to make the unhappy*

9

endings make sense. She sat up straight and sucked in a breath, regaining her composure, realizing she had a job to do—she had to get these parents some answers and, more importantly, get a child-killer behind bars before he struck again.

"Morgan Caldwell," Jenny said the second Zack answered the phone.

"Excuse me?"

"Morgan Caldwell. She's the person who was strangled."

"Isn't that the missing girl from Braddock?"

"Yup," Jenny confirmed, "That's her."

"How do you know?"

"Intuition," Jenny replied. "When I saw her face on the news I just knew."

At that moment the implication of Jenny's words seemed to hit Zack. "Oh, God. That's a real bummer. They're still hoping to find her alive."

"Yeah." Jenny made a partially-successful effort to remain unaffected. "I know."

"Have you called the police?"

"I just did," Jenny confessed. "But it didn't go very well."

"What happened?"

"Well, I told them I know that Morgan had been strangled in a remote area in the middle of the night by a man I could identify if necessary. They asked me how I knew, and when I told them I am a psychic who had a vision, they told me I was about the fifth one to call that hour. It seems every lunatic within a fifty mile radius has called them up claiming to be clairvoyant."

"Shit."

"Yeah, I should have known better. You know, I do remember Susan telling me she had a lot of similar problems before she made a name for herself as a reputable psychic." Jenny put her hand on her forehead. "I don't know what I'm going to have to do to get them to believe me."

"You'll just have to come up with some earth shattering detail that no regular person could possibly know."

"With my luck they'll view that as evidence that I did it and I'll find my ass in jail."

10

"Oh, yeah, hadn't thought of that. That would suck."

"Indeed it would." Jenny let out a deep sigh. "I'm going to go try to relax—see if I can inspire another contact. If that doesn't work, I'll go back to the lake tomorrow and paint some more. If neither of those things bring any answers, I'll make a trip out to Braddock tomorrow night. Maybe being closer to the action will help."

"I don't have to work tomorrow night. If you do go out there, can I go with you?"

"That'd be great, actually. I'd love the company. Besides, I'd feel more comfortable with you there if there's a killer on the loose."

After a nice long bath, Jenny climbed into bed, clearing her head of all active thought to facilitate a contact. Unfortunately she was a little too elevated, making relaxation an effort, defeating the purpose. Eventually she did feel waves of sleep taking over, and during one of those waves she had a brief but very clear image in her head.

Chapter 2

The air around her had the distinct crispness of a beautiful fall evening, the type of night she'd always enjoyed in the past. But there was nothing pleasurable about this particular night. She felt pain in her face; she'd been beaten. Her cheek bones throbbed as she tried to keep her bearings, knowing her life depended on it, all the while wondering if this was really happening or just a horrible dream. Her hands were immobilized, presumably pinned under the weight of her attacker. The barrel of a gun was pointed directly at her, and just beyond that she could see that same man using his teeth and his free hand to open a condom wrapper. He was going to rape her. She knew that. But hopefully once he was done he would let her go and this would all be over.

In an instant the image was gone, but it had been telling. Morgan was sexually assaulted before she was killed, but there would be no seminal fluid. No DNA. And the gun might have explained the lack of a struggle at the house; perhaps there had not been one. Maybe she'd gone peacefully after seeing the weapon.

Jenny jotted the information down on the notepad she kept by her bed, another strategy she'd learned from her mentor Susan. After the vision had been sufficiently described in writing, she lay back down, hoping to be enlightened a little more, but no other visions came to light.

In the morning, Jenny kept the television on while she packed up her painting supplies, ready to head back out to the lake. She knew local news updates recurred every half hour, so she made sure to be watching when the time came. Her heart skipped a beat when she heard the anchor begin.

Breaking news in the Morgan Caldwell investigation this morning. The body of a young woman was found in an orchard in Trent, thirty miles from the Caldwell home. While the remains have not yet been positively identified, police officials have reason to believe they could belong to Morgan Caldwell. Alex Mayfield is on the scene in Trent with the latest. Alex...

A live shot from the orchard-turned-media-circus appeared on the screen. A young man in a shirt and tie spoke eloquently into a microphone as many others did the same in the background.

Thanks, Pam. Police were called to the scene about an hour ago when the owner of this orchard made a grizzly discovery while heading out to harvest his pecans. The remains of a young woman were found just off of a service road on the property. Police are unsure of exactly how long the remains have been there, but based on the condition they believe it is possible that these remains belong to Morgan Caldwell. As you probably know Morgan disappeared from her home in Braddock three days ago and hasn't been seen since. A positive identification is expected later this afternoon, and we'll let you know the result as soon as it happens.
Reporting live from Trent, this is Alex Mayfield.

The announcer continued from the newsroom.

Morgan Caldwell is a sophomore at Monroe High School, where a vigil is scheduled to take place at seven o'clock Saturday night. A source close to the family says the vigil will go on as planned, even if those remains do turn out to be Morgan's.

The newscaster abruptly switched to the forecast, a concept which boggled Jenny's mind. How could she talk casually about the weather when something so horribly tragic had just occurred?

13

"Distance," Jenny reminded herself. "I've got to keep my distance." As cold as it seemed, Jenny needed to strive to be more like the newscaster.

At that moment her cell phone rang. She looked at the screen before answering, noticing Zack was the caller; she was sure she knew what the call was about. "I saw," she said instead of hello.

"This sucks," he replied. "But at least they found her. Now they can start investigating. Maybe the attacker left some clues behind."

"I hope so, but he seemed careful," Jenny said, recounting her vision from the previous evening. "He took steps to make sure he left no DNA behind."

"Well maybe she scratched the shit out of him and she's got some of his skin under her fingernails."

"Gloves," Jenny muttered, mostly to herself.

"What?"

"She was wearing gloves." Jenny closed her eyes to recount the first vision she'd had. She distinctly saw black leather gloves on her fists as she punched at the assailant. "I bet he made her put them on for that reason. I can't think of why else she'd be wearing gloves in October in Georgia. It's not that cold."

"Maybe there will be fingerprints on the gloves?"

"Maybe," Jenny said half-heartedly. She was preoccupied with thought. "What if I call the police and tell them they'll find sexual assault, no semen, and gloves. Do you think they'll believe I'm a psychic when I know all those details?"

"It's possible. I think you should call the police with what you have. Give them your phone number and your full cooperation. Hopefully soon they'll start to take you seriously."

Jenny sighed. "I guess you're right. Hey, are you still interested in a road trip to Braddock? Or even Trent? I think I may skip the painting today given the latest developments."

"I'm always up for a road trip," he replied. "What time?"

"I can be there in an hour. Will you be ready by then?"

"I was born ready. And while I'm waiting for you to come I'll find out where Morgan lives...lived. Maybe you can get a good contact if we get close enough to her house."

"That's excellent thinking," Jenny said. "See? This is why you're my partner."

Jenny spoke to a police officer and was able to convince him to at least write down her tip and her phone number. She was optimistic that Zack would turn out to be right; once her account started lining up with the facts, the police would be in contact with her again. Then she could work together with them and hopefully provide those poor grieving parents with some answers.

After a quick bite to eat she left to pick up Zack. "Where first?" she asked when he got into the car. "Braddock or Trent?"

"Braddock," Zack replied. "Not only is Trent out in the middle of nowhere, but did you see how crazy it was there? That place was crawling with reporters. We probably won't be able to get anywhere near the orchard."

"You're right," Jenny reasoned. "Have you got Morgan's address?"

"Sure do. Got it programmed." He held up his phone and waved it back and forth. "Time to rock and roll!"

Zack and Jenny discussed the clues they had so far as they drove out toward the Caldwell's house. The drive was short, only about thirty minutes, but before they could even come close to the house, they found the road was blocked off by police. Reporters and curious onlookers swarmed like bees. "Damn, dude," Zack said. "People are sick."

Jenny gave Zack a sideways glance. "We appear to be just as sick as they are, you know."

"We're here to help," he said, "not to stalk."

Jenny didn't respond as she turned her car around, looking for a place she could park within a reasonable distance. She was quite sure this quiet suburban road had never seen so much traffic, aside from an occasional graduation party or family reunion. A reflective glance at the well-manicured lawns and abundant minivans made Jenny wonder if any place on earth was safe from evil.

She found a space around the corner from the Caldwell house and parallel parked her car. "So what do we do now?" she asked.

"We get out," Zack replied, exiting the car. Jenny followed suit, and once outside he added, "and we get as close as we can."

Feeling like little more than an ambulance chaser, Jenny walked with her head down as she and Zack approached the scene. "Are you relaxing?" Zack asked her.

"No," Jenny confessed. "I'm not sure I can with all of this going on."

The crowd of people behind the police barricade had to have been in the hundreds, all with different motivations for being there. Teenagers were crying, women carried baked goods, and others looked as if they were simply satisfying a morbid curiosity. Members of the press stood just inside the police blockade, but even they were kept at a distance. Nervous excitement buzzed over the crowd, and while the noise was kept to a minimum, the energy level was extremely high—too high for Jenny to have any meaningful contact.

"I think I need to leave here," Jenny confessed. "I'm not getting anything."

"Okay. Where would you like to go?"

"Someplace quieter," she replied. "Close by, but quieter." Jenny looked around until her eyes fixed on the road beyond the crowd. "I want to be over there. On the other side."

"Are you on to something?"

"Don't know yet." Jenny always kept her answers brief when she was trying to receive a message. "But I want to be over there."

Zack pulled out his phone and looked for a way to get to the other side of the crowd. The entire street was blocked off, so they couldn't simply go through. "It looks like the streets form a grid," he said, examining at the map on his screen. "If we go this way and make a few lefts, we'll be on the other side." He pointed away from the crowd. "Do you want me to get the car?"

Jenny shook her head. "Walk."

Zack understood her need for brevity. He walked silently by her side as they rounded the block, passing groups of neighbors who were all discussing the same thing. Some were angry, others frightened, and still others were simply fascinated. No matter the reaction, there was only one topic of conversation on everyone's lips: Morgan Caldwell's murder.

As Zack and Jenny approached the crowd from the other side, Jenny stopped in her tracks. She turned slowly and began walking in the opposite direction with Zack wordlessly following her lead. They walked about a mile down the street and around an unfamiliar corner until Jenny stood frozen at a seemingly random spot on the side of the road. "Here," she said decidedly. "Something happened here."

They stood silently for a moment as Jenny tried to grasp what had happened. The location seemed too idyllic for anything bad to have ever transpired there. An average-sized house sat behind a bed of mums in full bloom; the lawn was well-manicured, and the mailbox had been hand-painted with care. Yet somehow this location harbored a horrible secret, although Jenny couldn't figure out what it was.

"What do you think happened?" Zack posed.

"Don't know," Jenny replied. She closed her eyes for several moments before shaking her head with frustration for the final time. "I can't get it. There's too much commotion." She pointed toward the ground. "But something definitely happened here. This is the spot, I'm sure of it."

Zack took out his phone and started typing, making a note of the address where they stood. He spoke as he pressed the letters. "15625 Armistead Lane. Got it," he remarked. "Do you want to try anywhere else?"

Jenny contemplated a moment before stating, "No. I don't think there's a point. There's too much interference. I guess we should just go back to the car."

They started the trek to the car silently until Jenny pounded her fists into her head. "Ugh. This is so frustrating. I can see him. When I close my eyes, I can totally see the man who did this. But I have no idea who he is."

"You're an artist," Zack surmised. "Why don't you paint a picture of him?"

A brief flicker of excitement was quickly overshadowed by reality. "I paint landscapes," Jenny declared. "I've never painted a face before. I'm not sure I could do it."

"How different could it be?"

"It's very different," Jenny declared. "For you to say an artist should be able to paint landscapes and portraits is like saying an athlete should be able to play baseball and football."

"Ever hear of Bo Jackson?"

"No."

Zack laughed. "Then I guess I shouldn't use him as a reference." He put his hand on Jenny's back and said in a comforting tone, "But I think you should try it. What have you got to lose?"

Jenny sighed, trying to ignore the twinge of excitement brought on by Zack's touch. "You're right. Worst comes to worst I can't do it."

"But if you can," Zack added, "then the whole world will know what Morgan Caldwell's killer looks like."

Jenny sat at Lake Wimsat with her canvas and paints. "Okay," she whispered under her breath. "Help me with this, Morgan. I can't do this alone." With that Jenny began painting, not allowing herself to think her way out of succeeding. She mindlessly let her hand take over, not pausing to look at the whole picture until it was completed. Unaware of exactly how much time had passed, Jenny took a step back to see the finished face she had created, and the image took her breath away. The likeness was amazing, right down to the piercing eyes.

She was staring into the face of a cold-blooded killer.

Jenny walked through the front door of her house with the painting tucked under her arm. "Hey," she called, signaling she was home. Greg was busy working on crown molding and didn't respond. Once she walked out of earshot from Greg, she sarcastically whispered, "Nice to see you, too, honey." She carefully leaned the canvas against a wall. "It's a painting of the murderer from my vision. I'm glad you asked."

She called Zack, eager to tell him she was able to capture the killer's likeness, but Zack had a bit of news of his own. "They officially identified the remains today," he said. "They are Morgan's. I saw it on TV a little bit ago."

Jenny contemplated the appropriateness of her comment before speaking, deciding her words were within reason. "Good. I'm glad. We already knew she was dead, so the sooner they determine it's her, the better."

"Did you finish your picture?"

"I did, actually, and it came out pretty good, if I do say so myself. Thanks for the idea."

"That's why I make the big bucks."

Jenny rolled her eyes. "I'm going to take a photo of it and print it out. A few times. Carrying around a canvas isn't exactly practical."

"Are you going to take it to the police?"

"I was debating on whether I should go in or wait until they contact me."

"I'd go in," Zack said. "As soon as you can. Imagine how you'd feel if someone else got attacked while you're sitting at home with a picture of the killer that you haven't shown anyone. They might recognize this guy right away as some scumbag they've already dealt with. You never know."

"You're right," Jenny said. "I would never be able to live with myself if I didn't do everything I can to get this guy caught."

"Atta girl," Zack said. "I'll keep my cell phone on. If they commit you to the loony bin, you can use me as your one phone call."

"Great," Jenny muttered. "Thanks."

Jenny walked nervously into the Braddock police station with the printout of her painting in her purse. She approached the information desk and said in a low tone, "Hi. I'd like to speak to somebody about the Morgan Caldwell case. I may have some information that will be useful."

"Okay," the woman behind the desk said. "What's your name?"

"Jenny Watkins."

"Okay, Miss Watkins, have a seat over there and I'll get a detective to speak with you as soon as one becomes available."

"Thank you," Jenny replied politely. She turned and sat on a bench with several other people, who she presumed had similar claims. This was going to take a while; she should have brought a book.

After thirty minutes her name was called and she apprehensively walked back with the detective who had addressed her. He didn't look very friendly; he looked tired and disheveled as if he'd been up all night, a likely scenario given the circumstances. She sat in the chair next to his desk as he looked pessimistically at her over his glasses. "So what have you got for me?"

His demeanor made Jenny want to go home, but at this point she was committed. "I believe I know who Morgan Caldwell's killer was, although I don't know his name."

The man typed as Jenny spoke. "Who do you believe it was?"

Jenny opened her purse and pulled out the picture, unfolding it in front of the detective. "This man. I painted his face."

When the detective looked at the paper, Jenny thought she saw a brief glimpse of recognition in his eyes. However, he simply regarded her with a skeptical expression and asked, "Is this a joke?"

That was not the reaction Jenny had expected. "No, sir. It's not a joke."

"And what makes you think this man is the killer?"

Jenny looked down at her lap and shamefully admitted, "I'm a psychic, and I saw it in a vision."

"You know what I think happened?" the detective asked, leaning forward on his elbows. "I think this guy promised he'd call you in the morning, and then he didn't. And now you're trying to get back at him. That's what I think."

"No, I swear…"

"Now you listen to me. We've got a real investigation going on here. We have a killer on our hands, in case you haven't noticed. We don't have time to be entertaining peoples' personal vendettas or their silly little fantasies that they can chit chat with the dead. Now I suggest you take your little picture and get out of here before I charge you with interfering with a police investigation."

Jenny opened her mouth to protest but thought better of it. Instead she folded her picture back up and placed it in her purse, wordlessly getting up from the chair and leaving the station. She wasn't sure whether to feel anger, shame or frustration, but she definitely brimmed with emotion as she climbed into her car.

Before calling Zack to confess her failure, Jenny dialed Susan, the only person who would fully understand her situation. "Hello?"

"Hi, Susan, it's Jenny." She started her car and pulled out of the parking lot.

"Well hello, Jenny. What's up?"

Jenny let out a sigh. "Do you remember what you went through before you met Bill?" Bill Abernathy had been the first cop to take Susan's psychic ability seriously.

"Oh dear."

"Yeah, I'm going through it now. On the Morgan Caldwell case."

"Really?" Susan asked. "Morgan Caldwell? Going straight for the high profile, huh?"

"I didn't choose it, believe me," Jenny confessed. "Morgan did. She gave me a very clear image of the killer's face, but nobody in a position to do anything about it will believe me. In fact, I painted a picture of him—a very good likeness, I might add—and brought it to the police department. The cop there actually got mad at me. I'm not exactly sure who this guy is, but he must be somebody important."

"I've lived in Georgia lot longer than you. If he's somebody important, maybe I'll recognize him. Can you send me the picture?"

"Absolutely. I'd love it if you could tell me who he is."

"Maybe it's a senator," Susan said in a gossipy tone.

"Nah, too young to be a senator."

"Alright, well, why don't you send me that picture and I'll call you back."

"Great." Jenny pulled over into a parking lot and photographed her picture, sending it to Susan. Within a minute the phone rang. "Recognize him?"

"No, I'm afraid I don't. He can't be that important."

"Okay, well, thanks anyway." Jenny's brief optimism faded. "If I get any more details I'll let you know."

"Sounds good. And good luck with this, Jenny. I know how frustrating it can be. Just do me a favor and don't do anything stupid, okay? You're dealing with a lunatic, here."

"I won't," Jenny replied. "I promise."

Chapter 3

"We should go to the vigil tonight," Zack said. "I've seen on TV that killers will often show up at those things. I think that's our best bet for getting a glimpse of this guy in person."

"I was thinking the same thing. Do you happen to know how to get to Monroe High School?"

"Yeah, I played more than one baseball game there back in the day."

Jenny cringed at the mention of high school baseball. All three of her brothers had played, and her father had always treated them like they walked on water because of it. Quickly dismissing such a trivial notion, she added, "I'd like to get there good and early. That way we are sure to see everyone who comes."

"Agreed. How about we plan to get there at six?"

"Six is perfect. I'll let my husband know he's fixing his own supper tonight."

"Good luck with that," Zack replied.

"Yeah," Jenny snorted. "I'll add that to the long list of things I do wrong in his eyes."

"Now that you bring it up," Zack began, "I've been wondering how he's been taking it now that you've gotten another contact."

"To tell you the truth, I'm not even sure. I tried to bring it up to him, but he essentially ignored me. He just changed the subject."

"Huh," Zack replied. "Is he upset that you're not helping him with the renovation?"

Jenny shrugged, although Zack couldn't see that through the phone. "I can tell he's not thrilled with it, but he hasn't actually complained. I don't think he can, really. He hasn't been shy about spending the money Elanor left me, and I think he realizes he can't have it both ways."

"Fair enough." Zack paused awkwardly. "Okay, then, I guess I'll get you at five thirty?"

"Sounds good. Thanks Zack." Jenny hung up the phone and sought out Greg, who was still upstairs struggling with the crown molding.

"Hey," she began, realizing she should probably offer to help but choosing not to. "I'm going to a vigil for Morgan Caldwell tonight. I'm hoping her killer will be there and I can recognize him."

"Okay," he replied, not missing a beat of his hammering. Jenny waited for elaboration that would have shown he cared, but as usual it never came.

"I'm not going to be able to fix dinner tonight. You'll have to fend for yourself."

"I'm used to that."

Jenny rolled her eyes and left the room, shaking her head. She wasn't sure why she was even bothering with marriage counseling. She was ninety-nine percent sure she wanted a divorce; she just couldn't bring herself to say it out loud. Every time Greg acted like this, however, the words inched closer to her lips.

As usual, Zack was late picking Jenny up. When he finally arrived, she hopped into his car quickly, hoping they could still get to the vigil early enough to see everyone in attendance. Once they were on their way, Jenny posed the question that had occurred to her while she was waiting for him.

"Hey Zack…how is it that you have the day off again? I thought you had once said that October is your busy season at work."

Zack bit his lip. "Umm…" He pretended to cough a few times. "I've been really sick?"

"No," Jenny said with wide eyes. "Did you really call in sick?"

"Kind of."

"What do you mean, *kind of*?"

23

"I mean I didn't call."

"You just didn't show up?"

Zack made a face, indicating she was right.

Jenny was dumbfounded. "Won't your father be furious?"

"Yup."

"I thought you had said you would be disowned if you didn't work for the family business."

"I most likely will be."

Jenny was still shocked. "But how are you going to get by?"

"On my looks?" Zack flashed Jenny a cheesy smile.

At that moment Jenny realized what was happening. Old Jenny was coming out—old, practical Jenny who always followed the rules and always did everything she was supposed to.

She hated old Jenny.

Her first client Elanor had taught her that people are in charge of their own happiness, and sometimes people have to step on some toes if they are going to be true to themselves. Jenny knew how much Zack hated his job, so she should have been happy for him that he'd quit. Instead, she couldn't get beyond the fact that he'd broken the rules.

"I'm sorry," she said. "I guess I was just surprised by your answer. I'm actually glad to hear you're playing hooky. I hate the idea of you working a job you don't like."

He smiled genuinely. "Thanks." After a pause, he added, "Although, I am quite sure I'm screwed. I have been living paycheck to paycheck, so I'll be homeless in no time." He let out a laugh. "I guess I haven't thought this through very well."

Jenny thought for a moment about the ridiculously huge inheritance Elanor had left her with the promise that she'd use the money to help others. "You know," she began, "if we are going to be partners in this crime-fighting arrangement we have, it seems to me you should probably be on a payroll or something…"

Zack was silent.

"What do you think is a fair salary?" Jenny continued, smiling at the flabbergasted look on his face. "How about if I match what you're making now, plus an extra ten grand a year for insurance?"

Looking close to tears, Zack said, "You'd do that for me?"

"Of course," Jenny replied. "I couldn't do any of this without you. We're a team, remember?"

Zack remained quiet for another moment, and when he did speak his voice reflected his shock. "I've always hated my job, but honestly—ever since our last adventure I've barely been able to tolerate it. I had so much fun working on Elanor's case, it was almost impossible to go back to designing houses after that." He wiped his hand down his face. "If I could do this…for a living. As my job…It'd be awesome."

Jenny understood completely; her marriage had been equally as difficult to return to after Elanor's case. "Well, you're hired. Effective immediately. You can go ahead and officially quit your other job if you'd like."

Zack's easygoing smile returned. "And search for another family while I'm at it."

"I hired you. You're pushing it if you think I'm going to adopt you."

Zack laughed. "Fair enough."

When they arrived at the vigil, a handful of people was already there. Jenny and Zack were greeted by a woman who handed them candles surrounded in paper cups to catch the wax. After a brief and solemn thank you they joined the small crowd.

"See anything?" Zack asked.

"No. You?"

"Not yet. We should position ourselves so we can see who comes in."

Without another word they moved to a strategic location in the crowd. As the start time of the vigil approached, however, people began to arrive in droves, making it impossible for them to see every face. "We'll need to circulate," Jenny proposed.

"Come on," Zack said, loosely guiding Jenny by the elbow. "Keep your eyes peeled." They walked through the masses of people to no avail, and then someone called for the crowd's attention.

"Thank you all for coming out tonight." The woman who had handed them the candles spoke first. "As you are all probably aware…" she had to pause due to being choked up. Sniffles and cries from the people in attendance bombarded Jenny's senses, making it difficult for her to remain unaffected.

25

You're here on business, Jenny thought to herself. *Stay strong. Do this for Morgan. She needs you.*

The woman speaking regained her composure and continued. "Morgan's remains were found in an orchard in Trent early yesterday morning." Quiet cries turned into sobs from the crowd. Jenny could hardly stand it. "We can take comfort in knowing she is with the Lord now, free from pain, shining her light down on us…"

Stop listening, start looking. Jenny bowed her head but scanned the crowd with her eyes, tuning out the sounds of mourning that stood to compromise her concentration. She noticed police officers around the perimeter doing the same, obviously looking for suspects as well. Seeing them provided her with an odd feeling of tranquility; she was actually at an advantage over them. At least she knew who she was looking for.

With that break in her uneasiness, Jenny felt a pull. She gently touched Zack's arm, indicating that she wanted him to follow her. She maneuvered through the tearful crowd, feeling disrespectful but knowing that she was being guided by Morgan herself. As she neared the outskirts of the group she felt compelled to look up. What she saw was horrifying.

She turned to Zack with wide eyes, gesturing her head in the direction she had just been looking, prompting him to do the same. After what seemed like an eternity, Zack zeroed in on what Jenny wanted him to see.

"Holy shit," Zack whispered. "He's a cop."

Chapter 4

"No wonder that detective reacted the way he did," Jenny said excitedly as soon as they got into the car. "I was accusing a cop of murder."

"You do realize this is going to make our job about a million times harder," Zack replied. "The police aren't going to want to help us target one of their own. We're going to need some pretty serious evidence if we're going to get them to believe us."

"Yeah, they're definitely not going to want to work with us, that's for sure." Jenny shook her head, wishing she had more control over when she got contacted. "Dammit! This is so frustrating."

"Well, maybe the evidence will lead the cops to him," Zack reasoned. "Just because one cop is crooked doesn't mean the rest are incompetent."

"True, but my concern is that there isn't going to be much evidence. Between the condom and the gloves, there may not be much to link him to the crime. He clearly knew what he was doing."

"Yeah, he's definitely an expert."

"Holy crap," Jenny proclaimed. "He's done this before."

Zack didn't reply, but the look on his face showed he wanted her to elaborate.

"Oh my God, I don't know why I didn't think of this earlier." Jenny turned her body toward Zack. "This can't be his first time. He was too good at it."

"Unless his experience as a cop taught him how not to get caught," Zack countered.

"Don't rain on my parade," Jenny said flatly. "Even if he never killed before, he probably offended before. I don't think people just wake up one morning and decide to murder someone. I imagine there must be some kind of progression."

"So what do we do? Look for similar unsolved crimes in the area?"

"I guess that's a start. We should be able to do that pretty easily from the comfort of home. Thank God for the Internet, huh?"

"No kidding."

Jenny began thinking about the Caldwell case. "But here's something I don't get...how did Morgan go from being asleep in her bedroom to being strangled in an orchard by a cop? Do you think he broke into her house?"

"Doesn't seem likely," Zack reasoned. "You did say something happened on Armistead Lane...maybe Morgan was there when she got accosted."

"But she was asleep in her house," Jenny replied.

"You were a really good kid, weren't you?" Zack surmised. "She was fifteen. She probably snuck out."

Indeed, Jenny had been an ideal child. "On a school night?"

Zack slapped his forehead with his hand, smiling. "Yes, on a school night. It happens."

"Where could she have been going?"

"Now that I don't know," Zack replied. "It might be worth looking into."

Jenny reasoned silently. "Do you think the cops are investigating that angle? That it wasn't a home invasion but rather a kid who snuck out?"

"Hopefully," Zack said. "I would like to think they'd be open to anything."

Jenny contemplated the Caldwell case some more before switching gears in her own head, suddenly feeling inadequate for all of the rebellious acts she'd never done. "Did you ever sneak out of your house as a kid?"

"Once or twice. But I'm reaching the age where I wish I hadn't."

Jenny laughed. "What does that mean?"

"It's just such a stupid thing to do. Look at what happened to Morgan; it just as easily could have been me. I'm beginning to realize

28

I did a lot of stupid shit when I was young—shit that could have gotten me killed. If I ever have kids, I would definitely not want them doing the same crap I did. That's for sure."

"Do you want kids?" Jenny asked.

"Sure," Zack replied. "I don't see why not. Although, I'll have to get a second date with a woman first. I haven't had one of those in a while."

"Technically, it only takes one date."

Zack laughed. "Actually, it doesn't even require a date. But that's not how I want to become a father. So what about you? Do you want kids?"

"Most definitely," Jenny replied, thinking to herself that she wished she'd had them already. "In fact, I believe that's why I married Greg. I hadn't had many boyfriends before him…well, none really to speak of. He came along and seemed interested in me, and my head went straight to weddings and babies. I may have wanted the life more than the guy."

Even though Jenny's confession made her feel almost naked, she viewed Zack's silence as an invitation to continue.

"If I'm going to be completely honest, I think that's why I'm afraid to say I want a divorce." Jenny physically felt the vulnerability growing under her skin; she hoped Zack wouldn't abuse it. "What if I divorce Greg and no other guys come along? What if this is my only chance at having a baby and I blow it?"

"Are you really worried about that?"

Jenny paused. "Well…yeah."

"Well, let me put your mind at ease. I can assure you that if you leave your husband, you won't stay single for very long. In fact, I'd be willing to bet guys will be lining up at your door."

Jenny felt a tingle of excitement grow within her, provided he was speaking the truth. "What makes you think that?"

Zack shrugged, clearly a little embarrassed. "Well, you're just a great girl. You're really easy to talk to. You're nice, funny, attractive…so many women out there are such high-maintenance bitches, but you're very down to earth. You are the kind of woman most guys my age are looking for."

Jenny was grateful for the darkness because it hid her reddened face. "That wasn't true before," she confessed. "I couldn't buy a date when I was younger."

"Well that's because boys are stupid."

Jenny laughed, but Zack added, "No, I'm serious. Twenty year old boys have no idea what they're doing. At all."

Jenny continued to giggle, but she took solace in his words. In the past she had tried to convince herself that notion was true, but she wasn't sure if she had just been fooling herself. To hear a guy actually voice it was very comforting. She also had to admit she was even more excited to hear those words coming from Zack. She couldn't deny her attraction to him, although she couldn't pinpoint why she felt it, either. He was a far cry from marriage material.

Perhaps that was his appeal.

Realizing their conversation was heading down a dangerous path, Jenny decided to bring it back to more innocuous topics. "So what were you doing when you snuck out?"

"That's just it," Zack replied. "Nothing spectacular. I was just sneaking out for the sake of sneaking out." He shook his head. "Stupid."

Jenny thought for a moment. "Do you think that's what Morgan was doing?"

"I wish I knew." Zack flashed a glance at Jenny. "Maybe she can tell you."

"I can't find anything," Jenny told Zack after hours of fruitless Internet searching. "I keep expanding the radius of my search, going further and further out from Braddock, looking for cases similar to Morgan's, but so far I've gotten zero results." She pinned her phone to her ear with her shoulder as she pulled some food out of the pantry. "You?"

"I'm having about as much luck as you are."

"Damn." Jenny closed the pantry door with her foot as she balanced crackers and peanut butter in her hands. "Maybe you were right. Maybe he learned all of his tricks from being a police officer."

"Or he could be new to the area," Zack surmised. "He could have a history, just somewhere else."

Jenny hadn't thought of that. "Boy, you're good."

"Currently I'm looking through recent articles about Braddock's police force, trying to see if there's a picture of him anywhere. I would think they'd put his name in the caption if they had his face in a photo. Unfortunately I haven't found many pictures of anybody. I'm beginning to think there are only a handful of officers that have contact with the press because I keep seeing the same people over and over again."

"That would make sense if you think about it."

"Yeah, I know it does." Zack's voice reflected his frustration. "This would just be so much easier if we had a name to go along with the face."

"I agree." Jenny spread peanut butter on her crackers. "I'll tell you what. You keep doing what you're doing, and I'll expand my search nationally."

"Sure thing, boss."

"Speaking of which," Jenny began, "did you tell your family you quit yet?"

"No, not yet. I'm putting that off as long as possible. It's going to be ugly."

"You might want to tell them so they can replace you."

"Fat chance," Zack remarked. "I'm irreplaceable."

Jenny sat uncomfortably at one end of the loveseat while Greg sat at the other. "How has this week been?" the counselor asked.

"The same," Greg replied.

"Actually," Jenny began, "it wasn't the same. This week was quite different. For me, anyway."

Greg shot a warning glance at Jenny, silently protesting the confession she was about to make. Jenny ignored him. "I received a contact this week."

"A contact?" the counselor asked.

"Yes," Jenny replied matter-of-factly as she pulled some papers out of her purse. "I haven't told you this yet because I realize it makes me sound like a crazy person, but I think you have to know this since it poses a huge problem for our marriage. I'm a psychic, and Greg hates it."

Greg lowered his head into his hand, rubbing his forehead.

Jenny handed the counselor some papers. "Here are our bank statements. As you can see, I've been making some sizeable deposits lately. Those come from Elanor Whitby's estate; Elanor was the founder of Choices magazine, so she was quite wealthy. I recently used my psychic ability to help her solve her boyfriend's murder from sixty years ago, and in return she left me an inheritance. A large one."

The counselor's eyes widened at the statements, but he didn't say anything, so Jenny continued. "That's the best proof I can offer. I hope you believe me, but it's okay if you don't. I realize it's a lot to swallow." Jenny sat back in the couch with her arms folded, satisfied with herself.

"Okay," the counselor began slowly, handing the papers back to Jenny. "So you're working as a psychic. Greg, is it true that you don't like it?"

Greg rubbed his temples slowly, still obviously annoyed that Jenny brought it up. "Now that you mention it, I'm not crazy about it."

"What bothers you about it?"

Greg leaned forward, resting his elbows on his knees. "Well, it made her irresponsible the last time. We're in the middle of a renovation at the house, so there's a lot to do. When she was working on her last…*case*," he made quotes with his hands. "She didn't show up for appointments and she would go running out of the house in the middle of a project because she had a contact. I couldn't count on her for anything, and I don't want to live like that."

"And I contend," Jenny interrupted before the counselor had a chance to respond, "there are plenty of people in this world with jobs who require them to be on call: doctors, detectives, medical examiners…they all get beeped at inconvenient hours. I'm sure their spouses deal with it."

"But I didn't marry a doctor. I married a teacher," Greg pled to the counselor. "A teacher who said she wanted to renovate this house with me, and now she says she doesn't want to. And she quit her teaching job. Now she wants to be a full time psychic, even though she knows I don't like it."

"First of all," Jenny said to Greg, "I didn't choose this. It just happened to me. And secondly, do you know how rare this gift is? You want me to pretend this isn't happening just because you don't like it? *Sorry, Morgan Caldwell, I'm not going to help solve your murder because my husband wants me to help put in hardwood floors.*"

The counselor put his hand up. "Now, let's remain civil, here."

"Sorry," Jenny said to the counselor, bowing her head in apology. "I take that back. But honestly I think there's more to it than what he's saying."

Greg looked skeptically at Jenny. "And what exactly do you think is going on?"

Jenny took a deep breath. "When Greg and I first met, he was an all-star running back for our college football team, and I was an insignificant elementary ed major. He was clearly the star of the show. Now the tables have turned. He's teaching math and is the assistant football coach at Lexington High—two very admirable jobs, but also two very ordinary jobs—and I have psychic ability. Now I'm the interesting one, and I don't think he can stand it."

"That's not it at all," Greg protested angrily.

"Then why do you hate it so much?" Jenny demanded.

"I already told you why."

Jenny silently shook her head, leaning further away from Greg on the couch.

"Okay," the counselor said, "I see this is obviously a huge source of contention. You'll have to see if you can come up with an arrangement that works for both of you."

"I think I should warn you," Jenny began, directing her words at the counselor, "I'm not willing to stop being a psychic. I'm not even willing to slow down."

"Marriage is about compromise," Greg said in a preachy tone. "You need to be willing to give a little."

"Look," Jenny began, "it's not like I want to spend all my time arranging flower baskets. *Lives* are at stake. My most recent contact has been from Morgan Caldwell, whose killer is still out there. How can I ignore that? He may strike again. I can't pretend it's not happening just because you can't handle it."

"I told you before, I can handle it. I just don't like having a wife who treats me like the last priority." Greg shook his head, returning to the same catch phrase as before. "I don't know how this marriage is going to work if you aren't willing to compromise."

"I'm not sure I want this marriage to work," Jenny replied before her brain was able to prevent her from saying it.

An awkward silence fell over the room, so Jenny elaborated, addressing the counselor because it was easier. "I feel like I'm a different person than I was when I met him. I was willing to be a silent sidekick back then, and that's not good enough for me anymore. I want to be my own person, and I feel like Greg is fighting me every step of the way." Jenny shrugged sadly. "I'm not sure I can reach my full potential if I stay married to him. I feel like at this point I have a choice to make: do what's best for him, or do what's best for me. I've spent the past seven years doing what's best for him, but now I need to look out for myself. And I don't think that's a bad thing."

"Is there any way you can do what's best for yourself and still operate within a boundary that Greg will find acceptable?"

Jenny shook her head solemnly. "I don't think so."

The counselor turned toward Greg. "Are you willing to be more accepting of your wife's new profession?"

"Not if it means she's only going to honor half of her promises to me."

The counselor leaned back in his chair. "I think right now you two are heated. After you get home and calm down, I'd like you to think about what you can do that will appease the other person. I'm sure you will be able to come up with some things that will require minimal effort on your part but will mean a lot to your partner."

Jenny folded her arms skeptically.

"Do you guys promise me you will do that?" the counselor asked.

"I promise," Greg said pompously. "Good luck getting her to do the same."

Jenny wanted to scream. Typical Greg—making himself look like a hero while simultaneously throwing her under the bus. The most disgusting part was that she was sure he would put in no such effort. Taking the opposite approach, Jenny decided to be honest in her response. "Oh, I'll do it," she replied. "If I'm not too busy with Morgan Caldwell's case."

Chapter 5

Jenny sighed with frustration as she sat back in her chair. Locally she could find no unsolved cases similar to Morgan Caldwell's; nationally she found too many. She rubbed her eyes which ached from all those hours of staring at the computer. A yawn followed soon after. The clock read seven, which meant she'd been at this for five hours straight. While the work lacked physical exertion, she certainly found it exhausting.

Suddenly she mechanically stood up and headed for her purse. Guided by the pull that was becoming increasingly familiar, she slipped on shoes and walked out the door without so much as a good-bye to Greg. She wasn't sure where she was going, but she knew she needed to maintain her concentration if she was going to get there. A confrontation with Greg stood to jeopardize that.

The car seemed to drive itself the same direction it had when she and Zack attended the vigil. Once inside the town of Braddock, however, she began to take turns that led her to unfamiliar territory. She finally ended up at a small watering hole called Billy's. She knew this was her destination, although she wasn't sure why.

As she got out of her car, she realized she didn't exactly look like a woman who had been planning to go out. Her hair was piled on her head in a sloppy bun, and her clothes were even less fancy than her hair. She pulled out the elastic holding her hair in place, letting her long brown locks fall in loose unruly curls around her shoulders. Using the car window as a mirror she made herself as presentable as possible, which was a far cry from beautiful. Self-conscious but undeterred, she ventured into Billy's, curious about what she would find.

A small crowd of people inhabited the restaurant, but Jenny's eyes immediately focused on the lone, sandy-haired man eating dinner at the bar. There he was, Morgan Caldwell's killer, enjoying a meal like he didn't have a care in the world.

With a quick invigorating breath and a glance toward the sky in a silent homage to Morgan, Jenny sat down a few bar stools down from the killer. She tried desperately to act naturally, although she wasn't sure how successful she could be with her insides doing cartwheels. "Hi," she said to the bartender, louder than she needed to, "May I have a menu please?" She hoped to attract the killer's attention, perhaps inspiring a conversation. A subtle glance in his direction revealed he hadn't even looked up from his plate.

Realizing she didn't exactly look stunning, Jenny accepted the fact that she might need to be the one to initiate a dialog. She had never been any good at flirting, but she couldn't let that stop her. She remembered her old college roommate's tactic whenever she wanted to strike up a conversation with an attractive stranger. *Well,* she thought to herself, *here goes nothing.*

"Excuse me," Jenny said to the killer. He glanced in her direction, and she felt sheer terror as she looked into his piercing eyes again. She wanted to run, but with Morgan as her inspiration she continued. "Is your name Neal by any chance?"

He shook his head and wiped his mouth with his napkin. "No, ma'am. Afraid not."

"Oh, I'm sorry. You just look so much like someone from my hometown. I should have known you weren't him, though. I'm not from around here."

"No, it's no problem," he replied, returning to his meal.

Crap, Jenny thought, *not the conversation starter I was hoping for.* She racked her brain for some other topic of conversation. Desperate, she eyed the menu for a moment before she said, "I've never eaten here before. Is there anything you'd recommend?"

The killer seemed to recognize that her previous remark wasn't a simple case of mistaken identity but rather an attempt at conversation. While she didn't look her best, she was a good ten years younger than this man, which in and of itself was probably flattering to him. His face lit up slightly as he turned his body toward Jenny, making her so nervous she wanted to vomit.

"I've always been a fan of their burgers," he replied.

"Burgers, huh?" she said. "That sounds good. I'll get a burger." With a quick glance at her own finger she realized she was wearing her wedding rings, something she figured she'd better address. "Although, I may be too upset to eat." She slumped her shoulders. "I just had a pretty big fight with my husband."

"Oh, yeah?"

Jenny was becoming increasingly aware of the personality traits of the woman she was portraying: dumb, flirtatious and talkative, which couldn't be more unlike the real Jenny. However, pretending this was an acting job made the task easier to swallow. "Yeah. I swear I don't know why I married that man." She made a dismissive gesture. "But enough about me. Why is a handsome man like yourself eating dinner alone at a bar?"

Dear God Jenny thought, *did I really just say that?*

"I'm too tired to cook," he said. "This is my first night off in a week."

"Wow. What do you do that takes up so much of your time?" The bartender approached at that point, and Jenny ordered a burger and a soda.

"I'm a police officer," he replied. "And we've all been putting in crazy hours lately."

"Is it because of that girl?" Jenny felt Morgan's spirit screaming inside her.

"Sure is. It's the first murder this town has seen in decades. We're not really staffed to handle stuff like this. Everybody has been putting in eighteen hour days."

Jenny's soda arrived. After a quick acknowledgement to the bartender, she said, "You must be exhausted."

"Yeah, I'm going home and going straight to bed after this."

I'm dumb, I'm forward, and I'm attracted to him, Jenny reminded herself. "Your wife must hate all those hours you put in." She spoke in a tone that, hopefully, made it obvious she was fishing.

"My ex-wife," he said with a laugh. "And, yes, she did. That's why she's my ex-wife."

Jenny flashed him a flirty smile that made her feel horribly dirty. She got up from her seat and moved closer to him, extending her hand. "Jenny O'dell," she said. There was no way she was giving him her real name.

"Tom Orlowski," he replied as he shook her hand. Her hand burned where he touched it, but she ignored the pain.

"Well it's a pleasure to meet you, Tom Orlowski." She sat down on the stool next to him. "So you're a cop, huh? That's very exciting."

"It's not always as exciting as it seems. Lots of paperwork."

"Have you been doing it long?"

"About ten years total. I've been here for about a year, and I worked in Connecticut before that."

"Where abouts in Connecticut? I have an aunt that lives in New Haven." That was a complete lie, and she hoped he didn't start asking her questions about geography.

"A town called Ivory Heights. It's pretty small; you've probably never heard of it."

"You're right," Jenny giggled. "I haven't." She leaned her elbow onto the bar. "So are you all getting any closer to figuring out who killed this girl?"

"Well, I can't talk about that. It's an ongoing investigation."

"I understand," Jenny replied, still playing dumb. "Although that isn't very fun." She showed renewed interest. "So what was the biggest case you had in Ivory Heights?"

"Cats in trees," he laughed. "Not much exciting happened up there. Like I said, it was a small town."

"You're starting to ruin my fantasy about police officers," she said playfully.

"It's hit or miss," he replied with a shrug. He popped a french fry into his mouth. "So why are you here by yourself?"

"Like I said, I had a fight with my husband. He pissed me off, and I needed to get out of the house. The thing is, though, we're new here, so I don't know anybody. I didn't really have anywhere to go, so I drove around until I found this place." She looked around, trying to divert attention from herself. "It looks like a cute place. Do you come here a lot?"

"I guess I'm kind of a regular," he said. "I'm friends with the owner."

"Would that be Billy?"

He laughed. "Good guess."

Despite her efforts at diversion, Tom asked a few more questions about her personal life. She managed to come up with a story that was an elusive but believable blend of fact and fiction. After several minutes of listening to Jenny's tale, Tom finished up his meal. "Well," he said as he pulled out his wallet. "It's been nice talking to you. I don't suppose it would do any good to ask for your phone number."

Nerves surged through Jenny, but she managed a flirty smile anyway. "I *am* married...technically. Although I'm not sure for how much longer. I still don't think that would be appropriate, though." She briefly stuck out her lip in a pout but then quickly turned it into a smile. "But if I just *happen* to run into you here again sometime, that would be okay, wouldn't it?"

"I like how you think," he said.

"You said you're kind of a regular here?"

"Yes ma'am."

"Well, I just may have to come back myself." She once again flashed a smile.

Tom paid his bill and got off the stool. He bid her goodbye and placed his hand on her back as he walked past her, bringing on that burning sensation again. Once he left the bar and was safely out of sight, she reached into her purse and pulled out her phone. Aware that the bartender was probably friends with Tom as well, she tried to appear casual, as if she was just texting a friend about nothing of importance. However, her text was directed at Zack, and it read: *The killer's name is Tom Orlowski and he's from Ivory Heights Connecticut. Look it up.*

After a moment her phone chirped. *For real?*

Jenny rolled her eyes. *Yes, for real.*

Her phone vibrated, indicating a call. As she suspected the caller was Zack, but she let it ring. Once the phone stopped buzzing, she texted him with *can't talk. Only text.*

Why? Where are you? You okay?

She smiled at his concern. *I'm fine. JUST LOOK IT UP.*

Jenny finished most of her food even though she was too nervous to have an appetite. She needed to look as inconspicuous as possible to the staff, and she appeared to be successful based on the underwhelming reaction of the employees. After what seemed like an eternity her phone chirped again, and she eagerly read the message.

Two unsolved murders, both girls, ages 15 and 21.

Jenny paid for her meal with cash and walked slowly out the door. Once she exited the building and rounded the corner she immediately dialed Zack. "Holy shit," Jenny exclaimed as soon as he picked up. "Are you kidding me?"

"I wouldn't joke about this."

"How long ago did these murders happen?"

"Three years ago," he said. "They don't know who did them, and nothing has happened since."

Jenny opened her car door. "What happened? Were they strangled?"

"Sure were. They were both plucked off the street and their bodies were found a short time later."

"Dear God," Jenny started her car but then she realized she didn't know where she was. To remain inconspicuous, she pulled out of the parking lot with the intent to only drive around the corner. "Were they together or were they separate incidents?"

"Separate. A few months apart. But that's about all I know. I want to look into this more."

"Are you home? Would it be okay if I swung by and looked with you?"

"My apartment's a mess," he confessed, "but you're welcome to come by."

"Why don't you text me your address? I'll be there as soon as I can, probably about a half an hour."

"Half an hour? Where are you?"

Jenny was a little afraid to admit where she was. "Braddock."

"Braddock? What are you doing there?"

"I was led here."

Zack sighed impatiently. "Is that how you found out his name?"

"Yeah."

"What happened?"

Jenny recounted the story to Zack, who got somewhat angry. "You approached him? Are you crazy? Why didn't you call me?"

"I didn't know I was being led to him until it was too late," Jenny protested. "Besides, we were in a public place, and I didn't give him my real name. I was careful."

"I still don't like it," Zack argued. "At all."

"I'm sorry," Jenny said. "Next time I'll send you a text. Speaking of which, I need you to text me your address so I don't have to just sit here in this parking lot forever."

"Okay. Just give me a minute." A few seconds later Jenny received Zack's address and headed toward his apartment.

"I've done a little more research," Zack said upon Jenny's arrival. She sat next to him on the couch as he thumbed through some papers next to his laptop. His apartment was indeed a mess. "The first murder occurred in July, three years ago. Her name was Allison Pope, and she was fifteen. Apparently her mother was a single mom and was sick as a dog in the middle of the night, so Allison walked to a convenience store about a mile and a half away to get her some medicine. She made it there, but never made it home."

Jenny shook her head.

Zack continued. "They didn't find her body until a few weeks later, and with the heat of summer there had been a lot of decomposition. She was in a wooded area, so animals got at her too. There was little more than a skeleton, and an incomplete one at that. A broken bone in her neck indicated strangulation, but as far as evidence goes, there wasn't a whole lot. At least none that was given to the press. From what I understand, they usually hold out on a few things so they know which confessions have merit."

"I've heard that too," Jenny said.

Zack flipped to another piece of paper. "The second murder happened in early November. Lashonda Williams was driving home from work late at night and got a flat tire. She called her roommate to come get her, but by the time the roommate got there Lashonda was gone. They found her body a few days later in a field. She'd been raped and strangled, but there was apparently no semen left at the scene."

"Because he uses condoms," Jenny said. "We knew that already."

"And what I've found definitely aligns with the fact that our killer was a cop. It would make perfect sense that these girls would willingly get into his car—especially Lashonda. She must have already known about the first murder; I would imagine she would have been pretty careful about who she'd accept a ride from. But a cop…" Zack paused. "You won't get a safer ride than that."

Jenny thought about the fear those girls must have experienced when they realized their savior wasn't what he'd seemed. How long did their terror last? Minutes? Hours? It must have felt like days. The notion caused her to shudder.

Zack's words rescued Jenny from her thoughts. "I've also started looking to see if they had any suspects. So far as I can tell, they can't come up with anyone who may have had a personal vendetta against Allison. She was an honor student who essentially kept to herself. Besides, nobody would have known she was going to be there at that hour, so they've pretty much concluded it had to be random. That means it could have been anybody." Zack looked at Jenny. "I honestly doubt they'd suspect one of their own in a case like that. There'd be way too many other people to consider…for all they knew it could have been someone just driving through."

"Even if they suspected Orlowski, do you think they would have gone public with that?"

"I doubt it. That's probably the kind of thing they'd want to keep quiet unless they were positive."

Jenny didn't say anything, her mind consumed with thought. Zack looked up a few more articles on his computer until he found one he liked. "It says here that they aren't sure the two cases are connected." Interrupting himself, he scrolled up the page. "This article was written shortly after Lashonda was killed." He found his previous spot on the page and continued. "The girls were different ages, different races…one was from Ivory Heights, the other was driving through town on her way home from work. With more than three months between them, they couldn't eliminate the possibility of coincidence, or even copycat."

Jenny grunted but remained otherwise silent.

Zack scanned the words of the article. "Lashonda did have an ex-boyfriend who came under fire. Seems he wanted her back but she wasn't interested. Apparently he couldn't let her go." Zack mumbled as he quickly read through the details, summarizing when he was finished. "The ex was considered a viable suspect when this was written. It seems he didn't have a good alibi for that night. He says he was home alone sleeping."

"It's possible at that hour. Didn't you say it was late at night?"

Zack regarded his notes. "She was a bartender at a night club. She left the bar around 2:30 in the morning."

"I'd be sleeping at that hour."

"But it's possible he was out killing his ex-girlfriend, too." Zack leaned back against the couch. "You got any gut feelings about this one?"

"I don't get *gut feelings* about any of them. I get visions when the victims are inclined to give them to me." She ran her fingers through her hair. "Unfortunately, I doubt I'll get anything from a thousand miles away."

Zack once again turned his attention to the computer, looking up more articles. Jenny curled her legs into her chest and rested her chin on her knee. Zack didn't notice Jenny's distance as she weighed the pros and cons of a plan she was considering. After a few moments, Jenny declared, "I'd like to go there."

Zack removed his focus from the laptop and turned toward Jenny. "Go where? Ivory Heights?"

Jenny nodded. "I think it would be a good idea."

"Do you think you would get good readings there?"

"Possibly," Jenny said. "I'm not sure. But now would be a good time to go. I don't think I'll be able to get many decent readings here…not for the next few days, anyway. There's too much excitement still." She let out a frustrated sigh. "When I was trying to figure out what happened on Armistead Lane, it was like I was trying to tune into a radio station that had too much static. No matter how hard I tried to listen, I couldn't make anything out. I know there was something being communicated, but the crowd gave too much interference. I won't be dealing with that up in Connecticut. I imagine most people have largely forgotten the crimes. Well, maybe not forgotten them, but at least have gone on with their lives. I doubt we'll encounter crowds of people at the crime scenes. If there is any message to be heard, I think I'll have a much better shot at receiving it up there."

"What if there's not?"

Jenny shrugged. "Then we turn around and come home. By the time we get back, hopefully some of the excitement will have died down here and I'll be able to get a better reading."

"Fair enough," Zack said with a smile.

"I'd like to go as soon as possible," Jenny added. "I don't want to waste any time. What's the earliest we can get out of here?"

Zack immediately began searching for flights, and soon his smile turned into a grimace. "There are no flights into Hartford, but there's one into Providence, Rhode Island at five thirty tomorrow morning." He scratched his head. "Damn. That's early."

"Book it," Jenny said decidedly. "That way we can spend the whole day there, and if nothing happens we can come back the day after."

"But we'd have to be up at, like, two thirty in the morning."

Jenny patted his leg. "Then you'd better get to bed. After you pack, of course."

"It's almost ten," Zack noted. "That's, like, four and a half hours of sleep."

"Yup," Jenny said standing up. "So are you going to drive to the airport or am I?"

"Actually, only four hours if you count packing time."

"You know what? I'll drive," Jenny said as she headed toward the door. "You're always late, and I don't want to miss this flight."

"I don't function well if I don't get enough sleep."

"While you're at it, can you book us a hotel in Ivory Heights for tomorrow night? Separate rooms, of course, but adjoining if you can arrange it."

"We'll need to stop for coffee."

Jenny paused just before she reached the door and turned toward Zack. "Are you even listening to me?"

"Flight into Providence, five thirty, you'll pick me up, I'm always late, hotel in Ivory Heights, separate but adjoining rooms."

She looked at the goofy, adorable man on the couch and smiled. "Be ready at three. I'll show up with coffee."

"Black," he replied. "At that hour I'll need it."

Chapter 6

Jenny sat across from Zack in a restaurant just over the Connecticut border as she referred to some notes she had written on the plane. "I was able to figure out where Lashonda Williams worked and where she lived, so I mapped out the route she most likely would have taken home. One of the articles said her car was found on Chamberlain Avenue, which appears to be a pretty major thoroughfare, and it's right along the route I suspected she'd take. When her tire went flat she apparently pulled into a dollar store parking lot where she called her roommate. As you know that's the last anyone heard from her. The roommate showed up and only her car was there. I've got the address of the dollar store already programmed into my phone. I figure it might be helpful to stop by there and see if I can get some kind of reading."

"Wow," Zack replied sipping his coffee. "You accomplished a lot while I was sleeping."

"It wasn't easy with you leaning on my shoulder," Jenny said with a smile, "but I managed. Anyway, I also discovered her boyfriend's name was Michael Boyd, and he apparently still lives in the area. While no charges have been filed, he's been taking some heat in the court of public opinion. It seems the town is divided as to whether or not they think he did it. I'm hoping Lashonda will be able to answer that question for me."

"That would suck if he didn't do it," Zack surmised. "Imagine living in a place where half the people think you're a murderer."

"Well, that's why we're here. We'll hopefully either clear his name or help put him in jail." Jenny tapped her pen on the table and referred to her notes. "I also found out what street Allison Pope lived on and what convenience store she was going to when she vanished. I mapped out her most likely route as well, but if she was on foot she may have taken some short cuts. I'll have to see it for myself when we get there to see if that's likely. But anyway, I'm having a tougher time determining if her family still lives there. I looked up the ownership history the house she lived in at the time of her disappearance, and her mother never owned it. She must have been renting, and I don't know if she still is or not. I'm not even sure how I'd find that out, other than knocking on the door."

At that point their food arrived. "Excellent," Zack said to the waitress. "Thank you." He turned his attention to Jenny. "You sure are thorough at five thirty in the morning."

"I have to be," Jenny said, spreading her napkin across her lap. "I feel like the clock's ticking. I don't know how long it will be before Orlowski strikes again. I can't stand the thought of someone else getting attacked because I couldn't work quickly enough. If I didn't have to sleep at all I wouldn't."

"Don't do that to yourself," Zack said. "You're doing the best you can, and that's all anyone can ask. Besides, if that sick bastard does strike again, nobody in the world is going to blame you for it."

"I will." Jenny poked at her scrambled eggs with her fork. "I'll always feel like there was something more I could have done."

"You went to the police, said *this is the man who did it,* and they laughed at you. If anyone dropped the ball it's them."

Jenny shrugged but didn't answer.

In an obvious attempt to change the subject, Zack posed, "So how did your husband take it when you told him you were coming here?"

Jenny made a guilty face. "I didn't tell him. I left a note."

"That sounds like something I would do," Zack took a big bite of pancake.

"It wasn't cowardice…necessarily," she argued with a giggle. "It was consideration. He was asleep when I got home, and he was still asleep when I left. I didn't want to wake him."

"Has he tried calling you?"

Jenny checked her phone. "Nope."

After an awkward silence, Zack said, "Forgive me if I'm overstepping my bounds, here." Jenny felt her blood run cold. "But I think you can do better than him. I know I've never met the guy, but from what I've seen and what you've said, I'm not impressed."

Jenny hung her head. "I'm not either." She took another drink of her coffee and said with renewed vigor, "So…where do you think we should start looking today?" Greg was not a topic she felt like discussing.

"At the police station."

"The police station? What do you think we will find there?"

"No. Not find. Show. You should go to the police, show them your picture of Orlowski, and tell them your story. For all we know he may already be a suspect. And if he isn't, I think these folks would find it very interesting that the murders followed him from Ivory Heights to Braddock."

Jenny snorted. "I'm not sure I'm ready for ridicule again. I guess I was hoping to find out something more concrete before I went to the police."

"What's more concrete than Morgan Caldwell?"

Sadness crept into Jenny's bones. "Nothing."

With Zack a step behind, Jenny approached the desk at the Ivory Heights police department. "Hi," she began apprehensively, "I'd like to speak to someone about the Allison Pope and Lashonda Williams cases. I may have some information."

The young officer behind the desk got very wide eyes. "Hang on a second," he said, disappearing through a door. After a moment he returned with a slightly overweight, gray-haired police officer who seemed much more sure of himself.

"Danny Fazzino," the older gentleman said, extending his hand.

"I'm Jenny Watkins, and this is my friend Zack Larrabee." Typical pleasantries followed.

"Please, come on back with me," Officer Fazzino said as he opened the door he'd emerged from. "I'll take your statements."

Jenny and Zack silently followed Officer Fazzino into a small room, presumably designed for confessions. The officer took a seat on one side of a table, gesturing for Zack and Jenny to sit on the other.

47

He wrote their names on paper, adding, "Do you mind if I record this interview?"

"Not at all," Jenny replied.

The officer pressed a button on a recording device and stated the date and Zack and Jenny's names. Then he said, "So what information do you have for me?"

Jenny let out a sigh. "I have the feeling I may know who killed Allison Pope. And maybe even Lashonda Williams."

"And who do you suspect it was?"

Another sigh. "You may not want to hear this, but I believe it was Tom Orlowski. He used to be a police officer from Ivory Heights."

"Yeah, I know who he is," Officer Fazzino replied, eyeing Jenny suspiciously. "What makes you think he did it?"

Zack interrupted before Jenny had a chance to respond. "I can answer this one." Jenny glanced over at Zack, and he smiled at her reassuringly. "She's probably too modest to say so, but she's a psychic. A good one. A few days ago she had a vision back in Georgia of a young woman being strangled. This was before she even knew anybody was missing. Come to find out a fifteen year old had been abducted and murdered a few towns over."

Officer Fazzino's face grew more serious.

Zack continued. "She painted the image of the man from her vision." He turned to Jenny. "Show him the picture." Jenny pulled the folded up picture out of her purse and showed it to the officer. "We found out later he was a cop in the same town as the murdered girl. We then determined he previously worked here, where two other girls had been murdered in a similar fashion. Now maybe that's just a coincidence, but I think it's worth looking into."

Officer Fazzino stared silently at the picture for what seemed like an eternity, his emotionless face giving Jenny no indication of what he was thinking. She wrung her fingers under the table, bracing herself for the same reaction she'd received in Braddock. Instead Officer Fazzino just slid the picture back to Jenny and said, "So what happened in Georgia?"

"They're still trying to figure that out," Jenny said. "The last time Morgan Caldwell was seen, she was tucked safely in her own bed. In the morning she wasn't there, and her body was found in a remote orchard a few days later."

Officer Fazzino remained silent once more, rubbing his chin with his hand, staring blankly at the desk. "It does sound familiar," he eventually whispered, the wheels obviously turning in his head. "It's like these girls just vanish into thin air."

Zack added, "It would make sense that the girls are being abducted by a police officer. Someone they trusted. These girls may have willingly gotten into his car, never realizing he had bad intentions."

At that point Officer Fazzino turned off the recording device, causing Jenny to wonder if Zack had just taken things too far. The officer looked Jenny square in the eye and then did the same with Zack. "Off the record," he began, "I've got to say...something never did sit right with me about that Orlowski kid. Don't get me wrong...All the young guns are overzealous. The rookies always come onto the force ready to take on the world...But Orlowski..." Officer Fazzino shook his head. "He was just a little too eager to use force, you know? He was the kind of kid who'd kick down an unlocked door. I was always afraid he'd end up shooting somebody." He let out a sigh. "I know we're not supposed to say stuff like this about one of our brothers, but it wouldn't surprise me if he did do it. He just had such an obsession with violence."

The officer looked sad.

In an attempt to distract Fazzino from his sorrow, Jenny spoke delicately. "I was planning on retracing the girls' footsteps today, seeing if I can get any sense of what may have happened to them. I can let you know if I get any more insight."

"Yeah, that'd be great." Fazzino shook his head and muttered, "I can't believe I'm pairing up with a psychic." The potential harshness of his statement dawned on him, and he quickly held up his hand and added, "No offense."

Jenny smiled. "None taken."

"It's just the other guys on the force would think I've lost it if they knew. But at this point I'm desperate. I'm willing to try anything. The people in this town want answers, and I haven't been able to provide them with any."

"Well," Jenny said assuredly, "Maybe the girls themselves will provide the answers."

Officer Fazzino smiled widely. "Nothing would make me happier."

Zack drove as Jenny's phone squawked the directions to the dollar store where Lashonda's car had been found. As the pair pulled onto Chamberlain Avenue, Jenny noted, "This isn't as much of a main thoroughfare as I thought it would be."

"It's a small town," Zack added. "The main drag won't necessarily be all that busy."

It made more sense to Jenny how an abduction could have taken place along this road without anyone noticing, especially at that hour. There was only one lane in each direction, and cars were sparse, even at mid-morning. Jenny surmised it must have been nearly deserted in the middle of the night.

Soon they approached the store and pulled into the lot. Zack parked in the space closest to the road, assuming that's where Lashonda would have parked with a flat tire. He put the car into park and declared, "Well, this is it."

Jenny stayed silent, which Zack respected. Her nerves tingled with anticipation, which she knew was detrimental to receiving a reading, so she did her best to relax. Soon she found herself getting out of the car and walking a few steps toward the building. Wordlessly Zack followed her lead, emerging from the car but keeping his distance.

"Here," Jenny said. "It happened here."

Zack didn't reply.

Jenny closed her eyes, furrowing her brow. "I feel fear."

Zack hung his head as Jenny continued to receive the message. She stayed quiet for a long time, focusing her attention on the image in her mind. "I see a ring," she added. "A diamond one." She squinted, shaking her head slightly, as she struggled to make sense of what she was seeing. "And there's something about a cell phone." After a moment she opened her eyes and added, "That's all I can get."

Zack rested his elbow on the open door of the car. "A diamond ring? Do you think Michael Boyd proposed to her that night?"

Jenny approached the car again. "In a dollar store parking lot? I wouldn't think so."

"Remember…they weren't dating. Maybe she wouldn't take his calls or visits. But if he was following her that night, she would have had no choice but to listen to him if she was stuck here with a flat tire."

Jenny shrugged. "Could be." She was distracted by a subtle tug that was beginning to stir inside her.

Unaware of Jenny's feeling, Zack continued. "The cell phone is a good point. These were all young women that went missing. I would think they'd have their cell phones with them. Why didn't they call people when they realized they were in trouble?"

"Give me the keys," Jenny said.

"What?"

Jenny walked around the car, holding out her hand. "Give me the keys."

Zack obliged, quickly running to the other side of the car and taking the passenger seat. Without a word Jenny turned the key and the two headed in an unknown direction. She turned down a series of side roads which were sparsely populated with modest old houses and generously sized yards. Eventually she stopped the car in front of a small white house with a large shed situated off to the side. She put the car in park and said, "This is it."

"Why are we here?" Zack posed.

"I'm not sure," Jenny admitted. "But this is definitely the place I was supposed to go to."

Zack looked out the window. "The house or the shed?"

Jenny silently shook her head as she climbed out of the car. She walked a few feet into the expansive yard with her hand on her chin. After a moment she informed an approaching Zack, "The shed."

"That shed's just about as big as the house," he noted. "You could live in that thing."

She stared at the run-down white structure, hoping to gain some insight, noting the wood piled against the shed's side and the old vehicles parked in front of it. Despite the sense of familiarity that undeniably nagged at her, she couldn't pinpoint exactly why she had been led to this place.

During Jenny's deliberation Zack had begun investigating the mailbox. "The name on the box says Hawkins," he noted. "Have you heard that name before?"

Zack's voice pulled Jenny back into the present. "Never."

Zack began typing the address in his cell phone. "Maybe we should give this information to Fazzino. It might mean something to him."

"Good idea," Jenny said as she pulled out her phone. "I'll do that right now."

"Fazzino."

"Hi, Officer Fazzino, it's Jenny Watkins."

"Hello Miss Watkins. Do you have anything for me?"

"Kind of," Jenny said. "I went to the dollar store where Lashonda's car was found, and I got a vision of a ring and something about a cell phone, although I'm not sure what it all means."

"Well," Fazzino replied. "We already know about the ring. Lashonda always wore her grandmother's ring, everywhere she went. When her body was found, the ring was missing. We put out BOLOs all over the place...oh, sorry, that means *be on the lookout*... We made flyers, put pictures of it on the news, made pawn shop owners aware of it...everything. We figured if we could find that ring, we'd have our killer. Unfortunately it didn't get us anywhere."

Jenny felt a twinge of disappointment, but she continued. "Do you know anything about the cell phone?"

"Her cell phone was found a few hours after her body during a grid search. It didn't give us any additional information. No fingerprints, no mysterious calls. Her last call was a brief one to her roommate, which we already knew about."

Wondering why she'd had these visions if they were of no use, Jenny felt a bit of reluctance to divulge the last detail, fearing it would be worthless as well. With a courage-gathering breath, she mentioned the Hawkins house. Officer Fazzino sounded as if he was jotting down the information when he replied, "That name's never come up in the investigation."

Jenny ran her fingers through her hair, feeling like a fraud. "I guess I'm oh-for-three then."

"Keep trying," Fazzino said kindly. "You might come up with something."

"Hopefully," Jenny replied. She looked as Zack as she added, "Maybe I'll get something a little more concrete from Allison."

52

Chapter 7

Zack and Jenny got out of the car in front of the house where Allison Pope had lived at the time of her disappearance. Jenny looked at the building, which appeared to have once been a single large house but over time became divided into two separate residences. She zipped up her jacket as she examined the place, taking a moment to see if she'd get any kind of reading, but she didn't feel anything. Stuffing her hands into her pockets, she turned to Zack and asked, "You ready?"

"Sure," he said. "Do you think it's okay to leave the car here?" He looked at the narrow, nearly deserted street, noting his rental car was the only vehicle along the side of the road.

"I'm not sure where else we would leave it," she replied. With a shrug she added, "Worst comes to worst we get a ticket."

"It must be nice to be made of money," Zack noted.

Jenny couldn't help but laugh. "I guess I'm getting used to my financial freedom. If I become a bitch let me know."

They started walking in the direction Allison would have headed to get to the convenience store. "I don't think you're capable of being a bitch," Zack noted.

"My husband would disagree with you."

"Your husband is an idiot."

Jenny bit her lip to stifle the smile brewing inside of her, although the conversation was heading in a direction she wasn't comfortable with. "I don't really want to talk about my husband."

With a nudge of her elbow, Jenny playfully demanded, "Instead, why don't you tell me a little bit about yourself?"

"Well, you already know I'm lazy, irresponsible, and incredibly handsome. What more do you need to know?"

"Dear God," Jenny said with laughter she couldn't suppress. "Tell me about your family."

"Well, both of my parents are still alive, and I've got a brother and a sister."

"That's right," Jenny said. "Your sister made those really good cookies in the model home."

"You remembered! She makes a damn good cookie, doesn't she?"

"Hell yeah she does."

"Her name is Donna. She's married with a couple of kids, and baking is her hobby. It's funny; she loves to bake, but then she always gives away the stuff she makes because she doesn't want the calories in her house. That's just fine with me, mind you. I'm always willing to help her out like that."

"You're a good brother."

"I know, right? The sacrifices I make for my family. Geesh." Zack giggled goofily.

"Is your sister older or younger?"

"Older. My sister is four years older than me, and my brother is right between us. I'm the baby of the bunch."

"What's your brother like?"

"Okay, picture me. Then picture the exact opposite. That's Tim."

"So he's energetic, responsible and ugly?"

Zack laughed. "Precisely."

"No, seriously, what's he like?"

Zack twisted his face, admitting with disgust, "He's just so *gung-ho*. When he was a teenager he couldn't wait to join the family business. He was usually the first one at the construction site and the last one to leave. Everything had to be perfect. If something wasn't done right, he would insist on doing the whole thing over again. Not me. I was often late to work, and as long as the house looked kind of square I was happy. Honestly, I never really did give a shit about the family business. It was never something I wanted to do."

"There's nothing wrong with wanting to do your own thing."

"Tell that to my father. He adores my brother, and he thinks I'm nothing more than a big, giant fuck up. And maybe I am." Zack shrugged. "All I know is I just want to be happy, and working twelve hours a day at a job I hate isn't my definition of happiness. I don't care if it would get me a lot of money. I'd rather live in my shitty little apartment and do something I like than live in a big house and work that job."

"We need to turn right up here," Jenny interrupted, pointing to the street they were quickly approaching. Zack didn't reply, nor did he continue with his story. While she was confused at first, Jenny laughed when she realized why Zack was being quiet. "I'm not getting a reading. I know we need to turn here because that's what the map said."

Zack, too, joined in the laughter. "I thought you were being led."

"Nope. Not this time." As they rounded the corner, Jenny looked down at her feet as she confessed, "If it makes you feel any better, I know how much it sucks when you feel like you pale in comparison to your siblings."

"The only way you would know that is if your inadequate sibling told you what it feels like."

With a roll of her eyes, Jenny replied, "No, silly, *I'm* the inadequate sibling."

"I don't believe that for a minute."

"Oh, believe it," Jenny replied emphatically.

"How could you have possibly disappointed your parents? You're, like, the perfect person."

"I was born a girl," she said. "And girls can't play professional baseball."

"So that's really what you did wrong? You were born a girl?"

"Well, it wasn't *wrong*. My father never came out and told me that he wished I was a boy. It was just painfully obvious that I didn't measure up to my brothers. His bond with them was clearly a lot stronger than it was with me."

Zack kicked a small rock as they walked. "I guess we're just a couple of fuck ups then, huh?"

"Yup," Jenny said. "A couple of crime-fighting fuck ups."

Zack laughed. "You make us sound like super heroes." He put his arm around her shoulder in a brotherly kind of way, pulling her in and giving a squeeze. "Well, hopefully I can make you feel better. If you want to see what a fuck up really looks like," he pointed to himself with his free thumb, "I'm your guy."

"You have a lower opinion of yourself than anyone I have ever met in my whole life," Jenny noted. "And yet you seem almost proud of it."

"Well, I've always said that *fuck up* is in the eye of the beholder."

"How profound."

"Isn't it?" Zack bragged. "I'm a profound kind of guy. But if you think about it, there's an element of truth to it. If you had asked Einstein's teacher, he would have said old Albert was a fuck up. He failed out of school, you know."

"That's a myth," Jenny said.

"It is totally not a myth."

"I'm a teacher...well, I *was* a teacher. And it was commonly known among us teachers that Einstein didn't flunk out of school, but he did fail a college entrance exam, which he was trying to take several years early." She smiled at him with a glance out of the corner of her eye.

Zack removed his arm from around Jenny's shoulder and complained, "You just bastardized my hero."

"Sorry, but you were operating under false pretenses."

"I was happy in my world of ignorance, thank you very much. But as much as I am *not* enjoying this conversation, aren't we supposed to be getting a feel for what may have happened to Allison?"

Jenny smiled. "Good point."

"Have you gotten any feelings yet?"

"No, but I haven't really been trying to. I actually wanted to walk from the house to the convenience store to see if there are any viable short cuts. Remember she didn't encounter trouble on the *way* to the store; she got abducted on the way home. I want to know what her most likely route home was, and when we follow those footsteps back I will focus on trying to get a reading."

"It doesn't look like there are any places she would have cut through. It's all houses."

"I think you're right. I guess she just took the road the whole time, which would make sense if Orlowski was going to stumble across her." Jenny pointed as they encountered an intersection. "We need to take a left."

As they rounded the corner, the convenience store became visible in the distance. "Is that what we're looking for?" Zack asked.

"Sure is. I'll want to hang out in there a while. Maybe you should buy something while we're there so we don't look like we're shoplifting."

"I'll have to put that on my expense account," Zack replied.

"Buy gum."

Jenny slowly wandered around the store while Zack picked up various magazines, nonchalantly thumbing through them and returning them to the rack. Jenny lingered by the medication aisle knowing Allison must have spent some time there, but she was unable to get any kind of reading. After several minutes of futile effort, Jenny approached Zack and spoke loudly enough for the cashier to hear. "Are you ready yet? You're taking forever."

Zack selected an automotive magazine and brought it to the register. After a quick transaction, the pair left the store. "Did you get anything?" Zack asked as soon as the door closed behind them.

"Nope. Nothing," Jenny confessed. "Hopefully we'll have better luck on the way back to the car."

The air felt chillier after the warmth of the convenience store, so Jenny zipped her jacket up a little higher and pulled her hood over her head. Zack remained quiet as they walked down the road, and Jenny made every effort to keep her mind free of thought. At one point she closed her eyes, loosely holding on to Zack's arm to guide her. Before she knew it they had arrived back at the car, and Zack posed, "Anything?"

Jenny's disappointment was obvious as she shook her head. "Nothing."

"Wow, that's a shame," Zack noted.

"Actually, it might not be."

"What do you mean?"

"Well, it's a bad thing for us, but I think it might mean something good for Allison." Jenny raised her eyes to look directly at Zack. "I think Allison may have crossed over."

Chapter 8

Jenny and Zack once again sat across the desk from Officer Fazzino. "I'd like to talk to Allison Pope's mother if she'll allow it," Jenny explained. "I can't offer her any information about her daughter's killer, but I do have an observation that might bring her some comfort."

"I'll give her a call," Fazzino said. "She'll probably be happy to hear there's some renewed interest in this case." He looked solemn. "I think she's becoming convinced it'll never get solved."

He picked up the receiver of the landline on the side of the desk. He dialed the number, which Jenny noted he knew by heart. "Hi, Natalie, Danny Fazzino…No, not quite. But I do have a woman here from Georgia who would like to talk to you. She says she's a psychic."

Jenny didn't like the phrase *she says.*

The officer continued. "Okay, thanks Natalie. We'll be there in a bit." He hung up the phone and stated the obvious. "She says she's willing to see you."

"Does she happen to still live in the same house that she did at the time of the kidnapping?"

"No," Fazzino said. "She moved a couple of years ago. She got remarried, and she lives in a bigger house on the other side of town."

Jenny didn't respond, but she thought of what a disadvantage that would be if she had been wrong about Allison crossing over. Perhaps a few quiet moments in Allison's old bedroom would have inspired the contact that had previously eluded her. Silence in her bedroom would have been equally as telling; it would have been evidence that Jenny's suspicions about crossing over were correct.

Fazzino continued, unaware of Jenny's thought process. "Why don't you two follow me there? I'd like to be there for this."

Natalie Easton opened the door and greeted her visitors with an expressionless face and tired eyes. "Hi Danny," she said without acknowledging Jenny and Zack.

"Hello Natalie," Fazzino replied.

"Come in," she recited mechanically. "You can take a seat in the living room."

Jenny crossed the room, immediately noticing two framed photographs above the fireplace, accentuated by candles on the mantle beneath. One picture featured a woman in her thirties that Jenny had never seen before, the other was a teenage girl Jenny recognized to be Allison from the pictures in the newspapers. Allison appeared much more alive in the large color picture than she had in the small black-and-white clippings. Jenny felt saddened by the image, knowing that the girl who posed for that picture was painfully unaware of the short amount of time she had left on this earth. *This should be just another picture in the house,* Jenny thought, *not the subject of a memorial.*

Upon Natalie's urging Jenny sat down, albeit uncomfortably, next to Zack on a floral loveseat. Natalie was not nearly as welcoming as Jenny had anticipated, appearing exhausted and skeptical rather than intrigued. Her demeanor reminded Jenny of the unpleasant officer she had originally encountered back in Braddock, invoking an uneasiness that made Jenny want to run away. *Your presence reminds this woman that she lost her child,* Jenny told herself. *What do you expect? Smiles and pleasantries?*

Jenny desperately hoped what she had to say would bring this woman some relief from the agony she clearly still endured.

Fazzino broke the painful silence. "Natalie, this young woman is Jenny Watkins and her friend is Zack Larrabee. Jenny is a psychic from Georgia here to work on Allison's case. She says there's been a similar crime down in her home town and she thinks the two might be related."

Natalie glanced skeptically at Jenny. "What makes you think my daughter's murder is related to a case in *Georgia*?"

Jenny swallowed. "I believe I may know who the perpetrator is down there, and he used to live here."

Natalie sat back in her chair and crossed both her legs and arms. "And just how do you know who the perpetrator is there?"

With a hint of shame, Jenny admitted, "I saw it in a vision."

Rubbing her eyes, Natalie let out a sigh.

"I know how it sounds," Zack chimed in. "But she has solved cases in the past; she's a legitimate psychic. And she saw the face of the murderer in a vision before she even knew there was a murder."

"So who do you think it was?" Natalie asked distrustfully.

Jenny glanced at Fazzino, wondering if she should disclose that she suspected it was a police officer. Fazzino had clearly been on the same page; he replied, "A stranger. We can't disclose his name quite yet, but she believes these were random crimes of opportunity."

"Didn't we know that already?" Natalie snapped.

The tension was palpable. Feeling remarkably uncomfortable, Jenny spoke softly. "I have come up here to see if I can prove the man who committed the Georgia murder...the man *I believe* committed the Georgia murder...also committed the crime against Allison and possibly Lashonda. I do feel like Lashonda tried to send me a message earlier today when I went to the dollar store parking lot. However, I haven't been able to get anything from Allison all day."

Natalie ran her fingers through her hair and drew in a deep breath. She was clearly struggling to understand the point of the visit, and her patience was running out.

Fearing she was going to be asked to leave, Jenny got straight to the point. "Mrs. Easton, I believe Allison has crossed over."

"Crossed over?"

"Yes ma'am." Gathering a breath Jenny added, "I have learned that spirits linger when they're feeling unrest of some kind, or if they feel like they have some unfinished business. I know Lashonda's spirit lingers because she was trying to send me a message earlier. Unfortunately I haven't been able to make much sense of her contact, but I'm working on that. But Allison...I haven't been able to get anything from Allison at all. That's what I mean when I say I think she's crossed over. I don't believe she is still here. I think she was able to make peace with what happened to her and she's moved on."

Tears began to fill Natalie's eyes. "Allison is with the Lord," she said with resolve. "I'm sure of that."

Jenny smiled compassionately and whispered, "I agree with you."

Clasping her hands, Natalie cleared her throat and began, "What you said...about Allison being at peace with what happened to her. It wouldn't surprise me. Allison was always such an easy going child. She rolled with the punches better than anyone I knew." An expression of both overwhelming love and sadness appeared on Natalie's face. "I always admired her for that. It figures she wouldn't hold a grudge against the man who did this to her." She shook her head. "That would be just like her."

"If it makes you feel any better," Jenny added, "from what I understand you'll get to see her again. Once you cross over, you get to reunite with all the loved ones who've gone before you."

"Oh, I believe that," Natalie said emphatically. "I realize not everyone does, but I do. Actually..." Natalie looked shamefully at her lap, "I used to be one of those people who didn't believe it. I used to think that once you died that was it. It was over. But if I'm going to wake up every morning, put my feet on the floor and go about my day, I *have to* believe I will see Allison again. Otherwise there's no way I could function."

"I'm glad you have that faith," Jenny whispered.

Natalie nodded. "I need my faith. And I have discovered that the Lord does indeed work in mysterious ways. I started going to church shortly after I lost Allison, and when I first started going they talked a lot about God's plan. I really didn't understand it at the time. Did God really plan for Allison to die so young? And so horribly? I couldn't buy into that. But just as I was ready to throw in the towel and stop going to church, I met Craig there. He has truly been a life saver. I can't imagine how lost I would be without him."

Sensing Natalie's need to vent, Jenny stayed quiet. "Craig had lost his wife in a car accident the year before." Natalie raised her eyes to the picture above the mantle. "She was only thirty two. So young. And poor Craig found himself in the unenviable position of having to raise his daughter by himself while coping with the loss of his wife.

"But when we met, we hit it off right away. Our personalities clicked, and our lives complemented each other nicely. We were like two broken puzzle pieces that happened to fit. We were both alone, and while he had a daughter who needed a mother, I was a mother who needed a daughter." With another loving glance up at the pictures on the wall, Natalie added, "I like to think that Sherry is looking out for Allison up in heaven, just like I'm looking out for her Savannah here on earth. We couldn't raise our own daughters, but God made sure we crossed paths so we could raise each other's."

"Are you out of your mind?" Jenny asked.

Chapter 9

The glares of the other three people in the room made Jenny aware that an explanation was necessary. "That's what I just heard in my head. *Are you out of your mind?*"

Jenny closed her eyes and held up her hand, signaling to the others to remain quiet and allow her to receive the message. "I'm seeing a boat," she said, squinting as if to try to get a better view of the image inside her own mind. "A small boat, like a row boat or a canoe or something. And I see a couple in the boat. It looks like the man is proposing to the woman." She remained silent as she made sense of the vision. "The spirit watching this is not happy about the engagement. The spirit is screaming, *Are you out of your mind?*

"It's desperate to communicate," Jenny went on. "It's frantically trying to tell the person in the boat that this is a bad idea." She shook her head. "I'm thinking rain. The spirit generated some rain to try to get the message across." Jenny struggled to process more, but the contact was gone. She opened her eyes and posed, "Does that make sense to anyone?"

"Me," Fazzino said, white as a sheet. All eyes in the room turned to the officer. "I was the man in the boat." He wiped his face with his hand. "And the spirit was my brother."

"My brother Jimmy was four years older than me," Fazzino began somberly, "And he kept me out of trouble, or at least he tried to." With a chuckle he added, "I probably shouldn't admit this being a

63

cop and all, but I was always up to something as a kid. And whenever I did anything stupid, my brother would say, *Are you out of your mind?*" Fazzino's slight New York accent became much thicker as he quoted his brother.

He shook his head and blinked back tears when he recalled, "Jimmy had epilepsy. For the most part he had it under control, but every once in a while he'd have a seizure. One day he went swimming by himself in my cousin's pool, and he apparently had a seizure while he was in the water. My aunt found him floating face down when she got home from work. He was twenty one years old."

Jenny's heart ached as she saw the pain on Fazzino's face. *Why is it always the young ones?* She thought.

"My entire life changed after that," he admitted. "I couldn't figure out why God took him and not me. He had always been the good one; if either one of us deserved to live it was him. But that's not how it happened." Fazzino hung his head but was able to quickly gather his composure. "After that I decided I needed to live right. I needed to be the man my brother never got to be. He's the reason I became a cop, you know. He always kept an eye out for me, making sure I did the right thing. I wanted to do the same thing for other people, so I joined the force. I figured it was the best way I could honor my brother."

The silence in the room was deafening. Jenny's eyes shifted over to Natalie, whose entire demeanor had changed. The skepticism and sadness had left her face, replaced by awe as she listened to Fazzino's confession. Jenny was hopeful that she had just gained credibility in Natalie's eyes.

Fazzino went on. "That girl in the boat was my first wife Mary. At the time I thought she was the greatest thing on the face of the earth, but it turns out my brother was right about her. I don't know how many times she cheated on me, and then she left and took half my money with her. Bitch." Suddenly aware of his surroundings, Fazzino raised his hand and said, "Sorry. Habit."

For the first time since they'd arrived, Natalie cracked a smile.

"But I remember that rain," Fazzino whispered. "We were out there in the middle of a lake, and it was a beautiful sunny day, but right after I proposed to her this freak shower came out of nowhere. Mary and I laughed because we thought it was a sign." Sadness filled his eyes. "And it was a sign; it was just telling us the opposite of what we believed. My God, I can't believe that was Jimmy." A tear leaked down his cheek. "He was still looking out for me, even though he was gone."

Another intense silence followed, which was broken by Natalie's gentle question. "Why do you think your brother's spirit lingers?"

"To watch after me," Fazzino said without a moment's hesitation. "It's got to be."

Natalie looked over at Jenny for validation, but Jenny had no answer, responding only with a subtle shrug and shake of the head.

"Wow," Fazzino cleared his throat. "This is intense. I'm sorry, but I think I need to go outside and get a little fresh air. I hope you don't mind."

"Not at all," Natalie said. "Let me get you a glass of water."

"That'd be great," Fazzino said as he stood up and walked shakily out the front door. Natalie quickly left the room in the direction of the kitchen.

"Nice work," Zack said to Jenny once they were alone. "Although the timing was a little rough."

"I didn't do it," Jenny replied. "All of the credit…and blame… needs to go to Jimmy."

"I've got to admit, this whole thing still fascinates me," Zack said. "What view did you have when you saw the people in the boat? Were you in the boat with them?"

"It was from above, like I was looking down at them."

"Could you hear them talking?"

"Not this time," Jenny said. "But sometimes I can. It's kind of like remembering dreams. Sometimes you can remember every detail, and sometimes you can only recall little snippets. This time it was just that one snapshot of the people in the boat."

"Incredible," Zack said.

"Unfortunately with Lashonda I'm only getting little feels for things. She wanted me to know something about a ring, something about a cell phone, and something about the Hawkins property, but I don't know exactly what."

At that point Natalie walked back into the room and sat down in the same seat as before. She looked fifteen years younger than the woman who had greeted them at the door.

"I want to apologize to you, Jenny," she began. "I know I wasn't exactly welcoming when you first got here. I have to admit I was very skeptical about you until I saw what just happened. That was amazing. You apparently hit the nail on the head. You should see Danny…he's really shaken up out there."

Jenny made a face.

"No, don't feel bad," Natalie said. "I think once the shock wears off he'll be delighted to know his brother is still in his life." She leaned forward and placed her elbows on her knees. "But what you're telling me about Allison…you're saying she has moved on?"

"I believe so."

"And that means she's at peace?"

"Yes ma'am."

"And I will see her again?"

"Yes ma'am."

Natalie sat straighter and took in a deep breath. She closed her eyes and placed her hand on her heart, pausing for a moment before snapping back into the present. "So what happened down in Georgia?"

"A fifteen year old girl named Morgan Caldwell was last seen in her own bed, and her body was found a few days later in an orchard. She'd been raped and strangled."

"Dear God," Natalie said shaking her head. "That's absolutely horrible. But what makes you think that case is related to Allison's?"

"Because Orlowski used to live here," Jenny blurted. Realizing what she had done, she bit her lip in an attempt to suck the words back in, hoping her comment would fly under the radar.

It didn't.

"Orlowski?" Natalie asked. "Orlowski," she repeated with a whisper, clearly trying to remember where she'd heard that name before. Suddenly her expression changed as the recollection hit. "You mean *Officer Orlowski?*"

Jenny winced and nodded slightly.

"I don't believe it. He worked on Allison's case. He was a good man." She looked up at Jenny. "You honestly think he did this?"

With a sigh Jenny confessed, "I don't know if he killed Allison or Lashonda, but I'm pretty sure he killed Morgan Caldwell."

"What makes you so sure?"

"Because I watched it happen."

Natalie's eyes were wide as saucers. "Did you actually watch it happen, or did you watch it in the same way you just watched Danny propose to his ex-wife?"

"The same way I just saw Officer Fazzino propose. It was in a vision. I got a very clear look at who killed Morgan because I saw the crime happen through her eyes." Jenny's voice softened. "It was as if he was strangling *me*."

At that moment Officer Fazzino walked in, and Natalie immediately announced, "Danny, she thinks it was Orlowski."

Officer Fazzino looked at Jenny in disbelief. "You told her?"

Natalie jumped in before Jenny could speak. "She didn't say this guy killed Allison, but she did say she saw him kill that girl in Georgia."

Looking defeated Fazzino said, "Yes, she does claim to have seen him murder that girl."

"Do you believe her?" Natalie demanded.

Fazzino stayed quiet for what seemed like an eternity. He looked at each person in the room, one at a time, his expression giving no indication of the answer. Finally, in a monotonous tone, he replied, "I believe it's worth looking into."

Fazzino's uninspired response had an apparent effect on Natalie. She took several breaths and spoke out loud, although it appeared she was talking mostly to herself. "You're right. I can't allow myself to get excited over this. I've gotten excited over too many leads in the past, and they all turned out to be dead ends. I have to assume that this guy didn't do it unless you can prove it to me." She shook her head. "But, damn, I had this man in my *house*. I expressed *gratitude* to him." She closed her eyes. "If it turns out he actually did this, I will be positively sick."

Jenny couldn't imagine how awful it would feel to be cordial to the man who killed your daughter.

At that moment the front door opened; a pre-teen girl with long braids bounded into the house carrying a soccer ball. Her father, wearing a shirt that said *coach,* followed. While the girl stopped in her tracks to look quizzically at the visitors, the father approached Fazzino with an extended hand. "Danny…good to see you again."

"You too, Craig. You're looking well."

"Natalie, who are these people?" the girl posed.

"Well, Savannah Banana, they're here to talk about Allison some more. They're still working on solving the case. Nothing bad is happening, I promise." With a smile she added, "How was practice?"

"Good," Savannah replied. "We scrimmaged and I scored a goal."

"Awesome job. I'll tell you what; why don't you run up and take a shower, and then by the time you're done we'll be finished here and we'll get a pizza."

"But I don't want to shower. I showered yesterday."

"And you just played soccer. You need a shower," Natalie stated flatly.

"Can the pizza be from Mario's?"

"I don't see why not," Natalie said. "Now go take that shower."

Savannah leapt up the stairs and disappeared from sight. Craig turned to Officer Fazzino. "Are there any new developments?"

"Kind of," Fazzino replied.

Natalie walked over to her husband and pointed at Jenny, "This woman is a psychic. You should have seen what she just disclosed to Danny. It was amazing."

"Was it about Allison?"

"No, but she has her suspicions about Allison," Natalie replied. "She thinks it might have been a cop."

Craig looked at Jenny. "Really?"

Before Jenny had the chance to respond, Natalie added, "She thinks it was one of the cops who worked on Allison's case. I've even told you about him. He was the one who found Allison's cell phone."

Zack and Jenny exchanged a bewildered look. "Did you just say he found her cell phone?" Jenny asked.

Natalie looked at Jenny, apparently surprised by the reaction. "Yeah, he found her cell phone. He prided himself on that, actually. It was in an area that had already been searched once, but it didn't turn up until he went back and took a second look."

"One of the messages Lashonda sent me had to do with a cell phone."

Natalie's eyes widened. "What did she say about it?"

"That's just it," Jenny said, "I haven't figured that out. The only thing I know is that it's important somehow."

"It seems a little suspicious to me," Zack surmised, "that a cell phone would just suddenly appear in an area that had already been searched."

"One step ahead of you," Fazzino replied, leaning his head toward the walkie-talkie on his shoulder. With the click of a button he said, "This is Fazzino."

A fuzzy voice blared through the device. "Anderson. What do you got for me Danny?"

"I want you to look up the file for Lashonda Williams and tell me who found her cell phone."

"Who *found* her cell phone?"

"Yes," Fazzino repeated. "Tell me which officer found her cell phone."

"Okay. Just give me a sec."

"Thanks," Fazzino said. He then turned his attention back to everyone in the room. "Now let me just make it clear that even if Orlowski turns out to be the one who found Lashonda's phone, that doesn't make him a murderer. It just might mean he's a cop with extraordinary eyesight and good instincts."

Craig put his arm around Natalie, who was clearly unnerved. As anxious as Jenny was to hear the results, she knew that Natalie's anxiety had to be immeasurably worse.

Fazzino continued. "And even if Orlowski is the perpetrator, this evidence will be circumstantial at best."

Natalie, as if oblivious to Fazzino's comments, put her hand on her forehead and posed, "Do you know what a fit I pitched when I found out the phone was in a place that had already been searched? I demanded to know who had been in charge of that area the first time so I could have his job." She chuckled in disbelief. "And it may turn out that the phone wasn't even there during the initial search. And the person I complained to...the person I regarded as a hero in all of this...the person I *complimented* for being the most competent person on the force... was actually her *killer*?"

"We don't know that yet," Fazzino reminded her.

Natalie sighed as she regained her composure. "You're right," she once again reminded herself. "We don't know that yet."

Jenny wanted to get Natalie's mind off of the wait. "Mrs. Easton," she began. "I was also led to a house, presumably by Lashonda. The name on the mailbox of that house was Hawkins, and

69

the house was on…" Jenny turned to Zack. "What was the name of that street again?"

"Old Schoolhouse Road," Zack said.

Jenny returned her attention to Natalie. "Does that name ring a bell?"

Natalie looked at Craig with a puzzled expression. Craig shook his head, giving Natalie the confirmation she needed to declare, "I've never heard of it."

"It seems nobody has," Jenny replied disappointedly.

Fazzino's walkie-talkie came alive. "I've got the file here. It's thick as hell. It's going to take me a while to figure out who found the phone."

Natalie's face deflated as Fazzino pressed the button and leaned toward his shoulder. "Don't stop looking 'til you find it."

The disappointment was palpable. Natalie left Craig's side and resumed her seat, turning to Jenny. "Have you spoken to Quinette?"

"Quinette?"

"Quinette Williams. Lashonda's mother."

"No ma'am," Jenny confessed. "I haven't done that yet."

Natalie pulled her phone out of her pocket as she spoke. "Craig, can you find out what our guests like on their pizza?" She dialed a number and put the phone to her ear. "Hi, Quinette…I'm doing well. Listen, I think you and Ty should drop whatever it is you're doing and come over. There's some pretty intense stuff going on over here…It's too much to say over the phone; you'll need to see it for yourself. And if I remember correctly, you like pepperoni and sausage on your pizza, right?"

Once the food had been delivered, Craig took Savannah upstairs under the transparent guise of a father-daughter dinner. Soon after, Quinette and Ty Williams arrived looking incredibly apprehensive. Without the typical pleasantries, Quinette immediately posed, "What's going on here?"

"Well," Natalie began, taking their coats, "this is Jenny, a psychic from Georgia, and her husband Zack."

Jenny didn't bother to correct her.

"She says she'd received some messages from Lashonda," Natalie continued.

Quinette and Ty exchanged a puzzled glance. "Messages?" Ty asked. "What kind of messages?"

The couple followed Natalie out of the foyer and into the living room. They both stared at Jenny, silently demanding an explanation. "Well," Jenny began, "I got a visual about her ring, and I distinctly got the impression that a cell phone is going to prove to be important."

"And get this," Natalie interrupted, but then she stopped herself. She shook her head. "Never mind. Keep going."

Jenny continued. "She also led me to a house on Old Schoolhouse Road. The people who live there are named Hawkins. I haven't been able to figure out what the connection is there, and I'm hoping you might know what it is."

"I don't know anybody named Hawkins," Quinette said flatly. "Okay, I..." she closed her eyes and shook her head. "You say..." She clearly had so many questions she couldn't pick just one.

Jenny stood up and walked over to the Williamses. She gently took hold of both of Quinette's hands and looked sincerely into her baffled eyes. "I understand," she whispered. "And I will tell you the whole story. Hopefully by the time I'm done this will all make sense, and then we can start trying to decipher Lashonda's messages."

Still looking lost, Quinette followed Jenny into the kitchen with Ty closely behind. They sat down at the table, and Jenny began the long process of telling the story from start to finish. Even Natalie had been unaware of some of the details, so she was just as entranced by the account as the Williamses.

Jenny noted the way the two women wordlessly took each other's hands when some of the more upsetting details were disclosed, providing each other with the silent solace that only a fellow mourning mother could deliver. These women clearly had a bond that most people would mercifully never understand, brought together by the most horrific of circumstances. As Jenny spoke to them she wished this friendship had never been forged and they were still perfectly happy strangers.

Sadly, that was not how their lives unfolded.

At the end of the explanation Quinette posed, "Do you have any idea if the same person is responsible for all three crimes? Nobody here knows if the Allison's and Lashonda's cases are related."

"I don't really know, unfortunately," Jenny confessed. "It would make sense if they were; the MO is the same. He seems like he's a crime-of-opportunity type of guy. If he sees a young woman alone in the middle of the night, he acts. But," she continued, "I know there's the added element of Michael Boyd in Lashonda's case. I don't really know anything about him other than what I've read online, and I'm not sure how reliable those accounts are. Do you have a feeling about Michael?"

"I wish I did," Ty said. "It would be so much better if we knew which direction to focus. Besides, if he didn't do it, he deserves an apology. But if he did do it, I'd like to go over there and kill him myself. Either way I can't bring myself to look at him. Not until I know the truth."

"Well, hopefully Lashonda can let me know one way or the other." Jenny leaned her elbows on the table. "Let me ask you this…Do you happen to live in the house she grew up in? I might be able to get a reading if I can spend a little time in her old room."

"No, we downsized once Lashonda moved out. She was our youngest, and we didn't need a house that big after the kids were gone," Quinette explained sadly.

"I see," Jenny replied.

At that point Fazzino's walkie-talkie blared. "Fazzino? This is Anderson."

"Fazzino. What'd you'd find out?"

"Orlowski found the phone."

The silence that followed spoke volumes. Fazzino briefly thanked Anderson, and then the quiet resumed. After a moment Ty noted, "That's pretty telling."

Fazzino held his hands up. "Let's not jump the gun. This may just be a coincidence."

Clearly the majority of the people in the room believed that it wasn't.

With a promise to keep investigating, Jenny and Zack said goodbye to the two families and Officer Fazzino. As soon as she sat down in the passenger seat Jenny succumbed to a series of yawns, the consequence of too little sleep the night before. "Thanks for driving," she said to Zack. "I'm not sure I could keep the car on the road."

"No problem," he replied. "I just want to stop at a store or something to get some munchies. Then I'll get you to the hotel so you can get some sleep."

"Thanks." Jenny closed her eyes and remained quiet during the ride to the hotel. She knew there was a lot to discuss, but she didn't have the energy to dedicate to such a serious conversation. There would always be tomorrow.

Once the pair arrived at the hotel and checked in, Jenny and Zack dragged their suitcases to their adjoining rooms. "Goodnight," Jenny said flatly as she slid the key card into the slot. "I'll see you in the morning."

"Goodnight, chief," Zack replied as he disappeared into his room.

Jenny walked into her hotel room, noting that it looked neat but not fancy. She looked longingly at the pillows as she plopped her suitcase on the king-sized bed, unzipping it to retrieve her toothbrush, toothpaste and pajamas. She did her nightly routine quickly, climbing between the sheets with an exhausted sigh.

Very quickly she felt waves of sleep wash over her. She nestled into the blankets, enjoying the warmth, feeling the events of the day disappear from her mind.

With a shot she sat up in bed. She ran quickly to the door that connected her room to Zack's, pounding mercilessly until Zack answered. He looked puzzled as he stood in just flannel pants with a bag of potato chips in his hand. "What's the matter?" He asked.

Jenny was frantic. "I know what happened to Lashonda."

Chapter 10

Without being invited in, Jenny pushed past Zack into his hotel room. "It was horrible," she recounted with a shiver as she sat on the edge of Zack's bed. "But at least now I know."

Zack sat down next to her. "So what happened?"

Jenny sighed to calm her nerves before she began. "Lashonda brought me back to that dollar store parking lot. She was sitting in the back of a car, feeling comfortable, presumably waiting for her roommate, but then the car started moving. She felt confusion at first, but that turned into panic as they continued to drive. She made a fuss, demanding to know where they were going. A male voice told her to shut up, and then a gun appeared in her face.

"She tried to reach for a door handle. She was fully prepared to jump out of the moving car and run for it. But there were no handles. The doors could only be opened from the outside."

Zack understood. "Because it was a cop car."

Jenny nodded. "Because it was a cop car." Jenny wiped her face with her hands, trying to shake off the fear that had gripped her throughout the vision. Her attempt was unsuccessful. "She knew, Zack. She knew she was going to die. Right there in the back seat she figured out that this was what had happened to Allison, and she was fully aware that she was about to meet the same fate." Jenny let out a shaky breath. "Do you know how horrifying that is?"

Putting his arm around Jenny, Zack replied, "I can't even begin to imagine."

"The next thing I knew I was in the midst of the attack, seeing it from Lashonda's point of view. It was incredibly dark. I couldn't see much of anything, including the attacker's face. He had me pinned by my forearms while he raped me." Jenny ran her fingers through her hair. "He seemed so angry, just like he had been during Morgan's attack. But I did get one piece of information that is very telling. Lashonda took off her own ring. It was apparently a little loose on her, and she was able to wriggle it off with her thumb and pinky finger even though Orlowski held her forearms."

"What? Why would she do that?"

"So she could leave a calling card. A little message that *Lashonda was here.* During a brief moment where she had that one hand free, she threw the ring into the distance. It made a clanking sound. It hit something. After hearing the sound, the man demanded to know what she had done, but she didn't answer, God bless her." Jenny looked squarely at Zack. "I think the cops need to stop looking for *who* has the ring and start looking for *where it is.* I think that will give them the answers they're looking for."

Zack frowned and nodded, showing how impressed he was. "That was pretty savvy of her."

"Yes, but unfortunately three years have gone by and no one's found it. Poor thing. She did everything she possibly could to leave a clue, and it's just sitting there."

"Do you think that's why her spirit lingers?"

Jenny looked down at her lap and whispered, "Maybe."

Despite her best effort to prevent them, tears filled Jenny's eyes. Zack noticed, and with his arm still around her, he asked, "Are you okay?"

Jenny nodded while wiping her eyes. "It's hard, that's all," she confessed. "I'm completely freaked out right now. And I'm so tired, but I know I'm not going to be able to sleep tonight. Not for a long time anyway. That image was just so horrible; I'm not going to be able to shake it any time soon."

"Well, you can sleep here if you want," Zack posed. Jenny looked around the room, noting the single bed, and then looked skeptically at Zack. "I'll be a gentleman, I swear," he added. "I just thought it might be comforting to not be alone."

Jenny realized as a married woman the correct response was to decline his offer, but the thought of going back into her room and

75

attempting to sleep alone was far too disturbing. "You know what? I think I'll take you up on that. It's the only way I'll get any rest."

"Okay, just let me clean up a little," Zack said, standing up and wiping chip crumbs off the comforter. "I didn't realize I'd have company."

Jenny smiled at his well-intended but feeble attempt at chivalry. Once Zack was done tidying, Jenny slid under the sheets and lay down, facing the outside of the bed with her back to the empty space that Zack would soon occupy. She was nervous and uneasy, but at least she wasn't frightened.

Jenny heard Zack brush his teeth and shut off some lights before he climbed into his side of the bed. He shut off the light on his nightstand and whispered, "Good night, honey."

Jenny smiled. "Good night dear." With the silence that ensued, thoughts began to swirl around Jenny's head. She relived the fear of Lashonda's final moments, her acceptance that she was about to die, and her determination to leave her mark behind. Jenny got the feeling that Lashonda had been a strong young woman—one who would not go down without a fight. Jenny hoped it was a fight she would ultimately win on Lashonda's behalf, and Orlowski would regret the day he ever decided to make Lashonda Williams his victim.

Disgust gripped Jenny's stomach as she thought of what a horrible man Orlowski was and how he managed to hide his disturbing true colors from so many people. How could he have fooled everyone for so long? She began to wonder why men like that even existed. If Natalie had been right, and God did have a plan, why did that plan include rapists and child killers? Did God make mistakes? Or was there simply no God at all?

"My brain needs an off switch," Jenny said out loud, although she was really talking to herself.

At that point Zack rolled over and put his arm around Jenny, pressing his body against hers and resting his chin on her shoulder. She could feel that he had an erection. "Are you okay?"

Jenny didn't respond. She knew she should be telling him to get back on his own side of the bed, or better yet she should have gotten out of his bed altogether and headed back to her own room, but she had to admit she enjoyed the feeling of his arm around her. Her uneasiness was quickly replaced by a tingle of excitement that she didn't want to end. As a result, she simply remained quiet.

The two lay motionless for quite some time before Zack started tracing his fingers up and down Jenny's arm. A tug-of-war ensued in Jenny's brain—she was enjoying his touch immensely, but she knew she shouldn't be allowing it. She was married. This needed to stop.

But why? She thought. Out of respect for her husband? The man who had never shown any respect to her? The man who was dead set against her having a life of her own? The man who was so concerned with his own image that he put her happiness on the back burner? Did she really need to stop doing this for him?

As if reading her mind, Zack whispered. "Just let me know if you want me to stop."

Jenny remained silent.

Zack traced his fingers up Jenny's arm, over her shoulder, and he began to tenderly stroke her cheek. She closed her eyes and drew in a breath, enjoying a feeling she'd never quite had before. Whenever she'd been with Greg in the past, she was always so consumed with feelings of inadequacy she couldn't fully enjoy herself. She was always worried that her performance wouldn't be good enough, or she didn't look good enough naked. None of those thoughts filled her head at this moment. She knew Zack wasn't judging her; he was simply enjoying her.

And she was enjoying him.

She felt his lips graze the back of her shoulder in a gentle kiss. Followed by another. And another. In an instant Jenny rolled over and wrapped her arms around Zack, engaging him in an incredibly passionate kiss. He held her tightly, giving her a feeling of security she desperately needed at that moment. He was there for her. He cared. He would make sure nothing bad happened to her.

Her husband would have thrown her to the wolves.

As they undressed Jenny felt no shame or embarrassment. Zack seemed truly excited by her, flaws and all, grunting with approval with every inch of her newly exposed skin. His reaction made her feel like the most beautiful woman in the world, a feeling she had honestly never had before.

After more than an hour of passionate exploring, Zack whispered, "I have condoms in my wallet." He kissed the tip of her nose. "If that's okay with you."

"Mmm-hmm," Jenny said approvingly.

Zack climbed to the edge of the large bed and felt around the nightstand for the lamp's on switch. When he found it the room became so bright Jenny had to squint. Zack climbed out of bed and crossed the room, heading for his wallet on the dresser.

As Jenny's eyes adjusted to the light she saw him naked for the first time. She giggled and covered her eyes, but not before noticing his slim but muscular build.

"Laughter is not usually the reaction guys go for when women see them naked," Zack said playfully.

"Sorry," Jenny said. "It's just so odd that I'm seeing you naked."

Zack opened his wallet and pulled out a condom. Holding it out, he exclaimed with a proud smile, "Look! It's not even expired. I exchanged them out a few months ago."

"That's fabulous," Jenny said with a snicker.

Zack walked back toward the bed, "I was never a boy scout, but I do believe in being prepared." He looked at Jenny, who had left herself exposed from under the covers, and suddenly his demeanor became serious. "And right now I'm really, really glad I do." He stood there and admired her for a second before saying, "Wow."

Jenny had never made a man say wow before.

Zack put the condom on and got back into bed with Jenny. Before too long he was inside her, and Jenny found herself living completely in the moment. No worries. No fears. No inadequacy. Just pleasure.

Suddenly Zack stopped and looked up at the ceiling. "Sorry," he said. "It's been a while."

"Are you done?" Jenny asked.

"No, but I will be if I keep going. I just need a minute."

Jenny giggled knowingly as Zack took several deep breaths with his eyes closed. "Okay," he said, "I think I'm good now. My God this is incredible."

And now Jenny was incredible.

After a few more similar incidents, Zack finally succumbed to his urge to release. This time Jenny had no doubt he was finished. He lay on top of her, depleted, breathing heavy. "Wow," he said again. "That was amazing."

Jenny smiled and traced her fingers gently up and down his back. After a moment, she tapped him with her pointer finger. "Hey…I thought you said you were going to be a gentleman."

Zack didn't look up when he breathlessly said, "Sorry. I've never really been a man of integrity, especially where beautiful women are concerned." After Jenny giggled, Zack added, "But I did try. Well, at least Big Zack did, anyway."

"Big Zack?"

"Yeah, I'm Big Zack. But then when I was lying in bed next to you, Little Zack got to thinking. It's always dangerous when Little Zack acts up. He's generally the brains of this operation, and once he gets started there's really no stopping him."

Jenny laughed through his explanation, and he continued.

"Funny thing. It turns out Little Zack likes you. A lot."

"Oh does he now?"

"Yup. He sure does. And when you were lying in bed next to him, he just couldn't help himself. He's a very determined little guy." Zack looked up and smiled at Jenny. He gave her a gentle peck on the lips and said, "And right now he wants his raincoat off. Just give me a minute, I'll be right back." He got out of bed and scampered to the bathroom.

Alone with her thoughts, Jenny began to realize the implications of what had just happened. She had just cheated on her husband, breaking the vow she took in front of God and her parents and everyone who loved her. She had always prided herself on being a good person, and now she has just done one of the worst things imaginable. Regret consumed her.

Zack walked back into the room, seemingly without a care in the world. He got into bed, sliding close to Jenny, but she simply proclaimed, "It's my turn to clean up." She got out of bed as quickly as she could, collected her pajamas, and rushed to the bathroom.

Her hands were shaking as she cleaned and dressed herself. She felt positively sick, desperately wishing she could go back in time and decline Zack's invitation to spend the night with him. She walked over to the sink where she splashed cold water on her face, trying to wash off the horrible feeling she had inside. As the water dripped from her face, she looked up into the mirror, disgusted by her own reflection. She was looking into the face of an adulteress, and no matter what she did from this point forward, every time she looked in the mirror she'd be staring at a cheater. She wanted to cry.

She reached behind her and grabbed a towel, drying her face before she looked back into the mirror. She stood up straighter this time, taking a deep breath, realizing she didn't have to be looking into the eyes of an adulteress. Taking a few steps closer to the mirror, she gazed at herself with a new-found respect. At that moment she concluded she wasn't looking at a cheater—she was looking at a woman who had just made the decision to leave her husband.

And that she could live with.

Feeling suddenly better with her situation, she slipped out of her pajamas and walked back into the bedroom with Zack. He was already breathing heavy; if he wasn't asleep, he was close. She turned off the lamp on Zack's nightstand and felt her way around to her side of the bed. Crawling in she felt Zack cuddle up next to her, throwing a heavy arm around her without saying a word. Jenny smiled. Zack was a good guy, after all. He wasn't perfect by any means, but he was genuine and kind hearted, and she was quite sure she didn't just get used.

She decided to demand her brain take the night off, and she enjoyed the sound of Zack's rhythmic breath and the feel of his body against hers. Before long she was able to drift off, finding herself in the midst of the best night's sleep she'd had in a long time.

She awoke to the feel of Zack's hands rubbing her stomach. "Hey," she said groggily but playfully.

"Hey," he replied, kissing her shoulder. "Sorry to wake you, but I couldn't resist." Still naked from the night before, Zack positioned himself on top of her. She could feel every inch of his skin, and it felt good.

But there was so much they needed to talk about. She thought they should come to some kind of agreement before doing this again—if they ever did it again. She started to protest, but as Zack's kisses reached her neck, a tingle of desire generated from deep within her. *Just go with it,* she thought to herself, *for once in your life just go with it.* She wrapped her arms and legs around him and pulled him in close.

The two lay looking at the ceiling, legs intertwined, Jenny using Zack's shoulder as a pillow. They silently enjoyed the moment for a long time before Jenny proclaimed, "I'm married."

"Yeah," Zack said flatly. "There's that."

"Yeah," Jenny repeated. "That little technicality."

"Can I just say something about that?" Zack asked.

"Of course."

"If I thought you were happily married, I never would have made a move on you. But I know you're not."

Jenny let out a sigh. "No, I'm not." She swept the hair out of her face. "I have to be honest…last night after we finished, I went into the bathroom and I felt awful about what happened. I couldn't believe I had been unfaithful. Me. Unfaithful." She shook her head. "It should have never happened."

"I'm sorry…"

"Wait, I'm not done," Jenny interrupted. "Then I realized there was only one way I was going to feel right about what went on between us. I have to leave Greg. I can't go back and act like his wife and pretend nothing happened. I have to go back and tell him that our marriage is over. Then I didn't really cheat on him; I just left him."

Zack didn't respond, making Jenny uneasy. She kept talking.

"I don't want you to be scared," she added. "I'm not saying I'm leaving him for you. I'm not roping you into a commitment or anything. I just wouldn't be able to live with myself if I slept with someone else and then went back to being married."

"I feel bad," Zack finally said. "I don't want to be responsible for ending your marriage."

Jenny flipped over and looked Zack in the eye. "Believe me. You're not the reason my marriage is ending. You're just the reason my marriage is ending *now*. Lately I've come to realize my relationship with Greg has been shitty from the start, and you didn't cause that." She smiled playfully. "Actually, you're doing me a favor. I've wanted to leave him for a long time; I just didn't have the courage to actually go through with it. Now you've given me the incentive I need to go home and say the words."

"Well, I'm glad I could do that for you. You know I don't like the way he treats you, and I think you deserve better."

Jenny blushed. "Thanks."

Zack wrapped his arms around Jenny's waist and looked at her sincerely. "And just so you know…you wouldn't be *roping* me into a commitment. That idea doesn't sound half bad to me, honestly."

Holy shit, Jenny thought. She hung her head and closed her eyes. "Thanks, Zack. I appreciate that. I truly do. But I have to tell you I can't even begin to think about commitment right now." She felt like a bitch as the words came out of her mouth, so she added, "I don't want to hurt you, believe me. That's the last thing I want to do. But I'm at a place in my life where I have to take things one minute at a time. If I start to think about any more than that, I'll lose my mind."

"That's fair," Zack replied. "I don't want to pressure you at all." He tucked her hair behind her ear. "I just wanted you to know where I'm coming from…that I'm not some womanizer who took advantage of you when you were vulnerable." Then he laughed out loud.

"What's so funny?"

"The thought of me being a womanizer. I would make the worst womanizer on the planet. My last set of condoms expired in my wallet. Do you know how sad that is?"

Jenny bit her lip. "I guess it has been a while, huh?"

"My last girlfriend was when I was twenty seven. I'm almost thirty. You do the math."

Jenny almost made the comment that she was surprised he'd been that long without a girlfriend, but in reality she wasn't. He wasn't boyfriend material, and that notion suddenly made her feel bad. Had *she* just taken advantage of *him*? That was a scenario she hadn't considered before.

To keep the conversation light, Jenny posed, "Has there been anything in between?"

"Expired condoms, remember?"

"Condoms," Jenny said. "Plural. How many of those things do you carry around with you?"

"Three."

"Three?"

"It's a tri-fold wallet," Zack explained, "so one for each section."

"My goodness."

"Well, here's my logic. I'm a morning person, and usually if there's a morning, that means there was a night before." Then he furrowed his brow. "But I guess that only makes two. I'm not sure why I carry that third one around. Wishful thinking, maybe?"

"My guess would be an ego issue," Jenny declared. She then patted him on the shoulder. "Well, I don't know about you, champ, but I'm pretty hungry. Do you want to get some breakfast?"

"Absolutely," Zack said. Jenny started to get up when Zack said, "But wait." She paused and he pulled her in for a slow, passionate kiss. "I know when we go downstairs we're going to go back to being business partners, and I just wanted to squeeze one more of those in."

Jenny smiled appreciatively, although inside she was terrified.

After quick showers Zack and Jenny walked down into the lobby for some breakfast, laptop in hand. They piled their plates high with free buffet food and took seats in the nearly empty dining area. After a few bites Zack posed, "You know, while I was in the shower I thought about your vision from Lashonda."

"Oh yeah?" Jenny posed. "What did you come up with?"

"Well, you said it was incredibly dark. And you also mentioned that when she threw her ring, it hit something. Do you think she was indoors?"

Jenny thought for a moment. "You know what? I do. When I was seeing things through Morgan's eyes, I could see stars in the sky. But with Lashonda it was pitch dark."

"Well, maybe the attack happened at the Hawkins' house."

Jenny's jaw dropped. "That would make perfect sense. I don't know why I didn't think of that. Maybe that used to be Orlowski's house."

"Only one way to find out," Zack replied, opening the laptop and beginning a real estate search. He referred to his cell phone for the address, making a puzzled face when he pulled up the record of the property. "It looks like the Hawkinses have lived there for eight years. Before that it was the Zimmermans, and before that the McMahons. There's no Orlowski anywhere on the record."

Jenny twisted her face. "That seemed so promising."

"Here's one for you. All three wives who owned the home were named Kimberly. What do you think the odds are of that?"

With a giggle, Jenny replied, "It is a little strange, but Kimberly isn't that uncommon of a name. If all three wives were named Esmerelda I'd be more impressed."

Zack shrugged in response. As his fingers pressed more keys on the computer, Jenny asked, "What are you doing now?"

"I'm trying to find out the date of Lashonda's murder. I want to see if it was a new moon or if it was cloudy, which might explain why it was dark. If it was a clear night, the darkness would be evidence the attack took place indoors."

"Very smart thinking."

A short time later Zack replied, "It says here it would have been a waxing gibbous that night, whatever the hell that means."

"More than half full."

Zack looked up at Jenny with awe. "How did you know that?"

"I used to be a teacher, remember? Teachers know everything. About everything."

"Apparently so." Zack continued to type, his brow becoming more furrowed with each passing minute. "Why is it so difficult to find out what the weather was like that night? Aren't there supposed to be records of this kind of thing?"

Jenny remained quiet as Zack searched. After a few moments she posed, "Even if it was cloudy, wouldn't the light of the moon shine through? I would think I'd have been able to see *something* if the attack happened outside."

"We may have to go with that theory," Zack surmised. "I'm not having any luck finding out what the weather was that night."

"And with the clanking sound," Jenny went on. "You're right. It sounded like the ring hit something metal. Maybe I was in a basement? That would explain the darkness, and there are always pipes and furnaces and stuff in basements."

Zack shrugged and nodded. "Could be." After taking a bite of his breakfast, Zack continued to search the computer. "Let me just take a look at what's happening down in Braddock. Maybe there are some new developments." A few moments later, he sat back in his chair and said, "Holy shit."

"What is it?"

"See for yourself." Zack spun the laptop around so Jenny could see the screen. She saw a mug shot of a baby-faced, brown-eyed young man who looked like a deer in headlights. The headline next to the picture said, in very large print, "Arrest made in Caldwell case."

Chapter 11

"What!?!" Jenny exclaimed louder than she had intended. The smattering of people in the dining room looked her way. She lowered her tone and added, "That can't be right."

"Let's see what it says," Zack replied as he turned the computer back to face him. He began to read. "Jeremy Stotler, 18, of 56 Hancock Drive in Braddock was arrested and charged with the kidnapping, rape and murder of fifteen-year-old Morgan Caldwell. Stotler is a senior at Monroe High School, the same school where Morgan had been a sophomore..."

Jenny shook her head in disbelief. "What proof could they have had?"

Zack scanned the article, noting "Cell phone records show she had plans to meet up with him in the middle of the night that night, and his DNA was apparently left at the scene."

"That's impossible," Jenny declared angrily. "He wasn't at the scene."

Shrugging, Zack said, "I'm just telling you what the article says."

"Cell phone records," Jenny muttered out loud. "I bet I know who found her cell phone."

Zack continued to convey the story. "Apparently this Stotler kid originally said he didn't see Morgan that night, and then he changed his story saying he did." Zack's eyes met Jenny's. "That probably screwed him."

Jenny rubbed her face with her hands. With a sigh she added, "This is horrible." She heard Zack's fingers typing, prompting her to ask, "What are you doing now?"

"Give me a second," he replied. A moment later, he added, "Yup. Just as I thought."

"What?"

"Well, clearly Morgan snuck out that night, and I figured maybe she walked to this Stotler kid's house, picked up a sample of his DNA—if you know what I mean—and then encountered Orlowski on her way home. And take a look." Zack spun the computer around so Jenny could see the screen, revealing a road map of Morgan's neighborhood. "The article said Jeremy Stotler lives on Hancock Drive. If you trace out the path she would have taken home from Hancock Drive, it would put her right on Armistead Lane, the place where you had that funny feeling that something had happened."

Jenny processed the information, trying to make sense of the swirls that occupied her mind. "Orlowski used a condom," she eventually whispered. "Apparently Jeremy Stotler didn't."

A long and painful silence followed. Pushing her half-eaten plate to the center of the table and leaning back in her chair, Jenny asked, "What time is the next flight back to Georgia?"

"You want to go back already?"

Jenny nodded.

After a moment of searching, Zack said, "There's a flight later tonight. It takes off at 7:30."

"That would be great, actually. That will give us some time to talk to Fazzino again today, letting him know what we've come up with. Then we can get back down to Braddock and make sure that poor kid doesn't spend any more time in jail than he needs to."

"Do you think that's the place we'll be the most effective? You don't think we stand a better chance here?" Zack, whose appetite remained unaffected by Jeremy Stotler's incarceration, took a bite of a muffin and added, "I'm not saying you're wrong, I'm genuinely asking where you think we'd be better off."

87

Jenny shook her head with disgust; the pathetic look on Jeremy Stotler's face had disturbed her deeply. "I don't know the answer to that. I guess we should hit the pavement hard today, gather as much information as we can up here in Connecticut, and then head back to Georgia tonight. And we'd better pray to God that Morgan has the strength to give me some more clues when we get there. Who knows how long it will be before Orlowski strikes again?"

At the police station, Officer Fazzino reviewed his notes. "So you think the attack happened indoors, and Lashonda left her ring behind?"

"Yes, sir," Jenny replied. "I don't think Orlowski knew what she'd done. The ring is possibly still there."

"Well, he didn't know what she had done *at the time*," Fazzino added. "But that missing ring was all over the news. I'm sure he was able to figure out what that clanking sound had been. It's quite possible he went back and got the ring the next day."

Jenny's shoulders slumped. She hadn't considered that scenario. "I guess that's why you're the detective."

With a smile Fazzino added, "So tell me a little more about this arrest in Georgia."

This time Zack spoke. "It appears Morgan made midnight plans with this Jeremy Stotler kid through messages on her cell phone. At first he denied meeting up with her, but he had left a little calling card behind, if you know what I mean."

Jenny rolled her eyes.

"I'm guessing you mean semen," Fazzino said flatly.

"Exactly," Zack replied. "Now Jenny clearly recalls Orlowski using a condom, so none of Orlowski's...*semen*...would be present. But what the cops are looking at down there is a body that had been raped and strangled, coupled with the semen of a boy who denied seeing her that night. I can see why they'd jump to the conclusion that Stotler did it...especially since there's probably a ton of pressure from the public for this case to be solved quickly."

"And you've also got Orlowski on the inside making sure the evidence points squarely at Jeremy Stotler," Jenny noted. "Is there any way you can call them up and tell them they have the wrong person?"

Fazzino let out a chuckle. "Unfortunately, no. But what I can do is call them up and let them know I've got two similar cases up here. I don't have to tell them I think they arrested the wrong guy; I can pretend I didn't even know anyone had been charged."

"Are you going to tell them to look at Orlowski?" Jenny posed.

Fazzino wiped the back of his neck with his hand. "Now that's a touchy subject. I'll have to tread lightly on that one. I'll throw out some feelers—let them know that Orlowski used to be one of ours— and see their reaction. If they act like his shit don't stink, I'll keep quiet. If they feel the same way about him that I do, I'll mention the possibility that Mr. Gunslinger may have had something to do with this. I'll have to play that one totally by ear."

While ideally Jenny would have liked a more definitive answer, she understood why it couldn't be that easy. "I appreciate anything you can do to set the record straight."

"Well, listen, I'm really impressed with your insight. I have to confess that the reason I was willing to talk to you at first was only because I was desperate. I've been working on this case for three years and I literally had nothing. I was so tired of having to tell Natalie and Quinette that I had no new leads about their daughters I was willing to try anything. But after seeing you yesterday...there's no way you could have known about Jimmy or about that rain shower. I have to believe you're for real. I never thought in a million years I'd be taking advice from a psychic, but I do honestly think you're a credible source."

"Thank you sir."

"But despite how I feel, I can't call up the people in Georgia and tell them they're wrong. I don't know what other evidence they have against this kid. For all I know they might actually have the right guy. I haven't seen enough proof for me to formally declare that Orlowski is a killer. Or a rapist. Or anything other than an overzealous cop."

"I understand." Jenny looked at her lap, aware that her disappointment was probably visible.

"Welcome to the world of police work," Fazzino said with another chuckle. "It's definitely a marathon, not a sprint. You've got to have the patience of a saint to be in this line of work."

"Patience has never been my strong suit," Jenny confessed.

"Well, my friend, that has to change."

Jenny didn't like that answer. "Zack and I have a flight to catch later tonight, so I'd like to make the most of today," she began. "Would it be possible for me to visit the place where Lashonda's body was found?"

"Sure," Fazzino said, "I can take you there. Do you want me to bring you by the place Allison's body was found too?"

"Maybe, if we have time," Jenny replied, "But I haven't gotten any messages from Allison so far; I'm not sure I'd get any today. I think I might want to spend the day focusing on Lashonda since I know she's trying to contact me."

"That sounds reasonable," Fazzino replied. "Let me grab my coat and I'll take you to the field."

The officer led Zack and Jenny through the tall, yellow stalks that covered the field. He seemed to know exactly where he was going, a concept which puzzled Jenny since there were so few landmarks to use as references. After a relatively long walk, the officer stopped and pointed to the ground. "Her body was found here," he noted. "She was lying face up with her head facing northeast." He gestured in that direction.

Jenny held up her hands. "Don't tell me anything else. I don't want any preconceived notions to cloud my mind."

Fazzino immediately stopped talking.

Jenny stuffed her hands in her pockets and took a few steps toward where the body had been located. She looked up at the sky, observing the same view Lashonda would have had from the ground. Jenny felt no fear as she had the other times Lashonda had contacted her. "Lashonda was never alive here," Jenny said mechanically. "She was killed in that other location and was already dead when her body was brought here."

Fazzino wrote frantically on his notepad.

"She was dragged," Jenny noted, "from that way." She pointed in the direction they had just walked. Closing her eyes for better focus, Jenny added, "She lost a shoe. She was being dragged from under her arms with her feet sliding along the ground, and one of her shoes fell off. It was along the path down there." Again Jenny pointed in the direction they had come.

Jenny was getting another message, although she was having a difficult time discerning what it was. She paced around, eyes still closed, trying to determine exactly what she was supposed to understand. She shook her head slightly and added uncertainly, "There's something significant about a bug. I don't know what. Just…a bug." After a moment, Jenny opened her eyes and declared, "That's all I've got."

"Well," Fazzino said, "You were right on target with the shoe."

"Was I really?" Jenny asked with a shiver. She pulled the hood of her jacket over her head.

"Yup. Her left shoe was found about 150 yards from her body. The broken grass blades indicated that she had been dragged to this location, and the missing shoe corroborated that idea. We weren't sure, though, if she was already dead when she was brought here or if she had been left here to die."

"There's no fear here," Jenny reiterated. "There was fear in the parking lot and absolute terror during the attack, wherever that was, but there was no emotion here. I have to believe she was already gone."

"That's good news," Fazzino said. "I hate the thought of someone being left out here to die. If it has to happen at all, the quicker the better, I say."

"So what about the bug?" Zack asked.

Fazzino shook his head. "That's a new one. I'm going to have to look into that. It did take a few days to find the body, so I imagine that the flies had found their way to her by then. It was an unseasonably warm fall that year, too, so perhaps the bugs were more of a factor than they usually would have been that time of year. I'll have to see if any notes were made about that."

"I'm freezing," Jenny said.

With a laugh, Fazzino posed, "Does that mean you want to head back to the car?"

"If you don't mind," Jenny replied. "Can we potentially drive to where Orlowski used to live? Maybe that's the dark place he brought Lashonda."

"Sounds good to me," Fazzino said as they filed away from the location. Jenny took one last look around as they left, noting the barrenness of the area, feeling a great deal of sympathy for Lashonda.

91

This was much too lonesome of a place for such a spirited young woman to be left. *Discarded like trash*, Jenny thought to herself as hatred of Orlowski consumed her.

With a glance to the sky, Jenny made a silent promise to Lashonda that she would do everything she could to make Orlowski pay for what he'd done.

Fazzino stopped the car in front of a modest, nondescript house near the center of Ivory Heights. "Here it is," he remarked. "This is the address we had on file for Orlowski."

Zack and Jenny stepped out of the car and stood at the edge of the lawn. Jenny studied the home carefully, doing her best to keep her own emotions out of the way. She shook her head as if to remove any thought from her mind, and with a sigh she closed her eyes, awaiting another contact from Lashonda.

She received nothing.

After several minutes of failed attempt, she opened her eyes and proclaimed, "I don't think she was ever here. The silence is speaking volumes."

Again Fazzino broke out his notebook. With a quick swirl of his pen, he asked, "So you aren't getting anything?"

"Nope. Not a thing. And like I said, if anything I would conclude that this is her way of telling me we're barking up the wrong tree."

"She seemed to be smart like that," Zack noted.

"Indeed she was," Jenny said sadly. "Indeed she was."

"So is there anywhere else you'd like me to take you?" Fazzino asked.

Jenny and Zack looked at each other, but neither had an obvious answer. "I might want to go back to the dollar store parking lot," Jenny suggested, looking to see if Zack had any objections. After noting Zack's silent approval, she turned to Fazzino. "But I know where that is. You don't need to come with us if you don't want. I'm sure you have a lot of other work you need to be doing."

"Always," Fazzino remarked. "But I do need to eat lunch, too. Would you guys like to grab a bite real quick?"

"Always," Zack replied in the same tone Fazzino had used.

"He'll never turn down food," Jenny added. "He's like a bottomless pit."

"Enjoy it now," Fazzino said, placing his hand on his slightly overweight stomach. "Once you get to be my age it catches up with you."

They all piled into Fazzino's car and headed to a local deli. While there, Zack and Jenny recounted the story of how they had come to work together and how, thanks to Elanor's generosity, they were now able to dedicate themselves to solving crimes full time. Fazzino shared some stories about his brother Jimmy, who seemed like he had been quite a character during his short life. Jenny felt both joy and sadness during Fazzino's accounts; as was the case with the other spirits she'd encountered, she wished she could have known Jimmy during his lifetime.

With a quick goodbye and a promise to pass along any new information, Zack and Jenny headed off in their rental car toward the dollar store parking lot. Once there, Jenny reclined comfortably in the driver's seat, leaving the keys in the ignition just in case she felt the sudden urge to go anywhere. Zack sat silently in the passenger seat watching the sparse traffic go by on Chamberlain Avenue.

A moment later Jenny turned the key to the car, pulling out of the parking lot as she and Zack wordlessly put on their seatbelts. She made familiar lefts and rights, once again landing in front of the Hawkins' house. She turned off the car and said, "Here we are again. Clearly we're supposed to be here for some reason."

Jenny looked out the window at the house. It was an older home, not in the best of shape. The shed was equally as run-down. "If Orlowski didn't used to live here, I can't imagine what the significance of this place would be," Jenny confessed. "It's just an old house."

Zack nudged Jenny's arm with his elbow. "Hey, check it out," he said. He gestured toward the side of the house where a gray-haired, heavy set woman in a thick housecoat appeared from the back yard. She walked exaggeratedly, indicative of hip trouble, as she carried some firewood in each hand. Taking note of the car in front of the house, the woman stopped for a moment, looking inquisitively, before she continued on her way through the front door.

"Do you suppose that was Kimberly?" Zack asked with a smile.

"You're a funny guy," Jenny replied flatly. At a loss, she shook her head. "I have no idea what's going on. This is the strangest thing ever. What does that old woman have to do with anything?" Jenny sat back in the driver's seat and closed her eyes. Her investigation was providing more questions than answers, and her frustration level was elevating.

"Three thirty seven," Jenny suddenly said.

"What?" Zack asked.

"Three thirty seven," Jenny repeated. "I just saw the number flash in front of me."

"What do you think it means?"

"I don't know that," Jenny confessed with a sigh.

Zack looked at the house number in front of them. "It isn't part of this address."

"Do you think it was a time?" Jenny posed. "Maybe the time of death?"

"It could be. Didn't you say she left work around two-thirty?"

"Somewhere around there," Jenny said. "Although, I'm not sure how knowing her time of death would help us." She looked at the clock on the dashboard of her rental car. "The numbers didn't look clock-ish, either. They were bigger. And black." She rubbed her eyes, trying to piece together the seemingly unrelated clues. *What could all of this mean?*

"Well," Zack began, "If we're going to return the rental car and make it to the gate on time, we'd probably better head back to the airport."

Jenny let out a frustrated sigh. "I guess you're right. I wish there was a way we could be in both places at the same time. I'd love to stay here and try to figure out what Lashonda is telling me, but I also want to get back to Georgia to figure out what's going on down there." She turned the key. "I wish I had a clone."

"Well, I'll give Officer Fazzino a call and let him know about three-thirty-seven. I'll also let him know that you were led here again so he doesn't dismiss the importance of this house."

"Thanks." Jenny turned the car around and headed out the way she came. "If only I could figure out *why* it's important."

"Patience, dear Jenny," Zack said as he pulled his phone out of his pocket. "Remember what Fazzino said about the marathon."

"Yeah, but while I'm busy running a marathon Orlowski might be plotting his next attack."

"Well, the people of Braddock will be more careful now that they know a killer is on the loose. Hopefully no girls will be out alone late at night."

Jenny glanced at Zack. "The people of Braddock don't think a killer is on the loose; they think a killer is behind bars. They probably believe Jeremy Stotler did it and all is right with the world again."

"Oh...right," Zack replied softly. "I forgot about that." He dialed the phone and held it to his ear. "Officer Fazzino, please...okay, thank you...Hi Officer Fazzino, it's Zack Larrabee..." Zack told the officer about the latest events and then remained silent for a long time. Jenny could hear the sound of Fazzino's voice on the phone, but she couldn't make out what he was saying. "That's great. Thank you for doing that. Can you actually text me that number? I don't have anything to write with at the moment. Great. Thanks. And I'll be in touch if we come up with anything...Okay, bye."

"What was that about?" Jenny was very curious.

"Fazzino called the authorities down in Braddock. He said he spoke to a guy named Johnson. He mentioned the similarities between Morgan Caldwell and the Connecticut cases. At first Johnson stuck to his story that Morgan's case was solved and they had ample evidence against Jeremy Stotler, but then Fazzino said there were unsubstantiated rumors that Orlowski may have been the culprit in Connecticut, and now he lived down there by Morgan Caldwell. Apparently this Johnson guy was open to the idea of looking into it, although as you might suspect it would be on the QT. Fazzino had mentioned that he had 'informants' down in Georgia, so Johnson gave him his personal cell phone number. You and I are to call Johnson directly if we get any new information. We are *not* to discuss this with anyone else on the force."

"Did he happen to mention that my *information* would be in the form of visions?"

"He didn't say," Zack surmised, "but I doubt it."

Jenny doubted it too.

During the trip back to Georgia, Zack and Jenny discussed possible explanations for the significance of the Hawkins house, the number 337, and any potential information an insect might provide. None of the theories they came up with seemed to be the silver bullet they had been hoping for; however, the conversation kept them busy during the entire flight and the first half of the drive home from the airport.

All that time, Jenny had managed to keep her mind off the unpleasant task that awaited her upon her arrival home. Once they drove past the high school where Greg taught, however, the memory of her failed marriage came flooding back. "Oh," she said with disgust. "I almost forgot about Greg." She put her hand on her forehead; she really didn't want to have to deal with that in the midst of everything else that was going on.

"Well," Zack proposed, "you don't have to go home tonight. You could always stay at my place if you want…"

Again, this was more than Jenny could handle. "I don't know," she said quickly, shaking her head. "I don't know if that's a good idea."

"Who said anything about it being good idea? I just said you could do it if you want to."

Jenny laughed at the absurdity of his comment.

"I'm actually serious," Zack replied. "Jenny, I know that you are a better person than me in, like, almost every way. There's so much you could teach me it's not even funny. But, there is one thing that I can teach you."

"Oh yeah?" Jenny asked with a smirk. "And what is that?"

"I can teach you how to have fun. I can teach you to be happy. I can teach you to live life."

"That's three things."

"Well, they're all related." Zack shifted in the passenger seat so he could face Jenny. "You are one of the nicest people I've ever met, but I almost think you're *too* nice. You're always so concerned with doing the right thing and making sure you don't hurt other people, which are both great qualities, but that means you're always putting yourself last. And I hate to see that."

Jenny remained quiet, focusing on the road.

"Don't get me wrong. This isn't about me pressuring you to come home with me. If you don't want to spend the night with me, just say so. That's a perfectly acceptable answer. But I don't want you saying no just because it isn't a good idea or it isn't the *right* thing to do. Sometimes you just have to say 'fuck it' and do what you want to do, not what everyone else wants you to do." Zack sat back in his seat and faced forward. "Isn't that what Elanor tried telling you, too?"

With that last comment, words that had already stung became almost unbearable to hear. That *was* the message that Elanor had tried to relay. Those *were* the words that Jenny had vowed to live by going forward. Yet, somehow, that concept continually eluded her. She always resorted back to being the same old Jenny. Doormat Jenny—the girl Elanor had warned her not to be.

However, this time her reluctance to accept Zack's invitation was not out of undue respect for Greg; rather, she was fearful that she would eventually hurt Zack, which was the last thing she wanted to do. She genuinely cared about him, and she didn't want to do anything that might ultimately cause him to leave her life permanently.

"You're quiet," Zack noted. "I've pissed you off."

"No," Jenny argued softly. "You just struck a chord, that's all." Lacking the energy to be anything more than honest, she confessed, "Zack, I think you're a great guy. I really do. But I can't guarantee that if we start something it will go on forever. It might end. And I might be the one to end it. I don't want to hurt you like that. That's why I'm thinking it might be better not to start anything at all."

"Okay," Zack began, "first of all, let me explain something to you. I'm a dude. And if I'm faced with either, A, never getting to have sex with a beautiful girl, or B, getting to have sex with her for a while until she puts an end to it…I have to say I'm going with B. There's really no question about it. It's B. Every time."

Jenny couldn't help but laugh.

Zack continued. "And if you're worried about hurting me long term, let me remind you that I'm the guy who just stopped showing up at my job one day. My job *with the family business.* I had absolutely no back-up plan and no idea how I was going to pay my rent. I just knew that I hated my job, and staying home felt good. Screw tomorrow. I'll worry about that tomorrow."

"I don't know how you can live like that."

"It's quite easy, actually," Zack said. "Although, I'm not sure I'd recommend taking it to the extreme that I do. It is a stupid way to live, come to think of it. BUT…a little bit of that attitude is good for you. If you spend your entire life worrying about tomorrow, you'll end up on your death bed realizing you didn't enjoy any of your todays."

Jenny knew his point was valid.

"So I'm going to ask it again. I'm not asking if you *should* spend the night with me. I'm not asking if Greg would approve, because who gives a shit about that guy. I'm not asking if the decision will ultimately end up hurting *me*. I'm simply asking if you, Jenny Watkins, *want* to spend the night with me tonight."

A tingle of excitement grew within Jenny. "Yes," she said softly. "I do."

"So then will you?"

Jenny stifled a smile. "Yes."

"Well, good, then," Zack said with a weak attempt at hiding his excitement. "It's settled." After a pause he added, "For the record, little Zack is very excited about this."

Jenny lay stretched out and naked, her body pressed against Zack's as he continued to sleep. The morning sun peeked through the window, adding to Jenny's feeling of invincibility. Having gotten a taste of what freedom felt like, she couldn't wait until it became a way of life for her. Soon enough she'd have that dreaded conversation with Greg behind her, the marriage would be over, and she'd be able to do as she pleased. She smiled and stretched, feeling younger and lighter than she had in ages.

Strangely she found herself looking forward to having that talk with Greg. That was the only thing keeping her from her new life.

That, and she had no place to live.

She heard Zack stir and draw in a deep breath. "Good morning," he said with a stretch.

"Indeed it is," Jenny replied.

Zack rolled over and pulled Jenny in close. "Easy, there, tiger," Jenny said. "I know you're a morning person, but I really want to get going on the case. While you and I are cozy in this little bed, Jeremy Stotler is sitting in a prison cell."

Zack rolled slowly back onto his side of the bed. "Yeah, that is kind of a mood-killer, isn't it?"

"A little bit, yeah," Jenny replied. "So do you want to shower first or should I?"

"You go ahead. I need a chance to wake up."

Jenny climbed in the shower and tried to determine what would be their best plan of attack. She would need to see the size of the crowds in front of the Caldwell and Stotler houses. Perhaps attention had shifted from Morgan's house to Jeremy's, and she'd be able to take advantage of a little bit of quiet at Morgan's. Maybe Morgan would be able to get through to her with a magic piece of evidence that would blow this case wide open.

Stop that, Jenny thought to herself. *It's a marathon, not a sprint. Stop feeling like you need to solve the case immediately. You're only setting yourself for disappointment.*

If only she didn't feel like she was playing beat the clock against Orlowski.

"Dammit," Jenny proclaimed when she saw the size of the crowd that still remained in front of the Caldwell's house. While there were fewer people there than the last time they had visited, there were still too many for Jenny to enjoy some quiet.

"I bet it's only worse at Jeremy's," Zack noted.

"I agree with you," Jenny added with a sigh. "I guess our best bet is to walk toward Jeremy's house. Maybe I'll pick something up along the way."

"Sounds like a plan." Zack parked his car, and the couple got out. Although it was warmer than it had been in Connecticut, Jenny was still chilly. She wished she had worn a warmer coat.

In an instant Jenny remembered what Elanor had told her about turning thirty. *At thirty you become cold all the time, and at forty you stop giving a shit. Mark my words. It'll happen.* Jenny had to smile; at twenty-six, it appears she was ahead of schedule, perhaps in both respects. With that thought a charge of mixed emotions ran through Jenny. She missed her deceased friend dearly, but she also felt the invisible support of one of her biggest fans. Elanor would have been cheering her on if she was there, inevitably with some swear words mixed in to the pep talk. With Elanor at her back, Jenny instantly felt stronger. She could do this. She could get Orlowski. There was no doubt in her mind.

"Are you ready?" she asked Zack as she pulled her hood over her head.

"Lead the way," he replied.

Having studied the map at length, Jenny already knew the way to Jeremy Stotler's house. She headed down the tree-lined street, keeping her head down, trying to drown out the buzz that the crowd, which consisted of press and curious onlookers, emitted. The excitement crackled like interference or white noise, but she tried not to get discouraged. The further she got from the crowd, the less racket she heard.

As they rounded the corner onto Armistead Drive, Jenny made an extra effort to remain calm. She imagined if a contact was to be made, it would most likely happen at the abduction site. Sure enough, as they approached the same spot as before she felt that familiar wave of recognition.

When she reached the location, she was once again directed to pause. "I don't feel fear here," she declared. "She may have gotten into his car here, but the attack happened elsewhere." She paced in small circles with her eyes closed, trying her best to receive additional information. Unable to gain any more insight, she wordlessly continued toward Jeremy Stotler's house.

As they got closer to their destination, Jenny could feel herself becoming happier with every step. "Her spirits were definitely high," she muttered. They continued along Armistead Lane until it intersected with Hancock Drive, where again the buzz of interference became a problem. When Jenny looked up, she figured out why. "Holy shit," she said. "It's a friggin circus."

The scene at Jeremy Stotler's house looked as chaotic as the scene at the Caldwell's a few days earlier. "I suppose getting a reading here is out of the question?"

"That's an understatement," Jenny replied. "Dammit! We should have stayed in Connecticut a few more days. Somehow I knew I'd make the wrong call."

"Don't be so hard on yourself," Zack said. "Besides, we don't necessarily need to be *right here* in order for you to get a vision. Correct me if I'm wrong, but you were at Lake Wimsat when you got the first message from Morgan."

Jenny let out a sigh. "Yeah, that's true."

"Maybe if we just go back to Evansdale and get the hell out of Braddock altogether she'll find you again."

Jenny rubbed her face in a failed attempt to wipe away the irritation she was feeling. "I guess."

"You are the worst marathon runner ever," Zack noted.

"I'm a sprinter. If I can't finish the race in about forty seconds, I am not happy."

"Sorry, chief, but this ain't no sprint."

Zack and Jenny headed back to their car.

Knowing what she needed to do, Jenny said goodbye to Zack and drove back to her house. Considering lunch time hadn't even arrived, she figured Greg would be at work when she got home. As she entered and called his name with no response, she felt a wave of relief that her suspicions had been correct. Now that she knew she was alone, she walked through the once beautiful building, noting the progress in the renovation that had occurred while she had been in Connecticut. She visited every room, gently touching the beautiful furniture that Elanor had ordered for the house. They were gorgeous furnishings and Jenny was going to miss them, less for their worth and more for the person who had sent them. But the furniture had been symbolic. Elanor had the pieces custom made to match Jenny's paintings—the paintings that had previously been sitting in a closet because, according to Greg, they didn't match the existing furniture. Elanor had bought an entire house worth of furniture as a subtle but unmistakable *fuck you* to Greg. Jenny couldn't help but giggle at the memory.

She knew Elanor would have been very supportive of what she was about to do. Yes, she planned to leave all that furniture behind, but the furniture was just stuff. Jenny was about to achieve her freedom, and she could practically hear Elanor cheering her on.

As Jenny exited each room, she took her painting with her. The furniture would stay behind, but the paintings would go. Those were hers, and they would go wherever she went.

Once she reached her bedroom, she packed her clothes, her laptop and some additional toiletries. She also packed a box with trinkets from a display in the guest room. Once she had filled a couple of suitcases and carried them down to the trunk of her car, she made sure her paintings were tucked safely in the back seat. Standing next to the car, she took one last look at her house.

This was the house Elanor had grown up in. Elanor had met her boyfriend Steve here, and they'd spent countless happy hours together at this very spot. Jenny had first discovered her psychic ability here when Steve's spirit contacted her.

But this had truly been Elanor's father's house—the man who was more concerned with social status than Elanor's happiness. Now the house belonged to Greg, another man who was more concerned with his image than anything else, including Jenny's well-being. It amazed Jenny how such a beautiful home could harbor such ugliness. No matter how well Greg would be able to restore the house's original grandeur, as long as he lived there the façade would be nothing more than a magnificent lie.

Jenny opened her car door and took her seat behind the wheel. Through the windshield she took one last look at the house. That house. That beautiful fucking house. With both hands she gave the house two emphatic middle fingers, started her car, and drove away.

Jenny pulled in to The Grove apartment complex, noting the sign in front of her parking space said "future resident." She hoped that was true. The last two apartment complexes didn't have what she needed.

Jenny walked into the office and approached the woman behind the desk. "Hi," she began. "I'm looking for an apartment with immediate occupancy and month-to-month lease option. Do you have anything like that available?"

"How many bedrooms do you need?" the young woman asked, typing into her computer.

"I really only need one, but I can be flexible."

After some more typing, she said, "I actually do have a one bedroom that is currently open. We do offer month-to-month leases; just be aware those are more expensive per month than our annual leases."

"That's fine," Jenny said with a relieved smile.

The young woman smiled at Jenny from behind thick glasses. "Would you like to take a look at it?"

Jenny brimmed with excitement. She knew it didn't matter what the apartment looked like; it was going to be her new home for the next few months. "Absolutely."

102

The desk worker disappeared into a small back room and came out with a key. She slipped on her jacket and grabbed her purse. "The building is quite a ways from here. Too far to walk," she explained. "And it's too cold to take the golf cart today. We'll use my car, if that's okay with you."

"That's fine," Jenny agreed. She followed the woman, who introduced herself as Maggie, out the door into the parking lot. Maggie was parked close by, and soon the women were on their way.

Jenny looked out the window in awe at the numerous identical buildings, wondering which was the one she'd soon call home. A strange feeling washed over her knowing that this foreign place would soon be familiar to her. Before long she would know this maze like the back of her hand. The thought was gratifying.

Soon Maggie parked the car and said, "Here we are. Now are you planning to live here by yourself?"

"I sure am," Jenny replied with a large smile.

"Well, I'm happy to report the apartment is on the third floor. I never feel right about women living alone on the ground floor. I feel like that's inviting trouble."

Jenny had never considered the prospect that she could potentially be unsafe living by herself. Although the thought had never crossed her mind before, she was indeed glad to hear she'd be on a higher floor.

The stairs to the apartment were in a covered breezeway between two halves of the same building. Her pulse raced as they reached the third floor and approached her door, which had a large 307 written at eye level. For a brief moment she considered the number 337 that she had seen in her vision. Could that have been an apartment number? She'd need to remember that possibility.

The door opened to reveal a small but clean apartment that faintly smelled of fresh paint. Jenny and Maggie initially stood in the small foyer which led directly into the open living area. "Go ahead," Maggie said. "You can look around."

Jenny smiled eagerly. "Thanks." After several steps she was in the center of the living room, which connected to a tiny dining area and kitchen. She noted the three rooms together could have fit easily into the family room of the house she shared with Greg. Undeterred she ventured into the galley kitchen, spreading her arms, touching both opposite walls without having to fully extend. Curious, she peeked out the small window that overlooked the parking lot below before returning to Maggie in the foyer.

"And here's the bedroom," Maggie added, referring to a room located directly off the foyer. Jenny walked in and examined the closet before checking out the bathroom. She found it odd that the apartment's only bathroom was located there; guests would need to walk through her bedroom to use it. Once back in the bedroom she peeked through the flimsy horizontal blinds to take another look at the parking lot below. She could see the dumpster.

"So what do you think?" Maggie asked.

Jenny came slowly back to the doorway. "It's perfect," she beamed.

"Great," Maggie said. "We'll just head back to the office and fill out some paperwork, and then you can call this place home."

Jenny looked around the apartment with awe. "Home," she whispered. "My new home."

Jenny hummed as she pushed her cart toward the camping section of the discount department store. So far she had picked up enough dinnerware for two, some pots and pans, and a few glasses. She remembered the apartment had a built-in microwave, which would inevitably prove to be helpful. She'd also chosen a pillow from the home section. Now all she needed was furniture. She threw two folding chairs into her cart, followed by an air mattress, an air pump and a sleeping bag. "Perfect," she said out loud as she left that department with satisfaction. A quick trip to the electronic section resulted in the selection of a small television. She inventoried her cart, trying to determine if she'd forgotten anything, but she couldn't think of anything else she'd need. She checked out, headed back to her apartment, and set up her new home.

Once the chairs were unfolded, the bed blown up, and her paintings hung lovingly on the walls, she opened the box of items she had brought from her old house. First she took out a framed black-and-white picture of young Elanor, placing it on the bar that separated her kitchen from her living room. Next to that she placed Steve's framed driver's license, the only photograph she had of him. The remaining items were the painting supplies Elanor had bought for Jenny shortly before she died, and those remained in the box.

Feeling satisfied, Jenny sat down in one of the folding chairs, resting her head back and closing her eyes. This would be her home until she could find a nice townhouse to buy. There was no sense in furnishing this apartment nicely only to turn around and have to move everything. She would simply live as a minimalist for now, and then she would have her real furniture delivered straight to her new house.

In the meantime, she was living the way Elanor had lived when she had first told her father to go to hell and ventured out penniless on her own. Jenny smiled when she remembered Elanor had said she ate nothing but peanut butter sandwiches for a month straight. Compared to Elanor, Jenny was actually living the good life; at least she could afford food and clothes. But she also remembered Elanor saying that penniless phase was the best thing that had ever happened to her. She had been born with a silver spoon in her mouth and a distorted perspective of what was important. Those months without material possessions taught her what happiness was truly about. While she no longer had nice things, she was out from under her father's thumb, and she had the freedom to enjoy her own life and make her own decisions. Elanor learned that stuff was just stuff; true happiness came from the inside.

If the feeling Jenny was experiencing at that moment was any indication, Elanor's conclusion was one hundred percent correct.

After a relaxing sigh, Jenny felt that familiar tug that signaled she was supposed to go somewhere. Without fully venturing into consciousness, Jenny grabbed her purse and her jacket and headed out the door.

Chapter 12

"Hello," Zack said when he picked up his phone.

"Hey," Jenny replied. "I'm calling from the street behind Jeremy Stotler's house."

"What are you doing there?"

"I got led here." Jenny looked beyond the house in front of her, focusing on the back of the Stotler's home, making sure she wasn't missing anything important. "I'm not sure why. Care to join me?"

"Sure," Zack said. "I can come out. What's the name of the street you're on?"

"I have no idea. You'll have to look at a map."

"Okay. I think I can handle that."

"Hey…can you bring some food with you? I haven't eaten and I'm starving."

"Sure thing, boss." After about a half an hour Zack's car pulled up behind Jenny's. He climbed in her passenger seat with a fast food bag in hand. "I hope a burger and fries is okay."

"Right now I'd eat my own foot if it was dipped in ketchup," Jenny confessed, eagerly taking the bag.

"So has anything exciting happened?"

Jenny shook her head as she took a bite of her burger. After she swallowed, she added, "Not a thing. I've been watching the house carefully, but so far nothing noteworthy has happened." She gestured toward the Stotlers' house. "There's still a lot of activity going on in front of the house, but I don't know why I was drawn back here."

The sun was starting to set, adding a layer of gray to the surroundings. Jenny wasn't sure how much longer she'd be able to see anything at all.

As Jenny held out the cup of fries for Zack to share, she noted, "I got an apartment today."

"What? Get out! Where?"

"The Grove."

"Holy shit. That's awesome. Have you talked to Greg yet?"

Jenny's face reflected her shame. "No. I wanted to have a place set up first so that I have somewhere to go after it all hits the fan."

"You could always lay low at my place. You know that, right?"

Jenny shook her head. "No offense or anything, but I don't want to go from Greg's place to your place. I want to do this myself. I have to do this myself. Besides, I don't want Greg thinking that you're the reason I'm leaving him. I want him to know that *he's* the reason I'm leaving him."

"I get that," Zack said. "But why the Grove? It's not exactly the nicest place. I imagine you could afford better than that."

"I could. But the Grove had immediate occupancy. Besides, I don't need fancy living accommodations. I'm not Greg."

At that moment something caught Jenny's eye. She nudged Zack with her elbow, pointing over his shoulder out the passenger window. A woman was hurrying out the back door of the Stotlers' house, run-walking through the yard between them, and she eventually got in her car which was parked a very short distance from Jenny's.

As this woman started her car, Jenny did the same. Zack buckled his seat belt while Jenny handed him the rest of her food. "Don't eat that. I'm still hungry," she commanded.

"No guarantees. It's food," Zack stated simply.

Jenny followed the woman's car for a couple of miles through residential neighborhoods to a split-level home, where the woman pulled into the driveway. Jenny stopped her car in front of the house, getting out quickly to be sure to catch the woman before she got into her house.

"Excuse me," Jenny called.

The woman, who appeared to be in her forties, turned to look quizzically at Jenny.

"Are you friends with Mrs. Stotler?" Jenny continued.

The curiosity on the woman's face turned quickly to anger. "You people are ruthless, you know that? The Stotlers have no comment at this time, thank you very much." She sped up her pace toward the house.

"Wait-wait-wait-wait-wait! I'm not with the press!" Jenny shouted all at once. Knowing she only had a few seconds until this woman disappeared into the house, she added, "I know who killed Morgan Caldwell."

With that the woman froze. After a moment she turned to Jenny, wordlessly inviting her to continue.

"And it wasn't Jeremy," Jenny added softly.

"Who was it?" the woman asked with shock.

Jenny let out a sigh. "If I tell you his name it would mean nothing to you. It was random. But if you give me a moment of your time, I can show you that there are similar unsolved cases in Connecticut, and the prime suspect in those cases now lives here."

"Why are you telling me this? Why aren't you going to the police?"

"I did go to the police," Jenny confessed, "and they wouldn't listen." Jenny took a few steps closer to the woman, hoping to appear friendlier. "Ideally I'd like to be able to talk with Mrs. Stotler. I am hoping we can piece some things together that will help clear Jeremy's name. Not only that, but there are some people down here that shouldn't be trusted. I need to let her know who those people are so she can be careful."

Jenny could see the wheels turning in this woman's head.

"But as you know," Jenny continued, "the Stotler house is a circus right now. I can't exactly go and ring her doorbell. But since you seem to be her friend, I'm wondering if you could help me get in contact with her."

The woman reached into her purse. "I'll give her a call and see what she says," she conceded. "If she does agree to meet you you'd have to go there, though. She won't leave her house. If she even steps out to get her mail those damn reporters swarm her like bees. They have no mercy. It's horrible." She pulled out her phone, pressed a button and put the phone to her ear. "Hi Abby. Sorry to bother you again, but there's a woman here who believes she may know who Morgan's real killer is and she'd like to talk to you…I don't know, she must have followed me from your house…Yeah, she seems okay…All right, I'll tell her. Thanks Abby."

Jenny held her breath until the woman replied, "She said it's okay for you to come over. You'd just need to use the back door."

Jenny smiled at the woman. "Thank you. Thank you so much."

The woman's voice became shaky. "Just get Jeremy out of jail, will you? That boy doesn't belong there. He wouldn't hurt a fly."

Jenny stepped into the Stotlers' house, immediately feeling the tension within. The lighting was dim, and thick blankets covered the windows, making the house seem even more somber. Abby Stotler, who greeted them at the door, looked as if she hadn't slept or eaten in days. She almost looked dead herself.

"Hi," Jenny said softly. "Thank you for seeing me. My name is Jenny Watkins, and this is my friend Zack Larrabee."

Abby nodded slightly. A man approached from the back of the room. "Evan Stotler," he said as he extended his hand, first to Zack and then to Jenny. "Please, have a seat," he said.

Zack and Jenny sat down on the couch as Abby immediately posed, "So who do you think did this?"

Jenny was reluctant to divulge her full suspicions right away. "A man from Connecticut. We just got back from there, actually. We were looking into two unsolved murders of young women up there whose circumstances are very similar to Morgan's case. The man we believe committed those murders now lives down here in Braddock."

Abby and Evan looked at each other before they turned back to Jenny. "Are you with the police?" Evan asked.

"Not exactly," Jenny confessed, still trying to avoid the word *psychic.* "We just investigate crimes as sort of our hobby."

"Have you told the police about this guy?" Evan asked.

Jenny shook her head. "I'm going to tell you something that cannot leave this room."

Evan and Abby hung on her every word.

"The man we believe to be responsible for this is a Braddock police officer." Jenny reached into her purse, pulling out one of her

109

pictures. "This man, in fact." She handed the picture over to the Stotlers, who looked at each other in disbelief.

"This was one of the men who came to arrest Jeremy!" Abby exclaimed.

"So you can see why this is a delicate situation," Jenny added.

Evan, who remained less emotional than his wife, posed, "What makes you think he did this?"

Jenny decided to stick with just the facts for the moment. "Like I said, there are two similar cases in Ivory Heights, Connecticut, where he used to be a police officer before he moved here. The first girl in Connecticut was walking to a convenience store in the middle of the night to get her single mother some medicine, and the second victim had a flat tire at three a.m. It's reasonable to think that if a police officer pulls up in either of those situations, the girls would readily get into his car."

"Especially the second girl," Zack added. "From what we can gather, she was pretty street-smart. She was twenty-one and completely sober, on her way home from work. You'd think that she'd be very reluctant to accept a ride from *anyone* considering the first murder from three months earlier hadn't been solved. She was probably quite relieved when a policeman showed up, not realizing he was the very man she should have been fearing."

Jenny continued. "Our theory in this particular case is that Morgan snuck out in the middle of the night to meet up with Jeremy. On her way back to her house, the officer offered her a ride home. It was probably chilly out, and she accepted. That was her fatal mistake."

Abby looked at Evan, addressing her comment to him. "That lines up perfectly with what Jeremy says happened."

"Yeah," Evan admitted with a tilt of his head. "It sure does."

"So what is the police's theory?" Zack asked. "What evidence do they have against Jeremy?"

Abby sighed, her eyes filling up with tears. She placed her hand over her mouth and looked away. With a pat on Abby's leg, Evan told the story. "Well, when the police first questioned Jeremy, there were a few things he didn't know. He didn't know Morgan was missing, and he didn't know they had cell phone records of texts between the two of them in the middle of the night. All he knew was that policemen had shown up at his school to ask if he'd been with

Morgan the night before. He thought her parents had found out and were planning to charge him with statutory rape, so he denied even seeing her. He claimed he was sleeping all night." Evan shook his head. "He's a kid for God's sake. He was afraid to get in trouble. I think if he had known that Morgan was missing he'd have done everything he could to help find her. His lies, though, were viewed as evidence of his guilt.

"They also found his DNA on her stomach and his skin under her fingernails. As you know, those things can result from consensual sex. However, there were signs of forcible rape on Morgan's body when she was found, and no other DNA was found besides Jeremy's. The police concluded that the sex between Morgan and Jeremy wasn't consensual."

"The killer wore a condom and she wore gloves," Jenny found herself saying before she had the inclination to stop herself.

Abby seemed confused. "What?"

Realizing she'd just revealed herself, Jenny hung her head. "Morgan. She was wearing gloves during her attack. And the killer used a condom."

"How do you know that?" Evan asked.

Jenny sighed and braced herself for ridicule. "I get visions," she replied.

Evan and Abby both remained quiet, inviting Jenny to elaborate.

"I saw the attack through Morgan's eyes while I was still unaware that anyone was missing. She made the contact with me before her story was on the news." Jenny swallowed and continued. "By the time the Amber Alert hit the air, I already knew she was gone. I can only receive messages from the deceased." She looked at her lap, trying to avoid eye contact with the couple sitting in front of her. "It broke my heart, especially when I saw the Caldwells pleading for her safe return.

"Although, during the vision Morgan did give me a good look at the person who did this. That was what enabled me to paint the picture I gave to you. However, when I brought it to the police, they got angry with me. I didn't know at the time I was accusing a police officer.

"Long story short, a little research showed this guy came from a small town in Connecticut with two similar homicides. I can't imagine that's a coincidence."

The Stotlers looked intently at Jenny, still silent.

"I realize I'm making an outrageous claim," Jenny added. "I understand if you're reluctant to believe me."

Abby broke her silence. "I'm willing to believe anything that will help exonerate my son."

Jenny nodded with appreciation. "Thank you. And now that you know the truth about me, I have to admit I was hoping to be able to go into Jeremy's room to see if I can get a reading there. Sometimes it helps to be where the victim actually was, and this was one of the last places..." Jenny decided against finishing her sentence.

Abby closed her eyes and whispered, "His room's downstairs."

"I'll take you there," Evan said as he stood. Zack and Jenny followed Evan down the stairs into a basement room that had clearly been inhabited by a teenager. Jenny didn't say anything as she walked in, swallowing the sadness that was creeping into her soul. Something about the way the room was decorated was especially upsetting to her: sports memorabilia, music posters, a guitar—typical teenage stuff. Jeremy's biggest concern should have been an upcoming math test or determining which girl to take to the prom. Murder should not have been touching his life in any capacity.

With a shudder Jenny physically shook off the sadness, reminding herself to remain professional. She had a job to do. She flashed a forced smile at Evan, hoping her sorrow hadn't been apparent. With a deep breath she ventured to Jeremy's bed, where she sat gently on the edge and closed her eyes.

She saw Jeremy's dimly-lit face appear before her, smiling, looking tenderly at her. Her spirits soared with his gaze, making her feel invincible and unmistakably alive. Pleasurable images flashed in front of her like short movie clips—laughter, hugs, kisses.

An itchy back.

She also felt herself being directed to the pile of Morgan's clothing that had been on the floor near Jeremy's bed. She inventoried the items, positive that there was something significant to be found there. As Jenny surveyed the clothes, she realized what she was supposed to notice. As soon as the insight struck, the vision disappeared.

Jenny paused for a moment after venturing into consciousness. Her sadness returned with a vengeance with the realization that things hadn't been as they'd seemed. These were children. First loves. These images in her mind should have been fond memories that both Morgan and Jeremy cherished for decades to come, not visions from a deceased girl seeking justice.

Fuck Orlowski, she thought. *Fucking asshole.* If he had been in front of her at that moment, she'd have killed him herself.

"Did you get something?" Zack asked.

Jenny nodded, hardly able to speak. She needed to get out of that room before the sorrow and anger swallowed her whole. "I'd like to go upstairs," she whispered.

Evan looked wide-eyed at Zack, who in turn approached Jenny and put his arm around her shoulder. That comfort was just what she needed, giving her the strength to walk out of the room and up the stairs.

During this time Abby had remained in the living room, and when the others returned it was obvious she'd been crying. Jenny purposely avoided looking at her in order to keep her own resolve. With a sigh Jenny sat down on the couch and began her account. "Things didn't go as far as you might suspect that night. While Jeremy did ejaculate, Morgan had remained dressed. Any evidence of trauma on Morgan's body was a direct result of what Orlowski had done to her. And Jeremy's skin under her fingernails was because she'd scratched his back. He had an itch."

Evan spoke softly. "That's exactly what Jeremy had said. He claimed they never had sex."

"I believe he was telling the truth," Jenny said. "And I can assure you that absolutely everything that went on in there was consensual." Looking down at her lap, Jenny added, "It appears Morgan was very much in love with your son."

With that Abby completely lost her composure. "That poor little girl!" she sobbed as she placed her head in her hands and folded over onto her lap. Evan rubbed her back as she went on. "She was an innocent child. How could anybody do that to a child?"

Jenny's resolve melted, and tears began to fill her eyes.

Abby looked up at Zack and Jenny with red eyes and tear-soaked cheeks. "I knew her. She'd been over the house a few times. She was such a sweet girl. I know she cared about my son, and I know he cared for her. Morgan's mother just didn't want them dating because of the age difference. She'd even called me to tell me that it wasn't personal—that she liked Jeremy and thought he was a good kid—but she didn't want her fifteen-year-old dating an eighteen-year-old. God, they were such a nice family. And I can't even call them and tell them how sorry I am for their loss because everybody thinks my son is responsible. I can't go to Morgan's funeral. *Jeremy* can't go to her funeral. I can't even *mourn* her for God's sake because I am so worried about my own son. I can't wrap my head around the fact that my son is in jail, let alone the fact that this beautiful little girl is gone. It's just too much."

Although Jenny wasn't looking at him, she could sense Zack's discomfort. The tension was palpable.

"The only thing this girl did wrong is that she wanted to spend time with my son," Abby continued. "How am I supposed to live with that? How is Jeremy supposed to live with that? And what if he gets convicted of this? What if he spends the rest of his life in jail for something he didn't do? What if he gets the death penalty?" Abby was becoming hysterical.

Business at hand, Jenny reminded herself. "Well, there was something else Morgan showed me that might be helpful in clearing Jeremy's name."

Abby immediately became quiet.

"She directed me to the pile of clothes on the floor. Her shoes were there, and her jacket, but no gloves. There were no gloves. And during Morgan's original vision of the attack, I distinctly saw her wearing gloves. That leads me to believe they weren't her gloves. They may have belonged to the killer. And I'm not sure if any gloves were found at the scene, but if they could determine the owner of the gloves, perhaps they'd be able to identify who did this."

"What did the gloves look like?" Evan asked. "Hopefully they weren't Jeremy's."

Jenny closed her eyes and covered her face, trying to recall images of the original contact. "It was hard to see, but black I think. Black and leather."

"Did they have fingers?"

"Yes, sir," Jenny said.

Evan turned excitedly to Abby. "The only pair of gloves Jeremy had were fingerless. And they might even still be here."

"I'll look for them," Abby said, immediately standing up and rushing off. While Jenny hated to admit it, she was glad Abby had left. Her sorrow had been way too contagious.

"Okay," Evan said, rubbing his temples. "Even if we do determine that she was wearing gloves that didn't belong to her or to Jeremy, who do we tell about this? The cops think they have the case solved. Not only that, but if we go to them and tell them that there were unidentified gloves at the scene, won't that make it look like Jeremy was there? How else would we know about the gloves?"

"Now you see what we're up against," Jenny proclaimed.

"Well," Zack added, "we do have the number of a man on the force who is open to secretly investigating this a little further. But you absolutely cannot tell anybody about that. Just let it help you sleep a little more soundly at night knowing someone on the inside is still not entirely convinced that Jeremy is the right guy."

"You don't know how much better that makes me feel," Evan said.

"Again, please, just don't say anything."

"Oh, I won't," Evan replied emphatically. "I won't do anything at all that could jeopardize this investigation. Believe me."

"I feel funny," Jenny announced. Something inside of her was screaming.

"Are you okay?" Zack asked.

Jenny felt anxiety and panic. If she could have jumped out of her own skin she would have. "Somebody is frantic. I imagine it's Morgan." She tried to make sense of the hysteria within her, but she wasn't able to sort any of it out.

Both men sat helplessly as Jenny turned her focus inward, trying to interpret the message. She eventually pointed at the window. "Something is going on out front."

Evan hopped up and immediately created a slight opening in the blanket over the window. He looked outside for a few minutes before proclaiming, "Well I'll be damned."

"What is it?" Zack asked.

Evan released the blanket, letting it fall back into place. He turned, white as a sheet, to Zack and Jenny. "That officer—the one you think did this—he's out there."

Chapter 13

Abby came quickly into the room, holding a pair of balled-up fingerless gloves. "Here they are!" she announced happily, but her look quickly turned to apprehension when she saw everyone's expressions. "What's the matter?"

"Now don't get upset," Evan said. "But the cop they believe is responsible for this…he's the one on duty right now."

Abby looked horrified, but Zack seemed confused. "On duty?" he asked.

Evan scratched his head. "Ever since Jeremy got arrested, they've had a cop stationed out there to keep the peace. There are a lot of press and neighbors milling about out there, and I imagine the cop is there to prevent things from getting out of hand or to keep people from harassing us." He continued to speak, but no longer to Zack and Jenny. He looked up at the ceiling and announced to no one, "I can't believe that fucking man has the nerve to sit outside of this house. I want to go out there and beat the snot out of him."

Mild, Jenny thought, compared to what she wanted to do to him.

"Actually, it's a good thing," Zack commented. When he received strange looks from the others, he elaborated. "He's accounted for. He can't be out there killing anyone else if he's spending the night in front of your house."

Evan looked defeated. "I guess you're right. I just hate the thought of that son of a bitch being anywhere near me." Suddenly he looked at Jenny with awe. "Hey…you knew he was out there."

117

"Yes, sir."

"That means you're for real."

Jenny smiled modestly. "Yes, sir, I am."

Once again Evan shook his head and said, "I'll be damned."

"I need to be able to get back to the car without him seeing me," Jenny stated nervously.

"He doesn't know you, does he?" Abby asked.

"Actually, he does," Jenny confessed. "Morgan led me to him once, and I had a conversation with him. That's how I found out he used to live in Connecticut. If she ever leads me to him again, I think he might offer me some more information. But if he sees me…that could ruin everything. He'd never tell me anything if he knew I was connected to you somehow."

"Um, not to mention your safety might be at risk," Zack added.

Jenny hadn't considered that before. Realizing the situation was worse than she thought, she hung her head.

"Well, it's dark," Evan said. "That'll help."

"I'll go out there," Abby declared.

The others looked at her. "What?" Evan asked.

"I'll go out there. I'll make a scene. I'll tell all the reporters to go to hell or something. And when I do, you two can slip out the back."

"Are you sure?" Jenny asked.

"Absolutely. I don't give a shit if the people of Braddock think I'm crazy. I want my son out of jail."

Although not a parent herself, Jenny imagined most mothers would have reacted the same way. "Okay, then," she said. "Let me get my coat. I'll go to the back of the house and wait for your cue."

"Wait a minute. Before you do," Abby came over to Jenny. "I just want to thank you. In a world where it seems everyone has already concluded my son is guilty, it's nice to know there are some people out there who believe he's innocent. And willing to fight for it."

"Actually, it's not me," Jenny confessed. "It's Morgan. She's the one desperate to clear Jeremy's name." Unsure if she should add the next part, Jenny continued anyway. "You know, it did occur to me that my first vision from Morgan came mid-morning, the day after she disappeared…probably around the same time the police were at school questioning Jeremy. I personally don't believe that's a coincidence."

Abby looked down at the floor as she processed the information. She didn't reply.

Jenny took Abby's hand. "I think Morgan will be able to achieve peace if Jeremy gets freed and Orlowski gets caught. I hope you can take some comfort in that."

Abby closed her eyes tightly and nodded.

"So," Jenny said with renewed vigor. "Are you ready to go out there and let them have it?"

Jenny giggled as she started the car. "Holy shit," she said. "Abby can sure put on a show, can't she?" The commotion from the front yard was heard easily from as far away as the car.

"Well, at least you know for sure Orlowski didn't see you."

"Yeah, that is a comfort," Jenny confessed. As the car pulled away, she added, "Damn. I'm exhausted."

"Well, you've had a long day," Zack replied.

"Indeed. I can't wait to go to bed."

"Do you even have a bed? Or are you planning on going back to your house?" After a pause he added, "Or my place?"

"I have an air mattress and a sleeping bag," Jenny declared proudly. "And that'll do."

"That doesn't exactly sound like luxury accommodations. Are you sure you wouldn't rather stay at my place?"

Jenny smiled. "Thank you for the offer, but I am going to sleep in my new place tonight. It's my first night there. That's very exciting."

"Okay," Zack said without bitterness. "Suit yourself."

"Hey, can you call that Johnson guy and tell him about the gloves?"

"Sure," Zack replied. "I get to be an informant. Now *that's* exciting. Are you sure you don't want to do it?"

"Nah, that's okay," Jenny said. "I don't even have the guy's number. I'll let you do the honors."

"What if he asks me questions? Like how we know about the gloves?"

"Why do you think I want you to be the informant?" Jenny said smiling.

Zack made a face at her before dialing the phone.

"Put him on speaker," Jenny said at the last minute. Zack obliged.

"Hello?"

"Yes, Officer Johnson. I was given your number by Danny Fazzino up in Ivory Heights, Connecticut. He told me to let you know if we have any insight on the Caldwell case."

"Oh, yes. Do you have anything for me?" Johnson asked.

"Yeah, one thing, Zack replied. "I am under the impression that Morgan was wearing gloves during the attack, but they weren't hers. They may have been the killer's. Maybe if you can get some of Orlowski's gloves and test them, you'll find Morgan's DNA."

"Well, that's a good thought, but there's a little something called *illegal search and seizure.* We'd need to have a warrant to secure any of his gloves, and we'd need probable cause to get a warrant. Right now we don't have that, unless you can give me something else." Johnson said.

"Um," Zack replied, "I don't have anything else."

"So what makes you think she was wearing his gloves?" Johnson asked.

Zack winced. "I'd rather not say." He bit his lip.

"Alright. So that's all you got for me?"

"Yes, sir. For now."

"Let me know if that changes."

"Will do," Zack said, hanging up his phone. "See? I suck at being an informant. You totally should have done it."

Jenny giggled. "You did fine," she said, although she didn't mean it.

Dressed in a t-shirt and a pair of sweat pants, Jenny turned off the light in her bedroom. Although she hadn't remembered to buy a lamp, there was enough light from the parking lot coming in through the open blinds she was able to see her way to the air mattress. She snuggled into her sleeping bag on top of her makeshift bed, happy to be tucked in for the night. Quickly, however, she realized just how quiet her apartment was.

She heard a banging sound, causing her to quickly raise her head up. She listened intently, hearing the sound again a short time later, determining it was simply the heating system making noise. *Orlowski is busy tonight,* she reminded herself. *He's in front of the Stotler's house. Besides, he has no idea where you live, and breaking and entering is not his MO. Nobody is coming to get you. Relax.* While the words made sense logically, Jenny found herself wishing she could watch television. That would have kept her mind off things. Although she had bought the television itself, she didn't have cable hooked up to it yet, so it was still useless. In search of another suitable distraction, she got back out of bed and retrieved her cell phone. While it was less ideal, it would have to do.

She put music on in the background and did a little investigating. She looked for the location of the orchard where Morgan's body had been found. She imagined the media frenzy had left that area by now and she'd have the ability to walk around in peace, hopefully gaining a little more insight from Morgan. She also searched for Orlowski's address, hoping to be able to make a stop there, wondering if he had ever brought Morgan back to his place. Her efforts were fruitless, however, which actually did make sense to her. She imagined a police officer wouldn't want his address easily accessible to anyone who spent a few minutes online.

Reading the latest news on the Caldwell case, she realized Morgan's viewing was scheduled for the following evening. Jenny decided she'd attend, not only to pay her respects, but also to try to receive a contact. There was a chance Orlowski would show up; she wondered if it would seem weird for him to see her at the service. *Would that make him suspicious? Should I try to mask my appearance?* She'd have to contemplate that some more.

Either way, she'd need nice clothes for the service, and those were all at the old house. While she could easily afford new ones, she knew that wasn't the answer. She needed to go back to the house and face Greg. Rolling over on her air mattress, she let out an aggravated sigh. This line of thinking was not going to help her fall asleep; her brain was proving to be her own worst enemy again. She'd have to switch focus if she stood any chance at all of drifting off.

Zack, she thought, and the image suddenly comforted her. She remembered how it felt to have him lying beside her, his arm pulling her in close. She imagined him there, and all of her worries seemed to melt away. Before long waves of sleep came over her, and she slept soundly through the night.

Rain fell gently from the sky as Jenny and Zack parked the car in front of the orchard where Morgan's body had been found. The exact location of the discovery hadn't been disclosed, but Jenny was optimistic that Morgan would lead the way. She was reaching for the umbrella she always kept between the seats of her car when she posed to Zack, "Did you bring an umbrella?"

"No," he replied. "I don't even think I own one."

"Do you want to share mine?"

"Nah," he said. "I'll be fine."

"Suit yourself." Jenny pushed the car door just enough to fit her umbrella through, opening it before she exited the car. "But the offer still stands if you change your mind."

They walked out of the car, heading toward the vast expanse of pecan trees. "Any idea where you're going?" Zack asked.

"Not yet," Jenny replied. "They had said she was found near a service road. I don't know if that helps us, though. This place is huge."

The two silently walked for a while, rain bouncing off Jenny's umbrella.

"I don't guess this rain does a whole lot for evidence, does it?" Zack finally said.

"I hope they've gotten all the evidence they need already."

"Unfortunately, they did—Jeremy Stotler's DNA."

Jenny shook her head at the thought of that poor boy still sitting in jail. She quickened her pace.

After walking for several minutes, Zack pointed off into the distance. "Hey, check that out."

Jenny looked in the direction he had pointed; through the trees she was able to make out a white tent. "Do you think that's where she was found?"

"I would imagine," Zack said. "I can't think of any other reason for a tent being out here."

Jenny wondered why she hadn't heard anything from Morgan thus far. She began to feel a little nervous that Morgan may have crossed over and her messages were a thing of the past.

That uneasiness dissipated, however, as they walked closer to the tent. With each step Jenny felt a growing sense of fear and dread. Her insides fluttered as she felt a desperate need to run. Walking toward the tent seemed counterintuitive—almost cruel—but Jenny knew she had to continue.

She held on to Zack's elbow as the feeling inside her grew more disturbing. "I feel fear here," she noted.

Zack didn't reply.

As Zack and Jenny crossed the service road, Jenny remembered the headlights that had illuminated Orlowski's face in her vision. She stopped for a moment in the middle of the dirt path, trying to get a feel for where the car had been parked. After venturing several steps down the road, she paused; she knew she had found the spot.

She closed her eyes and the sky became dark behind her lids. Orlowski's dimly lit face appeared before her. He handed her gloves, with a gun pointed at her face.

"Put these on," he demanded softly. "If you do everything I tell you, I won't hurt you."

Believing him, Jenny saw herself putting the gloves on.

Orlowski grabbed her by the shoulder and pushed her a few yards into the trees. He instructed her to lie down, and she did so. At that moment she heard the sound of rain falling heavily around her. Realizing the rain was in the present, Jenny discovered she'd lost the vision. "Dammit!" she exclaimed.

"What's the matter?" Zack posed.

Without looking at Zack she held her umbrella over his head and said, "I was having a vision but it got cut short. The rain interfered with it."

"What did you see?"

"Well, it was definitely Orlowski, and he did have her put gloves on. He forced her into the woods, and that's when it ended." She shook her head. "The bastard promised he wouldn't hurt her if she just did everything he said. You know as well as I do that he didn't mean it. He knew he was going to kill her, just like he did the others. It was just his way of keeping her quiet. Asshole."

123

"Sad," Zack noted. "You'd think you could trust a cop."

"You'd think," Jenny replied bitterly. A chill raced up her spine, but she was unsure whether that was due to the weather or the horror that had gone on under that tent.

The rain began to come down in sheets. Zack spoke loudly so he could be heard over the noise. "Do you want to go back to the car, or do you want to stay here?"

"The car," Jenny replied. "I don't think I'll be able to get anything like this."

The two huddled under the umbrella until they made it back to the shelter of Jenny's car. Once inside Jenny shuddered one more time, turning the car on and blasting the heat. "That was miserable," she commented.

Zack ignored her observation. "So why the switch, do you think?"

Jenny held her hands up in front of the heat vents, watching the water create a white curtain over the windshield. "What switch?"

"Well, he killed Lashonda in one location and dumped her in another. It seems with Morgan he killed her here, at the same spot he left her. Why do you think that is?"

Jenny shook her head. "I don't know. Do killers usually stick to the same pattern that way?"

"I thought so," Zack replied. "But I could be wrong."

"Do you think the gloves were the result of the whole 'Lashonda's ring' episode? I noticed during my vision the gloves were a little tight and hard to put on. I had to squiggle my hand around to get my fingers in them. There's no way I could have gotten them off easily to leave some sort of token behind."

Zack shrugged; he was preoccupied. "Could be. You know what confuses me the most, though?"

Jenny turned to look at Zack for the first time since they'd entered the car, and the sight momentarily took her breath away.

Zack looked very good wet.

Regaining her composure, Jenny casually asked, "What's that?"

Zack returned Jenny's glance, once again making her feel overcome with attraction. He looked intently at her and posed, "What took him so long to strike again? Why a three year break?"

Jenny could hardly pay attention to his words because she was so distracted by his appearance. "I don't know," she remarked. "What do you think?"

"I'm not sure. A three-year-long attack of consciousness? Temporary self-control? Were things going well for him at that time? Did these killings result from something shitty happening in his personal life? That's what's been bothering me. Is it really all about opportunity, or something more? If we can get an idea about what causes him to do this, maybe we can get an idea of when it's going to happen again."

Jenny turned back toward the windshield so she could focus. "Isn't the fact that he's a sick bastard what's causing him to do this?"

Zack snorted. "Maybe *cause* is the wrong word. I guess I'm talking about a *trigger*. If he gets in a fight with his girlfriend, does that inspire him to go out and kill some innocent girl? Or does he just see one of these girls out at night and something takes over him?"

"He had gloves with him," Jenny noted as the rain began to let up. "Doesn't that imply premeditation?"

"Maybe," Zack surmised. "But there are varying degrees of premeditation. He could have kept the gloves in the car for months waiting for the right opportunity, or he could have put them in his car that night because he was specifically hunting."

"Or maybe they were his gloves..."

"Well, you said they were small on you, and you—presumably—were a fifteen year old girl. Unless Orlowski has some serious bitch hands, I doubt they were his gloves."

"Bitch hands?"

Zack looked at Jenny as if it was absurd she'd never heard the phrase. "Yeah. Bitch hands."

Jenny let out a playful sigh; she couldn't believe she was genuinely attracted to this man. Placing her face into her hands, she said, "I don't know. I'm going to drive myself crazy with all this speculating. I wish I could get my hands on something irrefutable. Something that cries, 'Look, world, Orlowski did this!'"

"Well, the rain is letting up. Do you want to go back out there and see if you can get anything else?"

After thinking for a moment, Jenny said, "No. I've already seen what happens next, and I don't want to go through that again. If you want the truth," Jenny continued nervously, "I was thinking we could go back to your place."

"Uhh…." Zack seemed to be unsure if he had understood her correctly. "And do what?"

With a playful shrug, Jenny said, "Whatever comes to mind." She flashed him a look that left no question as to what she meant.

"Sure," he replied quickly. "You don't have to ask me twice on that one."

Jenny put the car in drive and turned it around. "I do have to confess that you look pretty sexy when you're wet."

"Okay, I'm going to stand outside every time it rains."

Jenny laughed as she drove. She couldn't believe how irresponsible she was being, but it certainly felt good for a change.

"Uh oh," Zack called from the bathroom.

"What's the matter?" Jenny stretched out, satisfied and naked, cozy under Zack's covers.

"Um, is this a bad time for you?"

Jenny didn't understand his cryptic message. "What do you mean *bad time*?"

"I mean," Zack said as he emerged from the bathroom, "is this a time when you could get pregnant?" He made a face. "The condom kind of…broke."

Flipping comfortably over on to her belly, Jenny remarked, "It's never a bad time. I'm on the pill."

"Oh, thank God," Zack said, hanging his head with relief. "Leave it to you to be the responsible one."

"Well," Jenny replied, "I'm not exactly sure I'd call myself responsible, all things considered, but I am grateful. I'd have an awful lot of explaining to do if I got pregnant."

Zack climbed back into bed, nestling up against Jenny. "What do you mean?"

"I *mean*, it would be very obvious this child wasn't Greg's. We haven't had sex in months."

"Really? Months?"

"Well, we've never christened our new house, and we've lived there for about three months now."

"Wow. No wonder Greg is cranky."

126

"He was cranky before I stopped putting out. It was cause and effect."

"So have you told him you want a divorce yet?"

"No, I haven't seen him," Jenny replied. With a giggle, she added, "I can't believe I'm lying in bed with the man I just had sex with, talking about my husband."

"Eh, shit happens." Zack rolled over on to his back.

"So do you have, like, zero respect for me?" Jenny posed.

"I have zero respect for your husband," Zack replied casually, "which is why I just had sex with his wife."

"You didn't answer the question."

He looked at Jenny. "Are you serious?"

"Yes, I'm serious."

"Of course I respect you," he replied sincerely. "I respect you more than I respect myself."

"Even though I'm cheating on my husband?"

"Hey, it takes two to tango. I'm just as guilty of this as you are."

"Yeah, but you aren't the one who took a vow."

Zack shrugged. "But I'm aware that you did, and I still hit on you anyway. And I am so irresistible, how were you supposed to say no to my advances? I really didn't leave you much choice." He looked at her playfully out of the corner of his eye.

"Yes, that was certainly unfair of you and Little Zack to gang up on me like that. I didn't stand a chance." She nudged Zack with her elbow. "On a totally different note, I want to go to Morgan's wake tonight, and I was wondering if you'd like to come with me."

"Are you asking me on a date?" Zack asked.

"Some date—a nice trip to the funeral home."

"I've had worse."

Jenny laughed. "Seriously, what is with you? It's like you've had sex and now you've lost your mind."

"Well, if my brain is housed in Little Zack like I think it is, I did just lose part of my mind."

Jenny smacked her hand on her forehead. "I hear you, but I'm choosing to ignore you. My question is whether you want to come with me or not to the wake."

"Sure, I'll go."

"Okay, next question. I was wondering if I should try to make myself look different when I go, just in case Orlowski is there. I may not want him to recognize me, especially if I'm with you. I was flirting with him pretty heavily the other night. It would be weird if I showed up with another guy."

"For all he knows, I could be your brother."

"That is true," Jenny thought out loud. "Actually, I did tell him I was married—unhappily so."

"So maybe I could go with you and act like I hate you. Then he'll think I'm your husband."

"Still ignoring you. But here's something to consider…why would I be at the wake? In my conversation with him, I didn't act like I knew Morgan."

"I'm sure at least half of the people who show up tonight won't know Morgan. They'll just want to pay their respects because of the way she died."

"I guess you're right. And if the place is as crowded as the vigil was, or even Morgan's own front yard, Orlowski might not even notice me at all. I might just be a face in the crowd."

"That's what I'm thinking."

Jenny let out a sigh and looked at Zack's alarm clock. "I guess I'd better head out of here. I need to go back to the house, get some funeral-appropriate clothes, and break up with my husband."

"Go get 'em, tiger."

"Oh…and I need to get a lamp."

Zack laughed out loud. "That's quite an interesting to-do list."

Jenny slid on her underwear. "And I need to call the cable company…"

Greg's car was in the driveway when Jenny pulled in. Butterflies danced around her belly as she approached the front door. She felt as if she reeked of recent sex, and Greg was going to notice as soon as she walked in.

Gathering a breath, she knocked on the door. A moment later, Greg opened it. "What are you knocking for?" he asked impatiently.

Jenny had forgotten that she was the only one aware of her new living arrangement. Unsure of how she should respond, she decided to simply ignore the question. She walked in, quickly passing Greg, remarking, "I really need to talk to you for a minute."

"You think?"

Ignore it, Jenny thought. *Don't let him get to you. Just do what you have to do.* She straightened her posture and declared, "I have come to the conclusion that our marriage just isn't working. I am here to tell you that I've gotten myself an apartment."

Greg let out a chuckle. "Oh yeah?"

Laughter was certainly not the reaction she had anticipated. "Yes, I have. And why do you think that's funny?"

"I just can't believe how far you're taking this." Greg shook his head. "But maybe this is a good thing. You'll go out, get your little apartment, and start living this life that you think will be so much better. I guarantee you'll fall flat on your face. Before you know it you'll be back here asking me to take you back."

Jenny's jaw dropped. She couldn't speak.

"But like I said, maybe it's a good thing. Then you'll get over this mid-life crisis, or whatever it is you're having, and you'll finally stop acting like I'm holding you back. You'll realize I'm holding you *up.*"

"Oh. My. God," Jenny said. "Oh my God. I cannot believe how blind I have been for seven years. This is how you are. This is how you always have been. You belittle me, making me feel like a failure, *on purpose.* And for all this time, I *believed* you. I believed that I was lucky to have you. That I wasn't worth anything on my own. How stupid could I have been? Isn't it obvious, Greg? Can't you see it? *You're* the asshole, not me."

"Keep talking," Greg said. "Keep talking like this and when you come crawling back to me, begging me to take you back, the answer is going to be no."

"No. *You* keep talking. Please. Because with every word you say it becomes clearer and clearer to me what a shithead you are. By all means, continue."

"You need to get out of here," Greg said sternly. "I see you've already taken your ugly, sad little excuses for paintings out of here, which I'm grateful for. I'm glad I don't have to look at those things anymore…"

"See? You're doing it again! You're trying to make me feel like shit! I'm totally on to you."

"I'm just speaking the truth…why do you think I kept those things in the closet for so long?"

"Because you're a shithead! And you were trying to make me feel inadequate. But that won't work anymore."

"You need to go."

"You're right, I do," Jenny replied. "I have places to go. I just need to get some clothes…and my easel. I forgot that before."

"Go ahead. Get your stuff. I don't give a shit."

"Don't mind if I do." Jenny bounded up the stairs, retrieving the items she needed. She quickly looked around for anything else she might want to take, but nothing immediately struck her.

She walked down the stairs and toward the front door where Greg was leaning against the wall in the foyer with his arms folded over his chest. "I give it a week before you're back."

Jenny looked at him with a softened expression. "Honestly, I think I'll be back before then." She opened the door, and before she walked out she added, "I guarantee there's something else I forgot."

She slammed the door behind her.

Chapter 14

"He makes me want to vomit," Jenny said as she pushed her shopping cart, her phone resting on her shoulder. "I can't believe I ever agreed to marry him."

"I take it things didn't go well?" Zack asked.

"I'm not sure if it did; that's the crazy part." Jenny surveyed the lamps in front of her. "I told him I got an apartment, and he just said, *you'll be back.* It's like he doesn't believe that it's really over."

"Well, that's not your fault. You told him, and if he doesn't believe you that's on him."

Jenny shuddered. "Ugh. I just don't understand what I ever saw in him. I want to go back in time, find nineteen year old me and shake some sense into her."

"You can't change the past," Zack noted. "You can only look forward. When time goes by and you don't go back to him, then he'll figure out you meant it. But really, that's all you can do."

She placed a lamp into her cart. "I'm bad at being patient."

"I've noticed that."

As Jenny moved to the electronics section, she said, "Alright, well, that time do you want to leave for the wake tonight? And do you want to drive or should I?"

"I can drive," Zack replied. "And the hours are from five to nine. Do you want me to pick you up around five?"

"What time is it?"

"A little after four."

"Better make it six." Jenny tossed a couple of DVDs into her cart. "I still need to shower."

Zack and Jenny exited the car at the funeral home only to find the line for admittance to extending out the door and disappearing around the side of the building. "Wow," Zack said. "I knew it would be packed, but it's still impressive."

"I think she's everybody's daughter right now," Jenny noted as they walked toward the back of the line. "Remember what the news report said—she went to bed in her own home and wasn't there in the morning. Isn't that every parent's worst nightmare?"

"Orlowski is every parent's worst nightmare."

The mention of his name caused Jenny to scan the crowd. While she didn't see him, there were two cops on the street directing traffic and lots of police cars in the parking lot. Whether the policemen were guests or were on duty remained to be seen.

Zack and Jenny waited in line for over an hour before they entered the building, only to notice the line continued for a long time inside. Police officers stood at regular intervals throughout the entryway, but Jenny didn't see Orlowski. Zack did nudge her, however, and directed her toward a stern looking older officer who monitored the line slightly ahead of him. "Do you see his name tag?" Zack asked.

Jenny squinted and shook her head.

"I think it says Johnson. That may be our informant."

"You're the informant," Jenny stated. "He's the connection."

"Tomato, to-mah-to," Zack replied. "Either way it might be him."

Jenny looked at the man, who seemed preoccupied. He kept glancing inside the funeral home, looking around a corner that Zack and Jenny couldn't see. "He sure is busy watching something."

"You think it's Orlowski?"

Jenny shrugged. "I don't have any feelings right now. I actually feel quite calm."

The two went back to remaining silent. As the line progressed, they were able to confirm the stern-looking officer was Johnson. A few moments later Zack peered over Jenny's shoulder to see what had grabbed Johnson's attention. "Yup," Zack said. "That's Orlowski. He's standing in the back corner."

"Don't stare at him," Jenny warned.

"Don't worry. He's not looking at me," Zack whispered. "That sick bastard. He is standing at attention as if he actually is showing respect."

"I wonder why I'm not getting any feelings. Her killer is in the same room with her."

"But so is everyone she loves, and then some," Zack noted.

Jenny glanced toward the casket and found some teenage girls kneeling, crying, saying their last goodbyes. She had to look away before the sadness overwhelmed her, but she surmised Zack's analysis was right—maybe Morgan was more focused on her friends than Orlowski right now. That notion gave Jenny some peace.

Curiosity got the best of Jenny, and she glanced up to see Orlowski for herself. He was looking toward the casket with an expression that could have been perceived as majestic, but Jenny saw it differently. He was proud of himself. He single-handedly affected every single person in this room, and he felt good about that.

Asshole.

She didn't know how long she'd been staring when his eyes met hers. *Shit,* she thought, but in an instant she turned on her flirty smile and waved subtly at him. He raised his chin in her direction in acknowledgement.

"Shit. He caught me," Jenny said through her teeth. "He caught me staring at him."

"And you told me not to stare," Zack said.

"I know. I blew it," Jenny admitted. "Look irritated. Like we can barely stand each other."

Jenny rubbed her forehead with feigned disgust. This reaction was easy to elicit for her—she only had to think of Orlowski and the repulsion rose to the surface.

Soon their turn at the casket had arrived. "One at a time," Jenny whispered. "I'd like a minute alone with her. You go first."

Zack traveled alone to the side of the casket, kneeling down, interlacing his fingers like a school boy. Jenny watched him there, remembering a similar image from Elanor's viewing. They hadn't known each other long enough to have already attended two funerals together. Although, in this line of work, they would probably attend a lot more. Sorrow crept into Jenny's bones.

Zack's turn at the casket was relatively short. Then Jenny approached, kneeling down, taking a long, silent look at the girl who should have been anywhere but there. The body in the casket didn't resemble the pictures Jenny had seen of a vibrant young woman, brimming with life. Although Jenny knew she wasn't looking at Morgan—she was merely looking at the body that had once housed Morgan—she spoke anyway. "I'll get him," she whispered. "Just keep working with me, and I will get him. I already know what happened—we just need to prove it. We'll clear Jeremy's name, and we'll put Orlowski in jail." Suddenly doubt materialized within Jenny, so she adjusted her words. "I promise you…I will either get Orlowski, or I will die trying."

Jenny hung her head, closed her eyes, and whispered in closing, "Once this ordeal is over, may you have an eternity of peace."

Jenny stood up, looking to her left, realizing it was time to face Morgan's parents. That could have proven to be more difficult than paying her respects to Morgan. Sorrow had always been contagious for Jenny.

Business, Jenny thought. *You're here on business.* She marched over to the Caldwells, first shaking Mrs. Caldwell's hand. "I'm so sorry for your loss."

Clearly exhausted, Morgan's mother answered somewhat mechanically. "Thank you. The support from the community has been overwhelming."

"We are all behind you," Jenny replied, before she moved on to Morgan's father. Once again she extended her hand, expressing her condolences, resisting the urge to point at Orlowski and tell Mr. Caldwell that this was really the man who had killed his daughter. *In due time,* she thought. Besides, Mr. Caldwell was better off being ignorant at this point. If he knew the murderer was standing mere yards away from him—and Morgan—it would have been too much for the grieving father to handle.

Zack looked somewhat pale when Jenny met up with him at the end of the receiving line. "That was brutal," he whispered.

Jenny kept her tears tucked safely away. "I know," she said. "Why don't we have a seat?"

Despite the length of the line to get into the funeral home, the seats were largely empty. Most people, it seemed, left after paying their respects. Zack and Jenny sat down as Jenny whispered, "I want to go say hello to him."

"Who? Orlowski?"

Jenny nodded.

"Are you out of your mind?"

Jenny glanced at him, unsure if he was aware he was quoting Officer Fazzino's brother. Sometimes he delivered humor with such a straight face it was difficult for her to tell. "I think it's what my character would do," Jenny confessed.

"Your character?"

"Yeah, the person I pretended to be when I talked to him. Flirty, kind of dumb...I think she'd go say hi."

Zack inhaled deeply and cocked his head to the side. "Okay," he said, "Knock yourself out. Just be careful."

Jenny stood up and walked sideways out of the row of chairs toward Orlowski. He seemed to recognize she was on her way to say hello to him; he watched her from the moment she looked up at him.

"Hi there," Jenny began, "Remember me?"

"Billy's, right?"

"Yup. Or should I say, yes sir? Look at you all fancy in your uniform. Are you on duty right now?"

"Unofficially," he replied. "We were all asked to come. You know, show our support, maintain crowd control."

"Well, you do look very handsome."

Orlowski looked over Jenny's shoulder toward Zack. "Is that your husband?"

Jenny rolled her eyes. "For now." She made a dismissive gesture with her hand. "Listen, I've actually come over here to tell you how impressed I am with how quickly you were able to solve this case. You guys really did a great job."

"Thanks," Orlowski replied. "It was pretty much open and shut."

"Well, it still wouldn't be solved without good police work."

"Thank you, ma'am."

"Ooh. Listen to you. *Ma'am.*" Jenny said. "I guess chivalry isn't dead."

"Not as long as I'm alive," Orlowski replied. Jenny was nearly overcome with repulsion.

"Well, I guess I'd better get back to my *husband.*" Jenny made a face as she said the word. "But maybe I'll see you around Billy's sometime?"

"I'm there all the time."

"Great. Maybe I'll see you soon." Jenny flashed a flirty smile and headed back to her seat.

With her back to Orlowski, Jenny whispered to Zack, "I want to puke."

"What happened?"

"Nothing, really. Just the man himself makes me sick, and the fact that I just flirted with him in a funeral home is even more disgusting." Jenny shivered. "I need a shower."

"I don't know why you wanted to go over there in the first place."

"I'm laying groundwork," Jenny said. "I mentioned I'm not happily married, and I also mentioned I might see him at Billy's again. He said he's always there...that sounded like an open invitation."

"An open invitation to hang out with a serial killer."

"An open invitation to *catch* a serial killer."

Zack scratched his head and made a face. "You make me nervous."

"I'm a big girl. I'll be okay. Although," she added, "I feel funny right now."

Zack looked up. "Well that's why."

Orlowski had left his post in the back corner of the room and walked by the casket, rounding the corner that led to the exit. Soon he was out of sight.

"I still feel funny," Jenny said. "I don't think he left."

"Do you think he got in line?"

"Possibly." Jenny rested her elbows on her knees and placed her head in her hands.

"Are you okay?"

Jenny nodded.

"Are you in pain?"

Keeping her head in her hands, she said, "Kind of. It's like there's a really, really loud ringing in my head...so loud it hurts."

"We can leave if you want."

Jenny shook her head. "No. I have to learn to deal with this."

Zack placed his hand on her back, rubbing her for support. While Jenny appreciated the sentiment, she moved his hand away. "You hate me, remember?"

Zack let out a sigh that was clearly rooted in frustration. Jenny knew what she was doing to him, and while she felt bad about it, it was the least of her concerns. She felt like she was about to explode.

The noise within her resonated louder and louder until Zack whispered, "He just rounded the corner. He's in line to pay his respects."

Already having drawn that conclusion, Jenny nodded subtly. Sweat began to drip down her face.

"You really don't look well," Zack said helplessly. "I think we should leave."

"No," Jenny whispered emphatically. "Morgan can't leave. This is her pain that I'm feeling. I can't abandon her."

Nausea gripped Jenny, and the voices in the funeral home echoed in her head. She began to feel distant, as if the room had just grown longer.

She looked up to see Zack—and numerous strangers—leaning over her. She was flat on her back between two rows of chairs.

"Hey!" Zack called, giving Jenny a gentle shake. "Hey! Are you okay?"

Confused, Jenny put her hand on her forehead. "Yeah," she said weakly. "I'm okay."

"It's her blood sugar," Zack explained to the crowd. "It gets too low sometimes."

Still too feeble to get up, Jenny surveyed the onlookers with embarrassment. She held her hand up to gesture that she was fine, adding, "I didn't eat enough today. That's all."

"Do you need us to get you something?" a kind stranger asked.

"No, we keep a soda in the car," Zack countered.

"We can stay with her if you want to go get it," another person said.

"I think the fresh air will do her good," Zack replied. "I'll just bring her to the car and take her home."

Jenny nodded from the floor. "He's right. I'll be fine." While she still felt too weak to do so, she sat up and pretended to be well.

The crowd began to dissipate as Zack helped Jenny to her feet. He held her up as they walked past Orlowski, through the entryway, and out the door. The crisp fall air did bring Jenny some immediate comfort; she breathed in deeply and felt a new sense of strength.

"I told you we should have left," Zack muttered angrily.

"I know. You were right."

"Are you okay?"

"Yeah, I'm alright."

Zack shook his head. "You scared the shit out of me, you know that?"

"Did I pass out?"

"Hell yes you passed out," he replied irritably. "One minute you're just sitting there and the next you're on the floor, out cold. I didn't know what to do."

Jenny laughed feebly. "Sorry about that."

"Do me a favor," he said a little more calmly. "Next time you feel like that, don't try to be a hero. Get yourself out of there."

"Okay, that's fair," Jenny concluded as she slowly lowered herself into the passenger seat of his car. Zack shut the door behind her and walked around to the driver's side.

Once inside the car, Zack asked, "Do you want to sleep at my place tonight? Not for sex, but so I can keep an eye on you?"

"I actually think that's a good idea," Jenny admitted. "Thanks for the offer."

The two were quiet for a while as Zack calmed down. Eventually he spoke, his voice reflecting a hint of sympathy. "You must have really been in pain in there."

Jenny nodded. "It was awful. One time I had a really bad hangover in college, and it felt like that, only fifty times more intense."

Zack patted her leg playfully. "A hangover reference. Nothing like catering to your audience. It's definitely a feeling I can relate to."

"Then you know how much that sucked."

"Indeed. Although, you said you had a hangover *once* in college. Did you really only have one hangover?"

"Are you really choosing this moment to point out how much of a nerd I am?"

Zack laughed. "No. I actually admire how good you are. I was hung over all the damn time when I was younger."

"Ick," Jenny said. "Why would you do that to yourself?"

"I was a boy," he replied. "And boys are stupid, remember?"

"Unfortunately, I don't have any of my stuff here," Jenny noted as she walked into Zack's apartment.

"What do you need?"

"A change of clothes, my toothbrush…"

"Well, little lady, you're in luck," Zack said. "Here, sit down on the couch. Get comfy. I'll be right back."

Jenny stifled a smile as she sat, wondering what Zack had up his sleeve. He emerged from his bedroom carrying a pair of sweatpants and a sweatshirt. "These may be a little big, but these are my smallest ones. Sweats are supposed to be big anyway." He plopped the clothes down on the sofa next to her and disappeared into his bathroom. "And," he called proudly, "the last time I went to the store, I thought maybe I should pick up an extra toothbrush." He returned, putting the sealed package on top of the clothes. "I figured if you were going to be sleeping over sometimes, it might be better if you kept one here."

Jenny blushed. "You did that for me?"

"Yup." Zack was clearly pleased with himself.

"Well, thank you. I really appreciate it."

"No problem." Zack locked eyes with Jenny, and they looked at each other longer than they should have. "I will say," he eventually continued, "you should probably get changed in my bedroom. If Little Zack sees you naked, it'll be all over, and that's not what tonight is about."

"Little Zack doesn't want to come out and play?" Jenny felt a twinge of disappointment.

"You were unresponsive on the floor an hour ago. I think tonight we should pass. Tonight you're here so I can keep an eye on you and get you some help if you need it."

Jenny felt a strange mixture of dissatisfaction and happiness. She had liked the idea of Zack finding her irresistible, but she knew logically that this was even better. The fact that he was willing to spend the night with her for the sole purpose of making sure she was okay was evidence that he genuinely cared about her.

Although, that concept was frightening.

Stop thinking, Jenny commanded herself. *Why must you over-analyze everything? Just enjoy it.* "Well, then," Jenny said, "I guess I should go put on these comfy clothes."

"That's the spirit," Zack said. "Do you want me to fix you something to eat while you're changing?"

"Oh, you don't have to do that."

"I know I don't *have* to. That's not what I asked. Would you *like* me to fix you something?"

Jenny was actually a little bit hungry. In an uncharacteristically self-serving move, she replied, "You know what? That'd be great."

"How does frozen pizza sound?"

Jenny smiled. "Perfect."

Jenny sat cross-legged in her oversized sweats, taking another piece of pizza. "Thanks for having me here. It is nice to not be alone tonight."

"My pleasure," Zack replied.

"I have to admit I am able to enjoy this a little bit more now that I've told Greg I want a divorce. The only thing that would make it better is if he believed me."

"Well that's his problem."

"His problem that becomes my problem." She took a bite. "I figure that once this case is solved, which is hopefully soon, I'll get a lawyer and serve him with papers. Then maybe he'll believe me."

"Are you worried that he's going to want to take half your money?"

"In a word?" Jenny replied. "Yes. But I've already thought of that. Even if he does take half the money, I'll still have enough to get by for the rest of my life. I don't plan to live extravagantly, and if I invest the money, I can live largely off the interest.

"I will say that I don't want him to get half the money, simply on principle," she continued. "It's not like I'm greedy and I want to keep it all for myself. It would just kind of suck that Greg gave me such a hard time about working on Elanor's case, and then when it results in a windfall, he gets to keep half of it. He doesn't deserve half of it. He doesn't deserve any of it."

"I agree."

"But if that's the price I have to pay for my freedom, I'll pay it. No sense losing sleep over it." Jenny took another bite of pizza. "The one thing I *am* losing sleep over, though, is telling my parents."

"You haven't told them?"

"Nope. And I don't know how I'm going to, either. They're thick-and-thin, til-death-do-us-part kind of people. I don't think they're going to be all that receptive to the idea. Throw in the fact that my father has heart problems—and has for years—I really, *really* don't want to tell him."

"I know how that goes," Zack confessed.

"Oh yeah," Jenny said, giving him a nudge with her foot, "did you tell your father that you quit?"

"I did."

"And how did that go?"

Zack shrugged. "About like you'd expect. He actually called me to ask me where I was, and I told him I wasn't coming in anymore. He went on and on about what an irresponsible piece of shit I am, and he asked how I planned to get by. I didn't tell him about this job; I just told him I'd manage. He doesn't need to know how I plan to get by, first of all. I'm almost thirty. And as far as I'm concerned he doesn't *deserve* to know what I do with my life. Not after calling me a piece of shit.

"And honestly," Zack continued, "I don't think he'd have any respect for what we do anyway. It's too vague, you know? He builds houses. Every afternoon there's concrete proof that he'd put in a hard days' work. He'd call this cream puff, hocus pocus kind of shit, I guarantee it." He made a dismissive gesture. "He's one of the most narrow-minded people I know."

"Sounds like it."

"I think he'd probably be happier if Orlowski was his son, as long as he built houses in between killings."

Jenny chuckled at the preposterousness of the thought. "That's awful."

"Awful, but I wouldn't be surprised if it was true."

Jenny hugged her leg into her chest. After a moment of reflection, she posed, "What do you think it was like for Orlowski growing up? Do you think his father was a hard-ass?"

Zack shook his head. "I don't know. That's a good question."

"I can't imagine what could possibly possess someone to follow this path in life. Was it abuse? Is his wiring just messed up?"

"I think that's the million dollar question. People have been trying to figure that out for centuries. If we knew what caused it, we could stop it." Zack thought about his own words. "Potentially."

"What's weird to me is that he is able to function so normally in society. How can somebody appear so…regular…and then have this horrible dark side? And how is he able to keep it hidden?"

"Did you ever hear of that BTK guy? That Bind-Torture-Kill guy who killed all those people in the midwest?" Zack posed, snapping his fingers. "What was his name?"

"Dennis Rader."

Zack looked impressed. "Okay, how did you know that?"

"I was a teacher." Jenny tapped her temple. "And teachers are smart, remember?"

"Are you mocking me?"

"Maybe."

"I admire that." He replied. "Anyway, BTK was, like, the most normal guy in the world. He was married with kids, not to mention a boy scout leader, a leader in his church…and a twisted serial killer. People were shocked to find out it was him. I do think I remember hearing that he harbored these sick thoughts from a very young age; he was just able to mask them well when necessary."

"Do you think that's why Orlowski became a cop?"

"What do you mean?"

"Well," Jenny said with a sigh, trying to come up with the most concise explanation she could. "Did you ever wonder why some priests molest children? In one of my psychology classes we discussed that being a priest doesn't cause you to molest children, people who are inclined to molest children often become priests. They figure if they just swear off their sexuality altogether, they will be able to fight off their demons. However, sometimes the demons win out, and the result is a child-molesting priest. Maybe Orlowski had a similar line of thinking—become the opposite of what his sick urges were telling him to be. Become a crusader for good, not evil.

"But there's another side to the coin, too. Sometimes these sickos become priests, little-league coaches—cops—because it puts them in a position of trust. It allows them unsupervised access to children, and the parents are completely unaware that they've entrusted their little ones to a monster. It could be that Orlowski specifically chose this career because he knew people would trust him, and they would put themselves in vulnerable positions around him."

"Either way he's a sick bastard," Zack surmised. "And I want him to rot in hell, even if he did choose to be a cop in an attempt to fight his demons."

"I wish I knew why he had these demons in the first place." Jenny tucked her hair behind her ear and rested her chin on her knee. "Do you believe in God, Zack?"

"Do I believe in God?" Zack repeated. "Is 'I don't know' an acceptable answer?"

"I think it's my answer," Jenny confessed.

"The reason *I'm* not sure is because I'm a lazy sack of shit and I've never really given it that much thought." He took a sip of soda. "So why are you on the fence?"

With another sigh, Jenny said, "Because of people like Orlowski. I was raised Catholic, and I never really questioned it before, but now I can't help but wonder why—if there is a God—He would make the Orlowskis and the Raders and the Bundys of the world. Does He screw up? I thought God was supposed to be omniscient. I would think the world would be a much better place if there was really a kind-hearted, all-powerful being up there supervising everything."

"Maybe one of your contacts will be able to clue you in," Zack said without judgment.

"Maybe," Jenny said solemnly. "But I think the answer is on the other side, and once the spirits cross over, I don't hear from them again."

"But at least you do know there is peace after you die. And you can be with your loved ones again."

Jenny smiled. "Yes, that's true. Maybe this life is a practice run. A try-out. Most of us pass, but the Orlowskis of the world fail, and they get separated. They end up in hell, while the rest of us enjoy heaven."

"Be careful, there," Zack said. "I'm not sure which way I'm headed."

With a laugh, Jenny asked, "Are there any bodies buried in your back yard?"

"Not that I'm aware of."

"Then I think you're fine."

Chapter 15

Jenny looked at the clock in her car. Five-thirty. It must have been dinner time.

She dialed her phone. "Hey Zack," she said, "I've been led to Billy's again."

"You're there now?"

"In the parking lot. I haven't gone in yet."

"It's in Braddock, right?" Jenny could hear Zack moving around. "I can be there in half an hour. Don't go in until I get there."

"Can't promise that," she said. "If he is in there, I don't know how much longer it will be before he leaves. I don't want to miss him because I'm sitting out here waiting for you."

"Shit, Jenny," Zack said. "Okay. I guess you should go in…but be careful."

"Remember," Jenny said as she fixed her hair in the rear view mirror. "When you do get here, you can't go in. He knows you now. You'll have to wait in the parking lot."

"Alright." The wheels were clearly turning in Zack's head. "I'll send you a text when I get there. Don't leave before then."

"Make sure the text is innocuous."

"English, please."

Jenny would have laughed if she wasn't so focused. "Make sure the text is innocent…about something trivial. I'll understand what it means."

"Okay, got it. And Jenny? Be careful."

"You've already said that."

"You haven't agreed."

"Okay, I'll be careful." Jenny smiled at his concern. "I'll be waiting for your text."

Jenny once again approached Orlowski as he sat alone at the bar. Swallowing her disgust, she cheerfully called, "Hey, stranger. Is this seat taken?"

Orlowski looked over his shoulder. "Hey," he replied, immediately lighting up. "If it isn't the fainter."

"Ha ha," she said playfully. "Very funny."

"Are you okay? You scared us all last night."

"Yeah, I'm okay." Remembering Zack's explanation, she added, "I just have low blood sugar is all. It happens from time to time if I don't eat enough." She climbed up onto the bar stool and plopped her purse on the counter. "And with all the stress that I'm under, I'm not eating like I should."

"Oh yeah," he replied. "Divorce. I've been there. It sucks."

"It sure does." Jenny asked the bartender for a menu.

"If it makes you feel any better, being divorced is much better than divorc-*ing*. Once you move out, or your husband moves out, it's a million times better."

Ain't that the truth. "I hope so. It's hard to live with a man I can barely stand."

"I remember those days, and I don't envy you," Orlowski remarked. With a chuckle, he then added, "Although, when I moved out I moved back in with my mother. That wasn't exactly ideal either."

"Moving back in with my parents is not an option," Jenny declared.

"That bad, huh?"

"Well, it's not that it's bad, necessarily. They just live in a different state." Jenny grinned flirtatiously. "That, and I haven't told them yet."

Orlowski made a face, causing Jenny to elaborate.

"They're firm believers that marriage is forever. They're not going to take it very well when I tell them we're thinking about splitting up." Jenny braced herself for the pain she'd endure, and then she nudged Orlowski with her elbow. "Come on, you must have had a tough time telling your folks, too." Her skin burned from the contact.

"Not at all, actually." He took a bite. "My dad's been dead for a long time, and my mother is on husband number six."

"Six?" Jenny asked with disbelief.

"Yup. Six. So she can't exactly say anything to me when my first and only marriage didn't work out."

Images of Orlowski's childhood started to form in Jenny's head.

"And let me tell you," Orlowski continued as he chewed his food, "each of my mother's husbands was worse than the one before."

"Really?"

He shook his head. "It was ridiculous. She'd finally break free from one asshole scumbag, only to turn around and marry another one. It's like she never learned. And it only got worse after I became a cop. Seriously, how does it look when you're a law enforcement officer and your mother is married to a guy with a criminal record?"

He seemed bitter.

"So I imagine you were shuffled around a lot as a kid." Jenny noted.

"At first I was," Orlowski explained. "But then husband number three died, leaving my mother with enough life insurance for her to buy a house outright. Mind you, it wasn't a glamorous house or anything, but she owned it. After that we stayed put, and the men came in and out." He let out a snort. "She should have installed a revolving door."

Something clicked inside Jenny's brain, and unfortunately she must not have masked it well. "Are you okay?" Orlowski asked. "You don't look right all of a sudden."

"It's the blood sugar," Jenny replied. That seemed to be a convenient answer for everything.

"Hey, Seth," Orlowski called to the bartender. "Bring her a Coke, would you?"

Within a few seconds a soda appeared in front of Jenny, and she drank it down quickly. The cold felt good to her. "Thank you," she said. "I've really got to start eating better."

"Or go to a doctor. That's really not good. What if you pass out at the wheel?"

"I keep a soda in the car." Jenny was impressed with her ability to lie. "If I start to feel funny, I pull over and drink it. It's worked every time so far."

"It's still scary," Orlowski declared. "I don't want to respond to a call one of these days and find out it's you with your car wrapped around a tree."

Jenny smiled. "Aren't you sweet? But I assure you, I'm fine." Jenny ordered a plate of fries from the bartender and turned back to Orlowski. "So, tell me, what brought you down here from Connecticut?"

"Well, it wasn't a direct trip. I made a stop in New Jersey for a couple of years first."

And how many girls did you kill while you were there? "That sounds like it has a story behind it," Jenny posed.

"You want to hear it?"

"I'm not going anywhere."

"Well, at first I just wanted to get out of Connecticut. Like I said, my marriage had shit the bed, and I was living with my mother and step-father. The first few weeks of living with them had been okay, but then I kind of had a falling out with my step-father. He essentially told me to get the hell away from him, and since it was his house I couldn't really argue."

"That's a shame," Jenny remarked. "What was the fight about?"

"Honestly, I'm not even really sure. It's just like one day he woke up and decided he'd had enough of me." Orlowski shook his head. "The man was a lunatic. I don't know what else to say. But anyway, not only did my step-father start giving me hell, I also came down with a case of Lyme disease."

"Lyme disease?"

"Yeah. You get it from deer ticks, which are all over the place in Connecticut. They're so small that they're difficult to see, but if you get bitten by one you get a red ring around the area. If you catch it quickly enough, you can avoid some of the more serious symptoms. Unfortunately for me, I got bitten on the back of my knee, so I couldn't see the ring. I mean, really…how often do you look at the back of your knee?"

"I don't think I've ever looked at the back of my knee."

148

"Exactly," he replied. "And it was winter time, so I wore pants all the time. No one else could see it either. So I ended up with a pretty bad case of Lyme. I got *very* sick."

Jenny made a face but remained silent.

"So I thought to myself, *you know what? Screw this.* I figured these were all signs that I needed to get the hell out of Connecticut." He leaned over to Jenny as if he was disclosing a secret. "I'm not sure if you're aware of this, but Lyme disease is named after a town in Connecticut. That's how common it is up there."

"I didn't know that," Jenny replied, although she actually did.

"Yup. Lyme Connecticut." Orlowski seemed proud of himself. "So anyway, I wanted to get out of Connecticut, but I was too sick to work. There was no way I could have supported myself. Right around that time the house I shared with my ex-wife sold, and we split the profit of it. It was enough money for me to move down to New Jersey and stay with one of my favorite step brothers—from marriage number four, I think." Orlowski looked as if he was doing some math in his head before asking himself, "Was it marriage number four?" He shooed the thought away. "It doesn't matter. Anyway, my step brother had just gotten a divorce, too, and he was faced with potentially losing his home. I gave him some money, and he let me recover at his place. It was a win-win for us both."

"That's great," Jenny said. "What part of New Jersey? Was it near the beach?"

"No, it was a town called Edmonton, just outside of Trenton. It's just about as far as you can get from a beach in New Jersey."

"Well that's a shame."

"I don't know about that. I was too sick to go to the beach anyway. It probably would have been a tease to be close to the water but be unable to enjoy it."

"I guess you're right. So how long did you live there?"

"About two years. Once I started to feel a little better, I got a job in a convenience store of all things. It wasn't physically demanding, so it was perfect for me until I started to feel one-hundred percent. After I got back to normal, though, I looked all around the country for vacancies on police forces. I did miss being a cop—it's my calling."

Jenny wanted to vomit.

"And Braddock had an opening, so I applied, and here I am."

"Well, we're happy to have you here, especially with all that's gone on. I really admire how quickly you all were able to solve the Morgan Caldwell case."

"It was pretty open and shut once we found her cell phone. She essentially outlined for us who she was with that night."

"Was her cell phone hard to find?"

Orlowski got a twinkle in his eye. "Can I let you in on a little secret?"

"Sure," Jenny replied excitedly, although she already had an idea what he was going to say.

"I'm the one who found it. It was about a hundred yards from her body at the orchard."

Using her best acting skills, Jenny replied with feigned excitement, "Wow! That's fabulous! Good for you. So you're, like, the hero in all of this."

Orlowski pretended to be modest. "I don't know about *that.* I just happened to be the lucky one who stumbled across it, that's all."

"Oh, don't sell yourself short." Jenny sickened herself.

"Either way, we were able to get our killer. That's the important part."

"That's right." Jenny held up her soda. "Let's drink to that."

Orlowski clinked glasses with her and took a drink. "It's not as fun when you're drinking water." He looked at his cup. "Through a straw."

"It's still deserves a celebration. We can all sleep a little more soundly now that the case is solved." Jenny took a drink from her nearly-empty glass. "Do you mind if I ask you a personal question?"

"Depends what it is," Orlowski replied with a smile.

Jenny's tone softened to serious. "What happened between you and your ex-wife?"

Orlowski smiled and looked down. "Kids," he replied.

"A source of contention, huh?" Jenny realized her vocabulary was probably a little too sophisticated for the character she was trying to portray; she'd need to tone it down. Fortunately it seemed to go unnoticed.

"Yeah. Things were fine until we started trying to have a family. That was about ten years ago."

"How long had you been married then?"

"About two years."

"So what happened?"

"Nothing," Orlowski replied, "For years nothing happened, and that was the problem. We couldn't conceive. I think she ultimately blamed me for that—decided I was the infertile one." He shrugged indifferently. "She ended up leaving so she could find someone who could give her a baby."

"You couldn't just adopt? Or do fertility treatments?"

"That's what I said. But she wanted a child of her own, the old-fashioned way."

Jenny slumped her shoulders. "Oh. That's too bad." Springing back to life, she cheerfully added, "I hope she gets remarried and finds out that *she* was the infertile one. Wouldn't that be a hoot? It would serve her right."

Orlowski only grunted, making Jenny realize she may have struck a nerve. Time to try a different tactic. "Are you guys on good terms?"

"I never talk to her."

Jenny smiled. "At least you're not fighting."

Orlowski returned her smile. "I guess that's one way to look at it."

"Did you fight a lot while you were married? The reason I ask you this is because I am trying to get a feel for my situation. See if I'm normal, you know?"

"No, I understand. Completely," Orlowski said. He squinted his eyes as he considered the question. "At first we didn't. I mean, she was clearly disappointed every month that went by and she wasn't pregnant, but we didn't fight about it. Not for years. But as time went on and she got older, I think the stress of not conceiving was getting to her. Her biological clock was ticking. Then she started to blame me for it, telling me it was my fault she wasn't pregnant, questioning my *manhood* of all things."

Jenny winced, wondering if this woman knew the repercussions of that challenge.

"She just wouldn't let it go, you know? So I eventually said to her *did you ever stop to think that* you *might be the problem?* Oh, that made her angry. After that, we did start fighting, and we fought up until I moved out."

"How long did that last?"

"A couple of years," Orlowski sighed. "A very long couple of years."

Jenny nodded silently in return.

"Do you and your husband fight?"

"We do now, but like you, we didn't at first." Jenny laughed. "I guess that's always the way. Things have to be good at first, otherwise you wouldn't get married to that person."

"True."

"But in the beginning I think I was infatuated with him. I'm not sure it was ever love. As the infatuation has worn off, I'm seeing a very annoying side to him. Things bother me when they didn't used to, you know?"

"Oh, I know."

Jenny looked at Orlowski out of the corner of her eye. "Do you think people are meant to be married forever? I mean, some animals mate for life. Do you think people are supposed to?"

"Clearly my mother doesn't think so."

Jenny laughed. "It sounds like you're right about that. But what about *you*? What do you think?"

After a little thought, he declared, "I guess if you meet the right person it should be easy enough. Finding the right person is the hard part, though."

"I sure didn't."

"Neither did I."

Jenny nodded to the bartender as he placed another soda and a ketchup bottle in front of her. "I know this may make me sound trashy, but I'm not so sure people are supposed to mate for life. I think that's why the feeling of new love goes away. We're supposed to be with a person as long as they make us feel that way, which is what, around three years? And then I think we're supposed to find someone else who gives us that new-love feeling again." Jenny's plate of fries arrived. "That's why I think we get that feeling."

"Interesting philosophy," Orlowski noted. "I'm sure a lot of conservative folks would disagree with you."

"Are *you* conservative?"

"Depends on the topic."

Jenny munched on a fry as she realized she shouldn't begin talking politics. She wasn't supposed to be that smart. Switching gears completely, she posed, "So what do you do for fun?"

It was not lost on Jenny that she just asked a serial killer what he did for fun.

"That's easy. Fishing."

"Oh yeah? You get a chance to do that much?"

"Quite a bit, actually. I work nights, so at six in the morning—while everyone else in the world is waking up to go to work—I'm heading home. That allows me to hit the river at sunrise, right when the fish are biting the most." A passionate smile appeared on his face. "It's great. On the weekdays I'm usually the only one there. It's just me and nature. You can't beat it."

"That does sound great," Jenny said, "but I'm not sure I could work nights."

"Oh, I love it. I volunteered for it, actually. I'm somewhat nocturnal by nature, so working by night and sleeping by day isn't that much of a stretch. I even did third shift when I worked at the convenience store in New Jersey." He gestured for the bartender to bring him his check. "Besides, I don't have a family, so it's easy for me to sleep during the day and work at night. Most of the other guys on the force are married or have kids, so I figured I'd let them have the day shifts."

"That's very kind of you."

"Well, it works for me. Besides," he added with a laugh, "the night shift pays better." Orlowski locked eyes with Jenny as he reached for his wallet. "As much as I hate to cut this short, I do have to start getting ready for work. So is it still useless to ask for your phone number?" The bartender offered the check to Orlowski, who handed over his credit card without looking at it.

"For now I'm afraid it still is, but I do know where to find you."

"But I don't know where to find you."

Jenny felt tingles, but she wasn't sure if those were her own nerves or if Morgan was stirring inside of her. Either way, she tried to mask her fear and remain focused. She batted her eyes and added, "I know you don't. Drives you crazy, doesn't it?"

"Well, it does give me incentive to come here to Billy's a little more often." Orlowski thanked the bartender, who returned his credit card. Orlowski signed the receipt.

"Good. I'd hate to come out here and not find you sitting at the bar."

Orlowski stood up from the bar stool and put on his jacket. "Hopefully that doesn't happen. I look forward to seeing you again."

"Me too." They locked eyes in a smile.

He once again placed his hand on Jenny's back as he walked past her, causing that familiar pang of pain. Once he was safely out the door, Jenny shivered, trying to shake off the feeling.

She continued to slowly eat her fries, waiting for the text from Zack. Eventually her phone chirped, with a message that said *I fed the dog.*

Jenny had to laugh. *He's gone.*

I'm still not leaving til you're in your car.

Smiling at her phone, Jenny asked for her check. *Lots to tell. I'll meet you back at your place.*

As soon as the door of Zack's apartment closed, Jenny said, "We need to look up the real estate records for the Hawkins property again."

"Why?"

"Just humor me. I want to see if I'm right."

Zack walked to his laptop and called up the records. "Alright, I have the site up. What am I looking for?"

"How much did the house sell for? From Kimberly to Kimberly…"

"It says zero," Zack said with dismay. "How can that be?"

"Because it wasn't a sale. It was a transfer. There weren't three wives named Kimberly; it was the same woman. She just got married a few times and changed her name."

Zack looked up at Jenny. "Okay, how did you know that?"

"Because that was Orlowski's mother."

Zack's eyes widened. "Kimberly Hawkins is Orlowski's mom?"

"I believe so. It clicked when he was talking to me at Billy's. He told me that his mother had six husbands, but that she owned her house. The men came and went, but she stayed. I remembered the Kimberlys, and it all made sense."

"Holy shit."

154

"And here's the kicker," Jenny said. "He moved in with her when he separated from his wife. He may have been living there at the time Lashonda was killed."

Still with wide eyes, Zack said, "We need to tell Fazzino this."

"We do, but there's more I haven't told you yet." Jenny sat down on the couch. "Do you remember how I had a feeling about a bug when I visited the place where Lashonda was found?"

"Yeah."

"Well, it was a deer tick."

"A deer tick?"

"Yup. Orlowski contracted a horrible case of Lyme disease, apparently not that long after he split up from his wife. He made a point of telling me it was winter, because he had a red ring where the tick bit him on the back of his knee, but nobody could see it since he was always wearing pants."

"Do you think he picked up that tick in the field where he dumped Lashonda's body?"

Jenny got a spark in her eye. "That's what I'm thinking. Wouldn't that be awesome?"

"Hell yeah it would be. Let's see if that's possible." Zack pushed some buttons on his laptop. After a short time, he laughed out loud and pointed at the screen. "Ha!"

"I guess it's possible?" Jenny asked.

"Not just possible. Probable. This site says early November is peak time for adult deer ticks, and about half of them carry Lyme disease. With all that tall grass, that field is just the kind of place they like to hang out, too, while waiting for their next host. Let me see something else…" He did another search and read his findings out loud. "*Symptoms of Lyme usually take several weeks to appear*. If he had the Lyme in winter, then he easily could have been bitten in early November…when he was disposing of Lashonda's body."

Zack and Jenny smiled at each other. "I guess Lashonda got the last laugh on that one, huh?" Jenny noted. "He was apparently sick as a dog for a long time."

"Good. Serves him right." He looked around. "Well played, little tick, wherever you are."

"Okay, Orlowski clued me in on one other thing, and it may give you the answer to your question."

"What question?"

155

"The-why-did-he-take-a-three-year-break question. He might not have taken a break at all. Can you look and see if there are any unsolved murders in Edmonton, New Jersey in the past three years?"

The joy faded from Zack's face. "Uh oh."

"Yeah," Jenny said. "He lived with a relative in New Jersey for a couple of years between Connecticut and Georgia. Something tells me we'll find some missing girls in his wake."

"Oh, God," Zack said with disgust. "I almost don't even want to look it up."

"I know. But if there are unsolved murders there, at least we might be able to give their loved ones some answers."

Zack tried a few searches, ultimately concluding, "I can't find any unsolved murders in Edmonton. It seems like a pretty sleepy town."

"How about Trenton? He said that was close by."

Zack gave a strange look to Jenny. "We'll probably find a million unsolved murders in Trenton."

"Girls," Jenny said. "Plucked off the street."

"I guess I can narrow it down by year," Zack said. "When did you say he moved there?"

Jenny let out a sigh as she did some calculations in her head. "Let me see," she began. "He said he left Connecticut shortly after her got the Lyme, so I guess that would be around December, three years ago. If he moved here about a year ago, like he claims, that means he left New Jersey around October of last year."

"Okay," Zack said, typing information in for his search. He looked at the screen with confusion. "There's a link here that says there are three unsolved murders of women, but they were prostitutes. Do you think that's Orlowski's work?"

"Well, it could be. He wasn't a cop in New Jersey. He needed some way to get these girls to get into his car."

Disgust emerged on Zack's face. "I guess you're right. Sick bastard."

"Go ahead and click on it." Jenny scooted over to Zack, looking over his shoulder at the link on the laptop screen.

With a quick glance at Jenny he said, "Alright, here we go."

"Wait, before you start, I want to take notes on this. Do you have some paper I could use?"

"Sure," Zack replied, getting up from the couch and rummaging through some piles on his kitchen table. "Do you need a pen, too?"

Jenny pulled a pen out of her purse and clicked it open. "Nope. Got one."

He returned to the sofa, handing Jenny a spiral notebook. She sat back against the corner of the couch while Zack placed the computer on his lap. He clicked on the link and began to read out loud.

It has been four months since Renee Podgewaite's body was found at the banks of the Delaware River. She was the last of three Trenton prostitutes to be found strangled within a ten month period.

"Wait a minute," Jenny interrupted. "When was this article written?"

Zack scanned the top of the page. "Um, let me see. January fifteenth of this year."

Jenny counted the months backwards on her fingers. "So she was found in mid-September."

"It looks that way," Zack replied. Jenny wrote down the information as he continued to read.

Podgewaite, 32, was found partially submerged in the river by a man walking his dog. Five months earlier, Angela Velasquez's remains were found alongside railroad tracks just over the Pennsylvania border. Paris Carter had been found last November behind a warehouse that was less than a mile from both Velasquez and Podgewaite's remains. All three women had worked the streets of Trenton as prostitutes, and all three appear to have been assaulted and strangled.

Police are uncertain if they are looking at separate incidents or the work of a serial killer.

Local authorities have come under fire for the lack of progress on the investigation. Family members of the victims claim the cases are getting less consideration than they deserve because of the lifestyles these women led. "Yes, they made some bad choices," says Paolo Velasquez, brother of Angela Velasquez, "but they were still people, and these murders should get just as much attention as any other murder would. But so far that hasn't been happening."

The police counter by saying they are taking these cases very seriously, but prostitute murders offer extraordinary challenges. "These women routinely venture to isolated areas with strangers," says Officer Kevin Levito of the Trenton Police Department. "They don't tell anyone where they're going or who they're going with. Unfortunately this lifestyle makes them easy targets for predators.

"Many of the prostitutes have problems with addiction, adding another dimension of difficulty to the case," Levito added. "They will often go on binges, disappearing for days at a time without raising any suspicion. In fact, none of these women had been reported missing before their bodies were found. This makes it difficult to pinpoint exactly when or where the crimes took place. For most people, disappearances are reported quickly and it is much easier to determine who was last with the victim or where the victim had been prior to the attack."

Toxicology screens revealed high levels of drugs in all three women's systems.

Jenny rubbed her eyes. "We're going to get nowhere with this."

Holding up his hand, Zack replied, "Now, don't be so sure. We might find something."

"Orlowski told me he's nocturnal by nature. For a while he didn't have a job, and the job he did eventually get was at a convenience store, working nights. That means he could have come and gone at all hours of the night, and his brother-in-law or step-brother or whoever the hell he was living with wouldn't have paid any attention. If the cops can't even pinpoint when the attacks took place, I don't think we have any chance at all of placing Orlowski with any of these women." Jenny let out a frustrated sigh.

"Let's not give up quite yet. Let's keep digging and see what we find, shall we?" He looked at Jenny with raised eyebrows and patted her leg. *"Shall we?"*

Grateful for Zack's ability to keep her grounded, she nodded with a slight smile. "Okay. Let's keep going. What else does the article say?"

Zack skimmed the article and paraphrased as he went. "They had a suspect after the second murder. Apparently the other prostitutes in the area had pinpointed a guy that had always been creepy to them. He used to spend a lot of time driving past them, looking at them, before he'd decide on which one he'd like to 'hire.' The guy's name was Robert Slocum. He was later cleared when his DNA didn't match any at the scene."

Zack and Jenny looked at each other. "DNA?" Jenny remarked with awe. "There was DNA?"

"Apparently." Zack's optimistic look quickly faded. "Wait a minute. They said it didn't match *any* of the DNA at the scene, not just *the* DNA at the scene."

"You think there was DNA from more than one person?"

"Well, these were prostitutes."

Jenny curled her lip at the thought. "Well, this guy got cleared because his DNA wasn't present. But what if it was? I realize that wouldn't make him guilty, necessarily, but it would at least establish that he'd been in contact with her, right?"

"Intimate contact, actually."

"And it would prompt the investigators to do a little more digging, right?"

"I would think."

Jenny chewed on her fingernail as she thought some more, verbalizing each idea that popped into her head. "Maybe some of that DNA was Orlowski's. Although, he managed to not leave any DNA at his other crime scenes. He used condoms, and he put gloves on Morgan. This whole thing could really backfire. If they do get a sample of Orlowski's DNA and it doesn't match what was left at the scene, he might get cleared like this other guy did. Then they wouldn't look at him anymore."

"I hate to break this to you," Zack said, "but there's a chance Orlowski didn't even do it."

"You're right. He may not have." Jenny tapped her foot as an outlet for her increasingly pent-up energy. "But these cases are kind of similar to the three we know of, don't you think? And the time is right."

"Oh, yeah. I still think it's quite possible he's guilty; I just don't want us to jump the gun, that's all. Our goal is not to pin

159

Orlowski with every murder we can; our goal is to find the truth, whatever it is."

"Well, either way, DNA would be helpful with that, wouldn't it?"

"Absolutely."

Jenny thought some more. "I can get a sample of his DNA."

Zack gave her a bewildered look.

"Oh, God, no," Jenny replied with disgust. "Not like that. Are you crazy? I mean with a straw from Billy's. I think he likes to go there before work, so he's not drinking beer from a bottle—he's drinking soda or water through a straw. If I can snag the straw after he leaves and submit it to someone, do you think they can get a DNA profile?"

"From what I've seen on TV, I think the answer to that is yes. But would they be willing to do that? Does he have to be an official suspect first? Or can someone from the street just walk into the police department and say, *I think this straw contains the DNA of a prostitute killer.*"

"I think we should talk to the people at the Trenton Police Department. Maybe they'll be able to answer that for us."

"You want to take a field trip?" Zack asked.

"I was actually thinking a phone call," Jenny replied with a smile.

Zack bit his lip. "Oh yeah. That's what I meant."

Jenny patted Zack on his shoulder. "At first I considered making a field trip, too, but then I decided against it. I just think it would be way too hard to get anything up there. With the Connecticut cases, there were places to look: the dollar store parking lot, the route from Allison's house to the convenience store. If we go to Trenton, where would we look? We have no idea where these women were when they got abducted. I think it would take us a really long time to find anything, and it's time we just don't have."

"Yeah, I hear you," Zack replied. "Hey, but if Orlowski gets arrested and is safely behind bars, would you be interested in going up there? You know, try to see if he was involved in those killings and get their families some answers?"

"Absolutely." Jenny smiled at Zack. Repositioning herself to write more, Jenny added, "Okay, what other information can you find?"

With further research, Zack and Jenny were able to determine that the first killing happened two Novembers earlier, which was about eleven months after Orlowski's arrival in New Jersey. Jenny surmised that he was probably beginning to feel better by then, and he may have been able to physically carry out the murder. The victim was Paris Carter, who had been last seen on November tenth and whose body was found five days later behind a warehouse by an employee who noticed a foul smell. She was partially dressed and had been strangled, showing very little by way of defensive wounds. She had extremely high levels of heroin in her system, potentially explaining why she failed to fight back.

She would have been a very easy target.

Paris was 28 years old, originating from a middle class family in the suburbs just outside of Philadelphia. She got pregnant when she was very young—in her teens—and at first she and the baby's father tried to make a life together. They got married and settled into an apartment, but soon Paris found that the life of a stay-at-home mom was not nearly as exciting as the life her friends were enjoying. On the weekends she began to go out and party, soon finding herself using recreational drugs. Once she discovered the lure of heroin, she couldn't resist it.

Over time, her partying became a nightly occurrence; she would head out the door as soon as her husband got home from his job with a cable company. Some nights she would not return, leaving her husband scrambling to find someone to watch their baby in the morning so he could go to work. Fed up, her husband filed for divorce and full custody of their daughter, which went uncontested by Paris. He took the child back to his home state of Wisconsin so he could be closer to his family, leaving Paris with no place to stay.

Paris moved to Trenton to stay with a cousin, who quickly discovered Paris's troubles with addiction. The cousin tried unsuccessfully to get her some help; however, she didn't want to be helped. As a result, the cousin simply gave Paris a key to the apartment, making sure she had a place to stay at night if she needed it, and watched helplessly as Paris spiraled completely out of control.

At the time of the murder, Paris hadn't slept at her cousin's place in six months.

The second victim, Angela Velasquez, had been a cheerleader at her suburban high school before she started dating the wrong boy.

He had introduced her to crack cocaine, and soon it consumed her. Her downward spiral ultimately ended with her living as a prostitute, barely eating, turning tricks so she could afford her next fix.

This all ended for her in mid-April, five months after Paris's murder. The exact date of Angela's disappearance was uncertain; she'd had no routines. Her last known sighting was April twenty-first. Three days later her body was found along the side of some railroad tracks across the Pennsylvania border. She, too, was partially dressed and strangled. She, too, had high amounts of drugs in her system. However, she was only twenty years old.

DNA was recovered from under her fingernails; pubic hairs from three different individuals were found on her body. No seminal fluid was found during vaginal swabs, which wasn't surprising; men generally didn't employ the services of a prostitute without protecting themselves. The DNA from her fingernails had been run through the national criminal database, but no matches were found. Until they could find a suspect to compare it to, the DNA sample was useless.

Renee Podgewaite, the last of the three victims, had a different story than the other two women. Her father had been absent from the start; her mother was incarcerated when she was just a toddler. She'd traveled through the foster care system for most of her life, never able to find a permanent home. Dissatisfied with the way her life was unfolding, she ran away at age fifteen, determined to make a life of her own.

Uneducated and underage, she had very few options. Prostitution and drug trafficking were her only means of making money. For seventeen years she worked the streets, sleeping where she could, turning tricks to support her various addictions.

Renee was last seen on November twenty-fourth. Her lifeless body was found the following day by a man walking his dog along the bank of the Delaware River. She was wearing gloves, and no DNA was found at the scene.

Nobody came forward to claim her body or provide her with a funeral. Members of the Trenton police force contributed enough money to afford her a service and a modest headstone.

Jenny surveyed the notes she had taken. "Gloves," she noted. "That's probably the best link we have to Orlowski. Maybe he started making his victims wear gloves after…" Jenny flipped through her notes, "Angela Velasquez got the DNA under her fingernails. Maybe she scratched the shit out of him and he wanted to keep it from happening again."

"That would be great if she did, wouldn't it? For more reasons than one."

"I'd like to talk to someone in the police department to see if we can request that DNA analysis of Orlowski."

"We should probably call Fazzino and Johnson anyway and let them know what we found out," Zack said. "Maybe we could ask one of them while we have them on the phone."

"Sounds good. Why don't we call Johnson first?" Jenny smiled. "Actually, why don't *you* call Johnson first? He kind of scares me."

"Great," Zack said in a lackluster tone. "I get to be the informant again."

"But you're so *good* at it," Jenny replied with a smirk.

"Easy, wiseass," Zack joked as he pulled his phone out of his pocket. He dialed Johnson's number and put the phone on speaker.

"Johnson."

"Hi, Officer Johnson. It's, uh, me again, calling with some information about Orlowski."

"Okay, what have you got?"

Zack took a deep breath. "Well, we discovered that he used to live in New Jersey. He spent two years there in between the time he lived in Connecticut and the time he moved here. While he was in New Jersey, three prostitutes were murdered not far from where he lived." Zack waited for a response that didn't come. "In Trenton."

"Oh yeah?"

"Yeah," Zack replied. "And one of the victims had DNA under her fingernails, but it didn't match anybody in the criminal database. I might be wrong, but I wouldn't think Orlowski's DNA would be in the criminal database."

"Probably not."

Zack's discomfort from Johnson's minimalistic answers was becoming apparent. "We were thinking that maybe if we got a sample of Orlowski's DNA, we could do a comparison. You know, maybe connect him to the crime?"

"We?"

Zack appeared confused for a moment, then said, "Oh, yeah. *We*. I am working with a partner."

"Okay, well, here's the problem. Just because a hooker has a guy's DNA under her fingernails, that doesn't mean the guy's a murderer. Any defense attorney worth a damn is going to argue that the guy did have sex with her, but she was very much alive and well when he left her. And honestly, any defense attorney representing a cop is going to go so far as to claim the sex was consensual…off the clock. He wouldn't even admit that his client used a hooker because that alone would be grounds for dismissal from his job."

"We'd actually thought of that," Zack muttered softly. "But it would at least tie him to the victim…wouldn't it?"

"It would, but I'm not sure it'd be enough to issue an arrest warrant. The case against him would still be largely circumstantial. Truthfully, even I'm not convinced he did it myself. I'm just open to the idea to make sure all of our bases are covered."

Zack made a face. "I understand." A long silence ensued. "So should we still try and get his DNA sample? I-I-I've seen on TV that if you get the DNA from a public place, then it's not illegal search and seizure. My partner sometimes has dinner with Orlowski and can get you a straw that he's used if you want."

"Well, if you bring me a straw with DNA on it, how do I know for sure it's Orlowski's?"

Zack didn't reply.

"I'll tell you what," Johnson continued. "The next time your *partner* has dinner with Orlowski, make sure it's in a public place. Let me know he's there. Maybe I'll just have to swing by and get a bite…you know, run into him by accident."

Zack and Jenny both let out silent sighs of relief. "Okay, we'll do that. Thank you Officer Johnson."

"Yup." Without another word, Johnson hung up the phone. Zack did the same.

Jenny looked squarely at Zack. "He definitely scares me."

"Yeah, he's not the most personable guy I've ever dealt with, that's for sure."

"Well, at least he's on board with the idea of collecting Orlowski's DNA. That's about all we can ask for, isn't it?"

"I guess so," Zack replied. "Okay, time to call Fazzino. This time it's your turn."

"I don't mind calling Fazzino," Jenny confessed. "He's not scary." Jenny retrieved her cell phone out of her purse and dialed Officer Fazzino's number.

"Well, hello, Jenny Watkins. How are you today?"

"Doing well, Officer Fazzino. How are you?"

"Great. And, please, call me Danny."

"Okay, *Danny.*" Jenny made a face as she said the name. "Well, I'm calling because I have some new information for you."

"Excellent. What is it?"

"Well, we think the Hawkins house belongs to Orlowski's mother and step-father."

"Is that so?" Fazzino asked.

"Yes, sir. And he may have actually been staying there at the time Lashonda was killed. He had just separated from his wife then."

"Huh," Fazzino said. "What do you know?"

Jenny also told him about the Lyme disease. "That's right," Fazzino remarked. "I do remember him being really sick right before he resigned. I didn't know it was Lyme, though. I figured he had the flu or mono or something."

"No, sir. It was Lyme disease."

"That's good to know," Fazzino replied. "Although I'm not sure that helps us with our investigation."

Jenny scratched her head. "I guess it doesn't, does it?"

"So do you have any other developments?"

Jenny mentioned the prostitutes in Trenton, disclosing that she was working with Officer Johnson to get a DNA sample. Fazzino agreed with Johnson's assessment that while a DNA match would be helpful, it wouldn't be the smoking gun they were looking for.

"But that's about it," Jenny concluded. "That's all I have for you."

"Well, it turns out *I* have a little information for *you*," Fazzino said proudly.

"Really?" Butterflies began to dance around Jenny's stomach.

"Yup. We always keep our cruisers marked with identification numbers on the rear quarter panel. We also keep a log of which officer has each cruiser on any given night. And guess what number cruiser Orlowski had the night Lashonda disappeared?"

Jenny felt her blood run cold. "Three-thirty-seven?"

"Bingo. While it certainly isn't anything concrete, it just adds more credibility to the argument that Orlowski's our guy. There's absolutely no way you could have known that without some divine intervention."

Jenny lowered her eyes. "I guess Lashonda made a note of that when she got out of the car. She sure did everything she could to protect herself, poor thing."

"And it may have paid off," Fazzino said happily, although Jenny failed to see it that way.

"Well, this is some good information," Fazzino concluded. "I'll see what I can do at the Hawkins house."

"Great. Thanks for looking into that."

"No," Fazzino replied. "Thank *you*."

Jenny curled up on her air mattress with her phone in her hand. She felt a sadness she just couldn't shake as she searched the Internet for more information about the three New Jersey victims. She wanted to know about them—who they were before they became bodies at dumpsites. She didn't imagine that their disappearances received even a fraction of the attention that the other girls' did. She didn't envision long lines at their funeral services. The last victim wouldn't have even *had* a funeral service if it hadn't been for the kindness of the police officers involved. That notion, above all else, bothered Jenny the most.

She looked up an article which featured photographs of the three young women, taken at happier times in their lives. Angela Velasquez was featured in her cheerleading outfit, posed on one knee with pom poms raised in the air. Her smile could have brightened any room. Jenny stared at the picture, looking at this beautiful young girl who had made the simple mistake of choosing the wrong boy. She probably started doing the drugs in an attempt to be accepted by him. Jenny thought about all of the concessions she personally had made when she was younger in order to impress Greg. Similar mistakes, very different outcomes. *There but for the grace of God go I*, Jenny thought as she felt an ache in her stomach.

Paris's picture showed her holding her baby daughter. She looked happy, like a proud new mother. Perhaps the monotony of motherhood hadn't sunk in at the time this picture was taken. At that

166

point she was still okay with making the sacrifices that young mothers make. Jenny's eyes focused on the baby, who was now growing up without a mother. She hoped that the father had gotten remarried to a nice woman who would raise this little girl as her own. The baby deserved that—the baby hadn't done anything wrong.

Jenny closed her eyes for a moment to pay homage to these two victims—privileged girls who held the world in their hands but let it slip through their fingers.

Unlike the others, the photograph of Renee Podgewaite was distant and fuzzy; it may have been the only picture they could find of her. That notion made Jenny even sadder. This woman truly hadn't mattered. She wasn't like the other girls who paid too hefty of a price for some bad choices; this woman never stood a chance. From the moment she was born, her heartbreaking fate had been sealed.

A flood of tears consumed Jenny. The emotion that she'd been suppressing flowed freely, giving her a huge feeling of release. All of her pent-up sorrow about the victims, her own failed marriage, and Jeremy Stotler's wrongful arrest found its way to the surface as she sobbed relentlessly into her pillow. After several moments she began to calm down, feeling a renewed sense of peace. Despite her overwhelming desire to always stay strong, she had to admit that sometimes there was nothing better than a good, healthy cry.

As the tears dried and her mood returned to normal, a distant memory popped into her head. She recalled men in suits coming to the door of her childhood home back in Kentucky to ask about a neighbor who worked in law enforcement. The questions had been routine and basic, rather unremarkable, except they asked about any extended periods of unaccounted for time. Maybe, just maybe, she could claim to work for the government and pull off a similar interview of Orlowski's relative in New Jersey. If only she knew who he was.

Step brother. He had said it was a step brother…from marriage number four. If Hawkins was six…Jenny used her phone to call up the real estate records of the Hawkins property, noting that two husbands before had been MacMahon. She needed to find a MacMahon from Edmonton New Jersey. A white pages search revealed several MacMahons in Edmonton. Somehow she'd have to determine his first name. Suddenly she knew what her next conversation with Orlowski was going to be about.

She flipped over onto her side, feeling relaxed, when she heard a banging sound. Once again she raised her head, listening intently, but the noise didn't return. *Orlowski's at work,* she reasoned, *a half an hour away from here. He doesn't know your real name. He doesn't know where you live. Relax.* Despite the voice of reason echoing in her head, she remained spooked. Too spooked to sleep.

"The DVDs," she remarked, hopping out of bed. She retrieved her laptop and a movie, setting up a makeshift entertainment center in her desolate bedroom. The distraction proved to be enough to allow her to drift off into sleep.

Chapter 16

As Jenny locked up her apartment on her way to meet up with Zack, she noticed an extra key on her key ring. She remembered this was her mailbox key, and she hadn't checked her mail since she had moved in. Instead of heading to her car in the parking lot, she walked to the mailboxes next to her building. She found the rectangular metal box designated for her apartment, inserting her key to discover she only had one piece of mail, a copy of her rental contract from The Grove apartments. "Oh yeah," she remarked. "I haven't changed my address yet. Gotta do that."

She looked up to see an older woman standing very close to her. Realizing she'd been caught talking to herself, Jenny smiled as she threw the envelope into her purse and walked to her car. If Jenny gave a shit, that would have really been embarrassing. It was a good thing she didn't care anymore. She hopped in her car with a giggle and drove off.

Soon Jenny was at Zack's apartment, ready to head together to Billy's. "Wow, you look hot," Zack remarked as she walked through his door.

Jenny smiled. "Thanks, but I'm not dressed up for you. I'm trying to keep the interest of a serial killer. The other two times I've met up with him, I didn't realize I was going until I was already there, and I kind of looked like shit."

"I wouldn't say that."

"Well, I made no attempt to make myself look good, let me put it that way," Jenny remarked. "But this time I know I'm going, so I figured I'd at least try to appear attractive."

"Well, it worked, but that scares me," Zack said. "I hope he doesn't try anything with you."

"We're going to be in a public place, and you'll be right out there in the parking lot." Jenny held up a finger. "*And*, if Orlowski does show up, we'll let Johnson know, and *he'll* come too. I really don't think I'm in any danger."

"I still feel like we're using you as bait," Zack countered.

"I'm not bait."

"I wish I could be as sure about that as you are," Zack commented as they walked together out the door.

Jenny sat alone at the counter at Billy's, watching the television that hung behind the stacks of bottles behind the bar. She'd been there for about twenty five minutes, so far to no avail. Suddenly she started to get the same funny feeling she'd had at Morgan's funeral. She knew without looking that Orlowski was on his way.

"Hey," Olrowski's voice called a few moments later. Jenny turned toward him with a smile. "Well, don't you look nice?" he commented.

With a bat of her eyelashes she replied, "Thank you. I was hoping you'd show up."

"And I was hoping you'd be here." He placed his hand on Jenny's back as he sat next to her, causing searing pain and a clatter inside Jenny's brain. She managed a smile anyway.

"Oh," Jenny said, shaking her head. "I just remembered something. Hang on a second." She pulled out her phone and texted Zack. *I fed the dog.* She turned back to Orlowski. "So how was work last night? Did anything exciting happen?"

"Not really. A drunken brawl, that's about it. It was a pretty quiet night."

Jenny made a face. "You know, I was thinking about something last night."

"Oh yeah?" Orlowski ordered a chicken dinner and a soda from the bartender.

"Yeah. You said something about moving in with a step brother in New Jersey. You also said your mother was married, like, a million times."

"Well, six, but that's close to a million."

"I rounded up," Jenny declared. "I'm just curious how many step brothers and sisters you ended up having."

Orlowski let out a laugh. "God, I don't even know. I'd have to think about that for a minute."

"That many, huh?"

"It was a lot, that's for sure. And I don't even count the ones that happened after I moved out the first time. Scott and Hawk both have kids, but I don't consider them step brothers and sisters. At all."

"Hawk?" Jenny asked.

"My mom's current husband. His name is Earl Hawkins, but everyone calls him Hawk. He's got a few kids—two sons and a daughter—but I do *not* consider myself related to them. They're a bunch of redneck fuck-ups."

Jenny winced.

"Unfortunately, this has been my mom's longest marriage. She's been with him for about ten years now. I guess she's getting a little too old to play the field these days, so she's finally settled down."

Jenny curled her nose. "I'm getting a nasty visual."

"Oh, God," Orlowski said, covering his eyes. "Don't even go there."

Jenny laughed. "Okay, so was this *Scott* character the husband before?"

"Yeah." The wheels were turning in Orlowski's head. "Let me see, I think he lasted five or six years, maybe? I guess I was about twenty one when they got married, so that seems right."

"Did he have kids?"

"Two girls, but they were older than me. I only met them a handful of times. They didn't live close by."

"Were they redneck fuck-ups too?"

"No, I don't think so. But their father was. All of my mother's husbands were."

"Including your father?"

"My mother never married my father."

Jenny's eyes grew wide. "She had six husbands and none of them were your father?"

"Nope," Orlowski said. "She got pregnant with me when she was young. My father never married her. I think he wanted her to get an abortion, truthfully, but she refused."

"That's terrible," Jenny said, although she couldn't help but think how much better the world would have been if his mother had gone through with it.

"It is what it is," Orlowski replied. His soda arrived, and he took a drink through his straw. Jenny felt the urge to grab the straw and run out the door, but she sat patiently.

"So how many different step-fathers did you live with?" Jenny posed.

"Four. But I barely remember the first one. He and my mom divorced when I was about five. I have seen pictures of him and his kids, but I don't really have any memories of them."

"It still must have been traumatic for you to have your father figure and your siblings leave when you were so young. You must not have known what was going on."

"I can't say," Orlowski surmised. "I don't remember it at all."

"Okay, so who was number two, and how long did he last?"

"God, you ask a lot of questions."

"I'm just fascinated by this, that's all. I grew up with one mom and one dad in one house. My life was boring compared to yours."

"I'm not sure if boring is the word I would use," Orlowski said. "Okay, let me see." He looked up at the ceiling. "His name was Paul, and I think he lasted from about second grade to maybe fifth grade? He had older kids, too. Teenagers, I think. They didn't really have too much to do with me. I was probably a pain in the ass to them."

"I don't know about that," Jenny surmised.

"I do. I was in middle school when husband number three arrived with his twin kindergarteners. God, they were a nightmare."

"Were they girls or boys?"

"Boys. Fortunately they weren't around that much. I think they spent most of their time with their mother. But then my step-father died in a car accident, so they went to live with their mother permanently. I never saw them again after that."

"Wow. I'm sorry to hear that. Were you devastated when he died?"

"Not at all," Orlowski said. "I know this sounds terrible, but I was happy to see him go. He used to hit my mom sometimes, and he'd swear at me a lot. I couldn't help but think he got what he deserved when he died."

How incredibly ironic, Jenny thought. "Yikes. But I guess that leads to husband number four...the one with the cool step brother?"

"Yup. Mike."

"Was Mike the husband or the son?"

Orlowski smiled. "Both. They were Mike senior and Mike junior. Mike junior was my age, and he was a good kid. We were both in high school, and we'd both had similar shitty upbringings. I think that's why we could relate to each other. He was the only one of my step siblings I ever hung out with, and I continued to hang out with him even after our parents split up. He ended up marrying a girl from Trenton, and he eventually moved there, which is how I came to be there."

"How old were you when that divorce happened?"

"We were both seniors in high school, but by that age you're old enough to hang out with who you want. Even though Mike moved out, we still got together. I don't think my mom liked that idea very much. She would have preferred a clean break, but I didn't give a shit what she thought. If *she'd* given a shit what *I* thought, she wouldn't have had a new husband every five years. But apparently she didn't care, so neither did I."

Jenny's phone chirped. She looked at the screen; it was a message from Zack which read *a guy is here.*

Although she assumed he meant Officer Johnson, she wasn't sure. She rolled her eyes and said to Orlowski, "Ugh. This is my husband. I guess I should see what this is about." She grabbed her purse and stood up off the bar stool. "Don't go anywhere. I'll be right back."

Jenny headed out the door and dialed Zack's number. "What do you mean?" she said as soon as he picked up.

"Johnson. He's here."

"Okay, that's what I thought you meant."

"I flagged him down in the parking lot," Zack admitted. "I wanted to talk to you before he went in to see if now is a good time or if he should wait a little while before he goes in."

"Well, now he should wait a minute, just because it might look funny if I get a call and then he comes in right away."

"Good thinking."

"But now I have to come up with some story about what this phone call was about. Orlowski may have seen the message that a guy is here. What guy are we talking about?"

"The ant guy."

"The ant guy?"

"You know what I mean. What are those guys called? Exterminators. That's it. The exterminator is here."

"Why would you call me for that?"

"I'm an idiot," Zack insisted. "Maybe I am wondering how to pay him, but you already have him on automatic billing."

Jenny covered her eyes. "That's just stupid enough it might work."

"I'm good at being an idiot. So how's it going in there?"

"Okay," Jenny said. "I got the name of the relative in Edmonton."

"Are you being safe?"

"Yes, I'm safe," Jenny insisted. "Okay, I'm going to head back in. Tell…the exterminator…to wait a few minutes before going in."

"Will do."

Jenny hung up her phone and went back into the bar. After her eyes adjusted to the dark, her blood froze at what she saw.

Orlowski was reading her rental agreement.

Chapter 17

Jenny knew she must have looked like a deer in headlights. "How did you get that?" she asked.

"It fell out of your purse when you left," he explained. "So you got yourself an apartment, huh?"

Think. "I did."

"Why didn't you say so?"

A response popped into Jenny's head. She allowed her demeanor to relax as she flashed her flirty smile. She sat back down on the bar stool as she playfully snatched the rental agreement out of his hand. "I haven't moved in yet. I just got it in case I needed it."

"Do you think you'll use it?"

Jenny shrugged. "Maybe."

"It seems far from here. Why did you get an apartment so far away? "

Jenny looked Orlowki in the eye. "Now what good would it do to move out of my husband's house only to get an apartment close by? If I'm going to leave him, I'm going to *leave.*"

"Well, I have to admit I'm encouraged by this," Orlowski added. "I'm looking forward to the day I can call you and take you out on a proper date."

Every nerve in Jenny's body tingled. "In due time."

At that moment Orlowski looked over Jenny's shoulder to the door. She turned around to see Officer Johnson entering the bar. Johnson approached them and extended his hand. "Tom," he said. "Good to see you."

"Ed." Orlowski grabbed Johnson's elbow and engaged him in a firm handshake. "I didn't expect to see you here."

"Well, I had a couple of friends recommend this place, so I figured I'd give it a try."

"The food is good, and the scenery has improved ever since she's started coming here." Orlowski gestured toward Jenny, who blushed modestly.

"Well, I don't want to horn in on anything. I'll just have a seat over there. But it was good seeing you."

"You too." As Johnson walked away, Orlowski leaned closer to Jenny and said, "That's Ed Johnson. He's on the force. To be honest, I'm glad he doesn't want to sit with us. He has the personality of a park bench."

Jenny giggled. She actually knew he was speaking the truth.

"Don't get me wrong," Orlowski continued. "He's a nice enough guy. He's just difficult to talk to."

"Well, *you're* certainly easy enough to talk to."

"You too," Orlowski replied with a wink.

After seemingly endless small talk, Orlowski once again excused himself under the pretense of having to go to work. Jenny tried to remain casual, although on the inside she was desperate for the bartender to not clean up his dishes. Fortunately the bartender was in the back, out of sight. Once Orlowski was safely out the door, Jenny looked over her shoulder at Johnson, who made eye contact with her. She glanced toward the straw, looked back at Johnson, and nodded slightly. The message seemed to be received clearly.

Johnson got up and walked toward the bar, sitting where Orlowski had just been sitting. He very quickly pulled latex gloves and an envelope out of his pocket, getting everything situated discretely under the bar. With surprising ease he removed the straw from the glass and slipped it into the envelope. Without a word, he sat back down in his seat and resumed his dinner.

"I screwed up," Jenny confessed nervously on Zack's couch. "I screwed up bad."

"Why? What happened?" Zack asked.

Jenny covered her face with her hands. "When I went outside to talk to you on the phone, my rental agreement fell out of my purse. Orlowski read it. He saw the address." Hanging her head she added, "And my real name."

"Are you kidding me?" Zack asked.

"I wish I was."

"Well, you've got to stay with me, then. There's no way you can stay there now that he knows where you live."

"Well, I told him that I hadn't moved in yet. It was a *just in case* rental."

"He still might stake it out, just waiting for the moment he can catch you alone."

Jenny shook her head. "I doubt it. Besides, I'll be careful."

"You said that before," Zack remarked.

"I know, but I mean it." Jenny continued to speak before Zack could argue. "It could take months for Orlowski to be caught—if he gets caught at all. I can't impose on you that long."

"You wouldn't be imposing."

Jenny smiled. "Thank you, Zack. Really. But I don't think it's a good idea for me to stay here. For a lot of reasons."

Zack seemed angry, but she wasn't sure if he was upset with her stubbornness or if his feelings had been hurt. Either way, she knew she couldn't move in with Zack, unofficially or otherwise. She didn't want to lead him on. Besides, she needed to take care of herself. This time in her life was clearly a test to see if she could make it on her own. She needed the answer to that question to be yes.

"The good news is that Johnson got the straw," Jenny said cheerfully.

"Good," Zack replied without an ounce of emotion. He was clearly still irritated.

"And the step-brother's name is Mike MacMahon Junior."

"That's nice."

Uncomfortable with the obvious tension, Jenny stood up. "Well, I guess I'll be going, while it's still early."

"Text me when you get home. And lock your door." Zack didn't look at her.

"I will," Jenny assured him. "Just so you know, Orlowski is working tonight. He can't possibly come out here. He'll be spending the evening in Braddock."

177

"Still lock your door."

Jenny had to admit she was a little nervous as she scooted through her door and locked it behind her. She quickly turned on as many lights as she could, once again wishing she had cable to keep her company. Remembering her promise, she texted Zack that she had made it home safely, but then she sat on her folding chair, unsure what to do next.

Her eyes shifted to the easel she'd brought from her old house. She could paint. Painting always made her feel better. She retrieved the box of painting supplies Elanor had bought for her, which included only a small canvas. It would have to do.

But what to paint? She'd need to think about that. "No I don't," she said out loud. She had vowed to herself that the next time she broke out her canvas, she'd paint freely and see where it took her. After setting up her easel, she squeezed her paints onto her palette, dipped her brush in, and allowed her hand to simply start painting.

The following morning, Jenny formulated her list of questions for Orlowski's step brother. She assumed he would be at work at that hour, and her phone call would need to be in the evening. That afternoon, Jenny continued to work on her painting until she heard a knock at the door. Her nerves surged slightly, even though she had been expecting the knock. She tip toed quietly to the door and looked out the peep hole. With a smile she opened the door.

"Hello," she said cheerfully. "I am so happy to see you."

The man from the cable company walked through the door. "I hear you'd like Internet and cable hooked up."

"That's the rumor," Jenny replied, shutting and locking the door behind him.

He noted the half-finished painting on the easel. "Huh. Are you making that?"

"Yes, sir."

He furrowed his brow. "What is it going to be?"

Jenny giggled. "It's two paths. The straight one leads to ugliness, but if you take the path that turns right it's all pretty."

The cable man looked around the nearly-empty apartment. "I think I get it."

With a smile Jenny remarked, "I'm sure you do."

While the man connected Jenny's cable box, she looked at him critically, realizing that he was a complete stranger that she'd just let into her apartment. She'd even locked the door behind him. For some reason she trusted him, but she had no reason to. He was larger than her; if inclined, he could have easily overpowered her. She considered Morgan, Lashonda and Allison, who had all actually been choosier about whom they'd trust, and they all ended up dead. This was another case of *there but for the grace of God go I.* Jenny felt panic setting in.

As fear began to consume her, Jenny heard the man say, "Listen, if you need a little help with your bill, I might be able to get you a discount." He sat back on his heels and looked around the apartment. "I know what it's like to start over, and it isn't easy."

With one single kind gesture, this man just restored Jenny's faith in humanity.

"That's very nice of you," she replied sincerely, "but I actually am doing okay. I have things…they're just not here." Jenny decided against mentioning the eight-figure bank account she was sitting on.

With a smile he added, "I'm glad to hear that." He got back to work.

Jenny smiled kindly as her nerves subsided; although, this episode made Jenny decide that as soon as she got her townhouse, she'd get a dog. A big one.

Jenny walked up the three flights of stairs with her grocery bags. She should have taken two trips, but she decided to tough it out and carry everything at once. She regretted that decision after the first flight.

Once inside the apartment, she dropped all of the bags in her foyer and locked the door behind her. She picked up one bag and headed toward the kitchen; before she even took ten steps there was a heavy pounding at the door.

Jenny froze. Had she been followed? Was this Orlowski? For a brief moment, she wished she'd heeded Zack's advice and just stayed at his place. Quietly placing the bag on the floor, Jenny walked as softly as she could to the door. She looked out the peephole once again, seeing a familiar but unwelcome face.

Chapter 18

Jenny opened the door. "Greg," she said with astonishment. "What are you doing here?"

"Can we talk?" he asked.

Jenny looked beyond him to make sure he was alone. Her primary concern was getting him inside and closing the door. "Sure. Come on in." He stepped inside and she immediately shut him in. Once the door was locked her focus shifted, and suddenly she realized she had just received a man she had no desire to see. "What are you doing here?"

"I just want to know how long you're planning to do this."

"Do what?"

"This." Greg extended his arms and gestured to the apartment. "I mean, you've made your point. You can come home now."

"I *am* home," Jenny replied.

"Come on, Jenny, look at this place. Stop doing this."

"I happen to *like* this place."

Greg snorted. "Please. I mean, really."

Jenny scratched her head. "Are you done here?"

"I'm the one who should be asking you that."

With a sigh to keep herself grounded, Jenny said, "Greg, you don't seem to understand this, but I am done. Done with the marriage. This isn't some kind of tantrum or stunt to get your attention. This is my new home now, and I'm actually quite happy here."

He looked skeptically around. "I find that hard to believe."

"I know you do. You can't possibly be happy unless you have…stuff. I don't expect you to understand that I can be happy with just my freedom."

Frustration clearly gripped Greg. "Okay, I guess this was a waste of time." He turned toward the door. "Listen, when you come to your senses, let me know."

"Hey," Jenny called as Greg's hand touched the doorknob. "How did you know I lived here? Did you follow me or something?"

Greg didn't answer as he left. Jenny immediately locked the door behind him, shaking her head, trying to grasp what had just happened. As the last two minutes registered in her brain, she became very much aware of how careless she'd just been. She hadn't paid enough attention to her surroundings as she returned from the store. Had this been Orlowski at her door, she could have been killed.

But she also couldn't deny the power shift she'd just witnessed. She was now the card holder in her relationship with Greg. Mister You'll-Be-Back had just come looking for her. She couldn't help but smile. It seemed at this point in her life she had her choice of three different men, although among them were an asshole and a serial killer. "Quantity, not quality," she muttered as she returned to the shopping bag on the floor. "You can't have everything."

Her day remained uneventful. She received several texts from Zack, asking if she was okay. She felt guilty about making him worry so much; her goal hadn't been to upset him. His concern was unfortunate collateral damage in her quest to be independent.

She spent most of her day painting, watching her newly activated television, and surfing the Internet. When the clock hit seven, she decided it was time to try her luck at Mike MacMahon. She took several deep breaths to calm her nerves and dialed the phone, making sure to press the series of buttons that would allow her number to remain anonymous.

"Hello?"

"Hi, my name is Elizabeth Fairbanks; I work for the police department down here in Braddock Georgia. I'm looking for a Mr. Michael MacMahon."

"This is."

"Hi, Mr. MacMahon. I am calling in regards to your step brother, Tom Orlowski. He's being considered for a promotion, and he listed you as a character reference. Do you mind if I ask you a few questions while I have you on the phone?"

"No, that's fine."

Jenny asked a few routine questions: how long he had known Tom, and in what capacity. She asked if Orlowski had hung out with anyone questionable or lived beyond his means financially. These had all been questions she remembered from the interviews regarding her old neighbor. Then she posed the question she had been waiting for. "While Mr. Orlowski lived with you, did he have any stretches of unaccounted for time or moments when his whereabouts were in question?"

"Well, I have to confess, I hardly ever saw him, even though we lived together. He was the ideal roommate, actually." Mike let out a laugh. "He worked nights, I worked days...we would occasionally cross paths in the morning or evening, but beyond that it was as if he didn't live here at all."

"Do you suspect he was involved in any questionable activity while staying with you?"

"No," Mike said, seemingly genuinely. "He's a good guy."

Jenny's heart sank. This seemed like it was getting her nowhere. She continued to ask some appropriate questions for a few more minutes before concluding the call. "Damn," she said out loud when she hung up. "That was a waste."

About a half an hour later her phone rang; it was Danny Fazzino. Jenny wasn't expecting this phone call, so she was very interested to hear what he had to say.

She picked up eagerly. "Hello?"

"Hi Jenny, it's Danny Fazzino. How are you?"

"Doing well. To what do I owe the honor?" She was anxious for him to get to the point.

"Well, I just wanted to let you know we searched the Hawkins' shed."

"Really? You were able to get a warrant that fast?"

"Didn't need one," Fazzino replied. "I went to the house in uniform and spoke to his mother, saying I wanted to look for evidence in an old case. I think she automatically assumed I was looking for some dirt on one of her exes, so she told me to go ahead and take whatever I needed. I spent all afternoon searching that shed with a fine-toothed comb, and unfortunately I came up with nothing."

Jenny's heart fell into her feet.

"Are you sure it was the shed I was supposed to be focusing on?" Fazzino asked.

Making a face she remarked, "I *thought* so, but I could have been wrong."

"You've just been right about so many things, and you were led to this place twice," Fazzino said. "I thought for sure I would find something."

Jenny hung her head. "So did I."

"Alright," Fazzino added, "maybe I'll go back and see if I can search the house."

"That'd be great," Jenny remarked in a dejected tone.

"Well, have a good evening."

"You too." Jenny hung up the phone and felt very empty. She sat in her chair wondering if she had any ability at all or if she had just happened to get lucky a few times. *Stop,* she said to herself. *Stop beating yourself up. You have been right about a bunch of stuff. So you got one thing wrong. It happens.*

Her pep-talk didn't make her feel any better.

The next two days came and went without incident. Jenny felt impatient, like a caged animal. She was having a difficult time enjoying her freedom when she really didn't feel like she could be free. On the few occasions she did leave her apartment, she constantly looked over her shoulder. She only felt truly comfortable in her apartment, where she was bored silly.

Chapter 19

Jenny woke in the middle of the night to that familiar tug which told her she needed to go somewhere. She grabbed a coat, her purse, and some shoes—all while remaining trance-like—and headed out the door. The cold threatened to rouse her into consciousness, but she refused to allow it. Something told her she was headed somewhere important.

She drove into Braddock, down some streets that were unfamiliar to her. Eventually she was led to a long, deserted stretch where she stumbled across a lone young woman who was staggering along the road's edge. Jenny knew this was where she was supposed to be.

She pulled her phone out of her purse and dialed Zack's number. She got his voicemail, which wasn't surprising at that hour. "Zack," she said. "I've been led to Braddock. I'm not entirely sure where I am, but there's a girl out here by herself. I think Morgan wants me to protect her. I'm going to try to get her in my car and take her home. Give me a call when you get this message."

Jenny considered calling Officer Johnson, as scary as he was, but she didn't have his number. "Damn," she said out loud. She definitely should have gotten that number from Zack.

She climbed out of her car and approached the woman, who was illuminated solely by Jenny's headlights. "Hey," Jenny called. "Do you need a ride somewhere?"

The young woman was crying. "No," she demanded. "I do *not* need a ride somewhere. I *need* my boyfriend to stop being an asshole." She slurred her words as she spoke.

"I'm sorry to hear that," Jenny said, trying her best to befriend the drunken girl. "Listen, why don't you let me give you a ride home, or at least call a friend for you?"

"No," she insisted. "I'm *fine.*" She stumbled but regained her balance.

"Come on. It's dangerous out here. There's a killer on the loose."

"I'll have you know," the girl replied, putting her finger in the air, "that the killer was caught, thank you very much. See what you know? You don't know *nothing.*" She spoke with closed eyes.

At that moment Jenny began to get that all-too-familiar feeling that signaled Orlowski was on his way. *Please, God, no.* "Listen," Jenny pleaded. "Please. Get in the car. I'll take you straight home, I promise."

"I *told* you, I don't need a ride. I don't even know who you are."

Screaming began inside Jenny's head. At that moment she could hear the sound of an approaching car; the world around her started flashing in blue and red.

Shit.

The sand and gravel alongside the road crunched under the police car's tires as it pulled over. Jenny's mind raced. What was she going to say to him? How could she explain being here in the middle of the night? She'd have to come up with something. The only thing she knew for sure was that she could not allow this girl to be alone with Orlowski. That would have been a death sentence.

The car door opened, and the officer emerged from his vehicle. "Is there a problem here?" Jenny heard Orlowski's voice say. She remained frozen, blinded by his headlights, seeing only his silhouette walking toward her. "Hey," he added. "It's you."

"Yeah, it's me," Jenny said. "Everything's fine, actually. This is just my cousin...she's had a little too much to drink."

"I am *not* her cousin!" the woman shouted.

Jenny tried her best to play it cool. "See what I mean?" she said to Orlowski.

"Officer," the drunken woman slurred, "this woman is crazy. I have never seen her before in my *life*."

For the love of God, Jenny pleaded silently, *please shut up.*

The drunken woman staggered over to the police car, pounding on the passenger window with an open hand. "I want in. I want *you* to give me a ride home, not this crazy bitch."

"Tom," Jenny said pleadingly. "I'm sorry. She gets like this. She actually has a bit of a drug habit, and she doesn't have any idea what's going on."

"I do *not* have a drug habit. Let me in." She continued to pound on the door.

"I'll tell you what," Orlowski said. "I'll bring her home. Thanks for trying, though."

Frozen with fear, thoughts swirled around Jenny's head. *If this girl gets into his car, she's as good as dead. Although, maybe not. He has a witness this time. I can place him with her. Maybe he won't take that chance. But what if he does? What if he claims he dropped her off safely in front of her house and that she disappeared sometime afterward? He's a cop. People will probably believe him.*

Orlowski turned around and walked toward the woman, who continued to lean against his car. Every step seemed to take an eternity, as if he was walking in slow motion. Jenny tried her best to come up with something—anything—before Orlowski put this woman in his car and drove off into the night.

I can always follow him. But what if he loses me? Then she'd be all alone with him. She'd be completely at his mercy. He has no mercy. He would probably kill her. Oh my God I could never live with myself if I let this girl die.

"Can I come with you?" Jenny blurted before she even knew what she was saying.

"No," Orlowski said. "That's probably not a good idea." He finally reached the woman, placing his hand on her back as he made a motion toward the door handle to the back seat of his cruiser.

Oh my God. He's going to leave with her. Jenny looked at the woman with despair, unable to wrap her head around what was happening.

At that moment Orlowski stopped, paused a moment, and walked back around to the front of the car. He turned to Jenny, and she was able to see his face illuminated by the headlights—just like she had seen in Morgan's original vision. The eerie familiarity was horrifying. He looked intently at Jenny, his piercing eyes fixated on her. "On second thought," he said with a slight smile, "Why don't you come with us?"

Chapter 20

Jenny quickly weighed the options in front of her. *There's no way he'd try to kill both of us, would he? That would be way too brazen. He could never pull it off. But that girl all by herself would be a sitting duck…*

"Okay," Jenny said, "I'll come along." She felt numb as she headed toward the car, as if she was having an out-of-body experience. Her nerves tingled, but her mind remained inexplicably calm and subdued. Something primeval inside of her was taking over—the survival instinct, she assumed. Jenny only hoped it would serve her right.

"There's just one thing," Orlowski said as he escorted her to the cruiser. "It's kind of a technicality, but I could lose my job for it. Civilians aren't allowed in the front seat, and we're not allowed to let anyone have a cell phone in the back. I'm afraid you'll have to give me your cell phones until you get home."

Now Jenny knew how he managed to get the girls' phones— why none of them called for help. She helplessly handed her phone over to Orlowski, who promptly turned it off. The drunken girl, who was still leaning on the police car for support, turned over her phone as well.

Orlowski opened the back door to the car. "Ladies, your chariot awaits," he declared as he gestured for the women to enter.

And he has the nerve to act chivalrous.

The sound of the door closing behind Jenny rang out like a bullet, causing her to jump. As Orlowski climbed into the front of his car, she immediately started to doubt her decision. She had just gotten into this car, like Allison, Lashonda and Morgan before her, and they all ended up dead. She shouldn't have done this. She should have just followed him. Fear engulfed Jenny as the car began moving.

This was too familiar. She'd experienced this once before, through Lashonda's eyes, but this time it was real. This was her own fear. She wouldn't wake up from this. She might never wake up again.

How did I end up here? Jenny asked herself. *I said I'd be careful. I promised Susan I wouldn't do anything stupid, and I promised Zack I'd be cautious. And yet here I am. I'm about to become another one of his victims. And I knew. I knew he was a monster, and I let him take me anyway. I have no phone and no way to call for help. There's a cage in front of me, and there are no door handles, so I have no way to help myself. I have nothing. Nothing at all.*

The drunken girl laid her head against the window without a care in the world. Her heavy breathing indicated she was out cold.

Brains. Jenny sat up straighter. *I have my brains.* She thought for a moment about the approach she should take, trying to determine what would give her the best hope for survival. Before too long a plan came to mind. With a deep breath and a quick glance to the roof of the car, Jenny felt the strength of all of Orlowski's victims seep into her bones. *I can do this,* she thought. *For all of those girls I will do this.*

"Hey Orlowski," Jenny called from behind the cage. Her tone was different than he'd ever heard.

Jenny could see his eyes look into the rear view mirror.

"I've got a question for you. You said you used to work in Ivory Heights Connecticut, right?"

"Yeah," he replied.

"And you said the biggest case you had up there was...let me see if I have this right...cats in trees, was it?"

Jenny once again saw eyes shift in the mirror.

"Yeah." His tone grew defensive.

"How come you didn't mention those murdered girls? Did you forget?" Jenny didn't allow a hint of fear to taint her voice. "I wouldn't think you'd forget *that.*"

After a pause, Orlowski replied, "I guess it slipped my mind."

"It slipped your mind. Wow. That's a pretty big slip." Jenny leaned forward. "What were their names again? Allison Pope and Lashonda Williams? Isn't that right?"

"Yes, that's right."

Jenny could tell she was striking a nerve, so she continued. "I wouldn't think you'd forget them considering you were the one to find their cell phones."

"How did you know that?"

"Oh, I know lots of things." Jenny sat back in her seat, folding her arms across her chest. "Lots and lots of things."

Orlowski remained silent as he continued to drive.

"Aren't you going to ask where my cousin lives? You've been driving, but we haven't told you where to go. Isn't that a little strange?"

Silence.

"You know what else is strange?" Jenny added. "When you lived in Edmonton, three women disappeared from Trenton. Angela Velasquez, Paris Carter and Renee Podgewaite, but you probably only know them as hooker one, hooker two and hooker three."

Silence.

"And now you're here. And what do you know? Another dead girl. Boy, you must be the unluckiest guy in the world, huh Orlowski?"

Fear grabbed Jenny by the throat as Orlowski started to pull the car over.

"You don't want to do this," Jenny said, remaining tough as nails. "I'm not Jenny O'dell, bimbo from Braddock. I'm Jenny Watkins with the FBI. And guess what? I'm wearing a wire, asshole. Everyone knows I'm with you. If you lay even one finger on me—or sleeping beauty over here—you're completely fucked."

"Shut up," Orlowski said. The car ground to a halt.

She knew she was getting to him. "It's all over, Orlowski. We know about you. We know about every…"

"I *said* SHUT UP!"

"Every single one of those girls. Or were there more? Was Allison your first? Or was she just the first one we know of?"

"I said SHUT UP!" Orlowski put a gun through the wires of the cage.

Jenny looked down the barrel of the gun, bracing herself for the end. *So this is it. This is how I'm going to die.*

"You're fucked enough," Jenny continued, trying desperately to spare herself. "Add killing an FBI agent to the list and you're sure to get the death penalty."

Jenny, still focused on the gun, heard the sound of sirens approaching and seized the opportunity. "See? They're here for you Orlowski. It's over." After a few tense seconds, red and blue flashes began to fill the car.

He pushed the gun further through the cage. *Oh, God, here it is.* She fixated her eyes on Orlowski, who looked like he was deliberating. Maybe she still had a chance.

"Do you really want two dead girls in the back of your car when they find you? Two *unarmed* girls?"

Orlowski squeezed his eyes closed tightly. Within a second he placed the gun in his mouth and pulled the trigger, spraying blood and bits of his brains all over the car. Jenny screamed and covered her face, trying to protect herself from the image that had already been burned into her memory forever. And this was *her* memory, not a vision. She'd have to carry this with her for the rest of her life, knowing it was undeniably real.

She could smell the metallic stench of blood, feeling it drip down her skin. Desperate to get out of the car, she knew she had to be let out from the outside. The next few moments were excruciating as she sat and waited to be rescued.

Swarms of police officers with guns drawn surrounded the car, illuminated by headlights and blinding flashes. She could hear they were shouting, but she couldn't make out the words because her ears were still ringing from the gunshot. Unsure if she was considered a suspect of some kind, Jenny placed her hands in the air and closed her eyes. Before long she felt a flood of cold air hit her body; the door had been opened.

She was quickly led by the arm to the safety of one of the pursuing police cars. "Are you hurt?" the escorting officer asked; his voice still sounded fuzzy.

"No, I'm fine," Jenny replied.

The cold air felt good to Jenny, who was able to take a deep breath and survey the situation as she stood next to the car. Two policemen carried the drunken girl by her arms to the back of a squad car, where she plopped down and continued her nap.

"How did you know?" Jenny asked the officer next to her.

"Some things have come up that have raised suspicion," he replied. That was all he said.

At that moment Officer Johnson approached Jenny. "Are you alright?"

"Yes, sir. Just a little shaken up, that's all."

"We're going to need you to come down to the station and answer a few questions. You're not in any trouble; we just need a statement."

Jenny nodded. "That's fine."

Johnson looked at the officer who had helped Jenny to the car. "Get her out of here, will you? She's been through enough."

"Yes, sir." The policeman opened the back door and gently guided Jenny into the car.

While the door was still open, Jenny remarked to the policeman, "Oh…" She rubbed her temples. "Orlowski has my cell phone."

"You'll get it back," he replied. "Just not yet." He closed the door.

Sadly, Jenny didn't know Zack's number to give him a call. If he'd gotten her message from before, he'd probably be panicked if he tried to call back and she didn't answer. She rested her head back against the seat and looked at the ceiling of the car. She really could have used him right about then. Just hearing his voice would have been wonderful.

The ride to the police station seemed surreal. Jenny watched houses go by, dark, the occupants sound asleep. It was just another night for them. Alarms ringing too early. Work in the morning. Maybe a stop at the gas station. Jenny admired the normalcy they got to enjoy. They would most likely never witness anything close to what she'd just seen.

A strange feeling began to come over Jenny. Happiness. Redemption. The culmination of tireless effort—not her own, but Morgan's. Jenny smiled as she once again leaned her head back against the seat. *Godspeed, beautiful Morgan. It'll all be alright now, thanks to you.* Jenny blew a kiss to the ceiling of the car, knowing that this was goodbye. Morgan had better places to go, and she was off to enjoy them.

Jenny emerged from the car mechanically when they arrived at the station. Once she walked inside and the bright lights hit her, she was able to see the blood that covered her upper body—the blood that had coursed through the veins of a killer, nourishing a sick and demented brain, fueled by the coldest of hearts. She felt sickened by it. She wanted to jump out of her own skin.

"Is there anywhere I can wash up?" she asked.

The officer directed her to the ladies room, and while Jenny was able to get her skin clean, her clothes remained stained with rust-colored blood. The notion of staying like this was intolerable.

As if reading her mind, the police officer greeted her outside the bathroom with a blanket. She draped it around herself, covering the blood stains so she wouldn't have to look at them. "My purse and my keys are in the back of Orlowski's car," Jenny noted softly. "I am going to need those."

The police officer spoke into his shoulder unit, instructing someone from the scene to secure Jenny's purse and car keys. It was ridiculously trivial, all things considered, but Jenny was appreciative nonetheless.

Jenny gave her statement, near the end of which Officer Johnson came into the room. She finished talking, and Johnson once again asked if she was okay.

"Yes. I am. I'd like to get a hold of one of my friends, though. I think he might be worried about me."

"Are you talking about my informant?" Johnson asked.

Jenny smiled meekly. "Yes."

"He already knows. I called him. He's on his way here."

"Thanks," Jenny said. "Although he's going to kill me."

"And rightly so," Johnson remarked. "Knowing what you know, what the hell were you doing in the back of Orlowski's cruiser?"

"It was the girl," she explained. "She was hell bent on getting a ride from Orlowski, and I knew she was as good as dead if she went alone with him. So I went with her."

"Well, it worked out, but only because we already had the situation under control."

Jenny looked up at Johnson. "How? How did you know?"

"Well, your informant friend called us in a panic, saying that he feared Orlowski was going to strike again. We already had a GPS device on his squad car, so we had some officers tail him."

Zack, Jenny thought. Tears burned the back of her eyes as she acknowledged he had just saved her life.

"But how did you know to have a device put on his car?" Jenny asked.

"We got a call from Officer Fazzino yesterday. It seems he did a search of Orlowski's mother's shed two days ago and found nothing. But yesterday morning Orlowski's step-father showed up at the police station up in Connecticut claiming he knew what Fazzino had been after. He produced one of the dead girl's rings."

Jenny covered her mouth with her hand. "Oh my God."

"That was the tangible piece of evidence we needed to connect Orlowski to the killings."

"But if the step-father had the ring, why didn't he come forward with it a long time ago?"

"Officer Fazzino asked him the same thing. You see, we're talking about a guy with a criminal record. He was afraid if he showed up at the police station with a dead girl's ring, claiming a police officer had done the killing, nobody would believe him and he'd end up in jail on murder charges." Johnson cocked his head to the side. "You know what? He was probably right."

Jenny thought about the conversation she'd had with Orlowski where he disclosed that his step-father seemed to wake up one morning and suddenly hate him. That must have been the day that Hawk had found the ring. He knew. All this time, Earl Hawkins knew Orlowski was a murderer. But he couldn't do a damn thing about it.

Jenny closed her eyes and thought about the four lives that could have been spared had Earl Hawkins been a more reputable member of society.

"We were waiting to get a warrant for Orlowski's arrest," Johnson continued. "We should have had it tomorrow." He looked at his watch. "Actually, later today. But in the meantime we put the tracking device on his car so we could keep tabs on him, just in case. It's a good thing we did."

"Yes," Jenny said breathlessly. "Thank you. I don't think I've said that yet."

"No problem," Johnson replied. He leaned in closer to Jenny. "So tell me this. How do you know so much about Orlowski?"

Jenny thought about all of the stories she could make up, but there didn't seem to be a point. "I'm a psychic," she said flatly. "Morgan Caldwell contacted me, as did one of the girls in Connecticut."

He looked at her with awe but didn't say a word.

"So what about Jeremy Stotler?" Jenny asked. "Will he be released from jail?"

"Soon, I'm sure," Johnson said. "Unfortunately it's not that simple. We need to find some kind of evidence connecting Orlwoski to Morgan's murder."

"Gloves," Jenny muttered. "Small, black, leather ones." Jenny wriggled her fingers as if to illustrate. "If you can find the gloves, you'll find your connection."

Johnson smiled. "Got it."

At that moment Jenny heard a commotion from outside the interview room. Johnson stepped out into the hall, returning to Jenny to declare, "I think your friend is here." Jenny only smiled, but then Johnson added, "You can go see him if you want."

Jenny emerged from the room into the lobby. Zack rushed over to her, throwing his arms around her. "Jenny," he whispered. "Thank God you're okay." He was shaking all over.

"Yeah, I'm okay." Jenny returned his tight hug, and they stayed in a wordless embrace for a long time.

Once Zack let go, he put his hands on Jenny's shoulders, looked her squarely in the eye, and said, "I thought I'd lost you."

Jenny looked down at her feet. "No. You didn't lose me. But Orlowski's dead."

"So I heard."

"That's an image that's going to stick with me for a long time."

Zack pulled Jenny in for another hug. He kissed her on the top of the head and said, "He got what he deserved, is all."

"I still have his blood on my clothes. I want to go home and throw this outfit away."

"Can I convince you to stay at my place tonight?" Zack asked. "Or at least let me stay with you?"

Jenny nodded. "I think we should stay at your place." With a snort she added, "I'm not sure my air mattress is big enough for both of us."

Once a policeman arrived with Jenny's purse and keys, Zack gave her a ride back to her car. After a stop back at her apartment and a long, hot shower, it was nearly sunrise before Jenny arrived at Zack's. They both seemed to be on the same page as they headed straight to the bedroom. They plopped into bed and snuggled up together. Zack traced his fingers through Jenny's hair as he said to her, "I'm so glad to have you here."

"It's nice to be here," she replied.

"I was thinking about something before you came," Zack said. "I want you to hear me out before you say anything."

"Okay," Jenny replied, instantly becoming nervous.

"I want us to live together."

Jenny's whole body tensed. "What?"

"Not like a couple," Zack replied. "But in like a duplex or something. Or a house with an in-law suite. I've got it all figured out. I'd pay you rent, and I'll take care of the yard. I could fix things that break around the house. I'd be good to have around, you know."

Jenny's mind raced.

Zack lifted up onto one elbow. "You are planning to buy your own place anyway. I figure you could just as easily buy a place that has some living quarters for me. That way I can make sure you're okay, and we don't have any more episodes like we did tonight." He kissed her shoulder. "I couldn't handle another night like tonight. Ever."

Jenny remained silent as she contemplated Zack's argument.

"And how about this," Zack continued. "I'd even promise to never have sex with you again if that's what it took for you to agree to this. That's how serious I am." He stroked her chin with his finger. "I love you, and I don't want anything to happen to you. Even if it means I have to give you up."

The L-bomb. This was much more than Jenny could handle, although she certainly had to admit she was flattered.

"You're asking me to make a life-altering decision on a night when my emotions are running very high. Can I give this some thought and get back to you?" Jenny asked.

"Of course you can," Zack said. "I don't expect an answer right now."

To lighten the mood, Jenny added, "I had actually decided I shouldn't live alone, too, but the solution I came up with was to get a dog. A big dog, like a German Shepherd or something."

"I'm better than a German Shepherd," Zack said playfully. "I come housebroken. I don't shed. I won't chew up the furniture. I won't bite any visitors, or sniff anyone's crotch…"

Jenny giggled. "Okay, okay, I get your point."

"I might hump your leg, though, from time to time. Especially if you're dressed real pretty."

She gave Zack's ribs a playful nudge.

He lay back down and nestled his chin against her shoulder. "Seriously, are you doing okay? As scary as my night was, yours had to be a million times worse."

She reached her hand around and placed in on Zack's arm. "I'd be lying if I said it wasn't going to haunt me for a long, long time. I saw a man kill himself tonight. Even if he was an asshole, it was still a tough thing to witness."

"I'm sure."

"And knowing it was real and not a vision…" Jenny shuddered.

"Not to mention how scared you must have been when you were in his car. Did you think you were going to die?"

Jenny sighed. "Yes. A few times. Especially there at the end. I thought for sure he was contemplating killing me."

"I can't imagine how that must have felt."

"I believe horrible might be the word."

"So why do you think he offed himself instead of killing you?" Zack posed.

"I told him we were on to him," Jenny confessed. "I told him I was an FBI agent and we knew he was guilty. I said the cops would be coming after him, and shortly after I said that they showed up, by some miracle. When he saw the police come, he knew he'd been caught, and I guess he wanted to take the easy way out."

"The coward's way out."

"I'd thought of that, too. The families of the victims won't ever have the chance to look at him and tell him what a piece of shit he is. I mean, in one sense it's good that he's dead and will never hurt anyone again. But I hope the families don't feel cheated."

"I think after all this time they'll just be grateful to have answers. But I've got to say I'm impressed with your quick thinking. You just may have talked your way out of certain death."

"It was the only defense I had. He took my phone. I couldn't get out of the car. I had to come up with something."

"But claiming you were an FBI agent…that's pretty good."

"I'm a teacher, remember," Jenny said with a smile. "And teachers are smart."

Chapter 21

"Hi Susan," Jenny said as she picked up the phone.

"Hey Jenny. I see you made the papers again."

"Did I?" She couldn't help but smile. "It's been six weeks."

"It's an article about Jeremy Stotler's release from prison, but you're mentioned in it."

"I am so glad that kid's out of jail," Jenny replied. "I can sleep so much more soundly now."

"So is there anything else new. Anything that hasn't made the papers?"

"Well, I actually got a call just yesterday that the DNA from Angela Velasquez's fingernails came back as a match to Orlowski. Officer Johnson spoke to a detective from Trenton, who said the families of all three victims are satisfied that Orlowski was their guy, even though there was only evidence linking him to one of the murders. It would have been too much of a coincidence that the murder spree lasted only while he was in town if he wasn't the one doing it."

"Are you going to go up there?"

"Maybe. I'm not sure," Jenny said. "If the families are happy with the results—like it appears they are—I may not. Oh…" she added. "I almost forgot. I also got a call from Officer Fazzino in Connecticut. He interviewed Orlowski's ex-wife, and she had something interesting to say."

"Oh yeah?"

"It turns out our little friend Orlowski suffered from impotence. It wasn't a problem when they first got married, but as the years went on he had more and more trouble performing. He eventually reached a point where he couldn't achieve an erection at all...*except* when the sex was violent. Then he could see it through."

"Really? That's pretty telling."

"Indeed. It certainly gives us a motive," Jenny reasoned. "You know, I think back to a conversation I had with Orlowski where he talked about *infertility* being an issue in his marriage. He said his wife left him so she could be with a man who could provide her with a baby. Knowing what I know now, I would bet his wife left him so she could be with a man who could have sex with her without choking her."

Susan laughed. "I never questioned why she left."

"Actually, as much as I hate to admit this, I could see how he might be a perfectly regular husband or neighbor. If you didn't know he was a serial killer, you may have never been able to guess it. He seemed so...normal."

"That's what makes this so frightening," Susan noted.

"I know."

"So how is house hunting?"

"It's okay," Jenny replied. "It's hard to find exactly what we're looking for. There aren't too many places around here with a full-service in-law suite. In fact, we've decided to try to move a little closer to my family and a little further from his. I want to be near my dad because of his heart, and Zack wants to be away from his dad because of his attitude, so we've switched our focus to Tennessee."

"Moving out of state together? You sound like a couple," Susan remarked.

"We're not a couple. We're just friends."

"Jennifer..."

"Okay, so maybe we've had a few *liaisons*. But we're still just friends."

"Mmm-hmm," Susan replied skeptically. "We'll see how long it is before that in-law suite is empty."

Jenny giggled. "I don't know about that. He's a great guy and all, but he's very irresponsible. He might just be a really good fling."

Jenny heard her phone beep, so she pulled it away from her ear and discovered her mother was calling. "Susan, I hate to cut this short, but this is my mom calling. She never calls in the middle of the day. I can't help but think something is wrong."

Susan, a mother herself, said, "I totally understand. Call me back whenever."

"Thanks, Susan." Jenny switched lines, her blood running cold with anticipation. "Hi Mom," she said nervously. "Is everything okay?"

To be continued in *Shattered.*

To receive more information about upcoming releases and to be entered into drawings for giveaways, like the Facebook page:

www.facebook.com/jennywatkinsmysteries

Made in the USA
Middletown, DE
26 September 2020

20568953R00116